TAKE THE SUB AND RUN

CLUB ALIBI
BOOK 2

LILA DUBOIS

COPYRIGHT

Published by:
Farm Boy Press,
Sacramento, California, United States of America.

First electronic edition: May 20, 2025
This edition: May 19, 2025

Copyright © 2025 by Lila Dubois, all rights reserved.

Cover design by Lila Dubois
Copyedits by Nanette Sipe
Book formatted by Farm Boy Press

ISBN: 978-1-941641-89-7 ebook
ISBN: 978-1-941641-90-3 print

Without limiting the rights under copyright reserved above, no part of this publication may be reproduced, stored or introduced into a retrieval system, or transmitted, in any form or by any means (electronic, mechanical, photocopying, recording, or otherwise), without the prior written permission of both the copyright owners and the above publisher of this book, except for the use of brief quotations in a book review.

Publisher's note:
This book is a work of fiction. The names, characters, places, and incidents are products of the writer's imagination or have been used fictitiously and are not to be construed as real. Any resemblance to persons, living or dead, actual events, locale or organizations is entirely coincidental.

This ebook is licensed for your personal enjoyment only. It may not be re-sold or given away to other people. If you would like to share this book with another person, please purchase an additional copy for each recipient. If you're reading this book and did not purchase it, or it was not purchased for your use only, then please purchase your own copy. Thank you for respecting the hard work of this author.

For everyone who put it all on the line, and didn't get the result they wanted. We tried, and sometimes that's all we can do.

ALSO BY LILA DUBOIS

Checklist: *BDSM Erotic Romance written as L DuBois*

- A is for…
- B is for…
- C is for…
- D is for…
- E is for…
- F is for…
- G is for…
- H is for…
- I is for…
- J is for…
- K is for…
- L is for…
- M is for…
- N is for…
- O is for…
- P is for…
- Q is for…
- R is for…
- S is for…
- T is for…

Club Alibi: Contemporary BDSM Romance with Heist Movie Vibes

- To Catch a Sub
- Take the Sub and Run

Orchid Club: *Contemporary BDSM Romance*

San Francisco

- San Francisco Longing
- San Francisco Lost
- San Francisco Love
- *Complete trilogy:* Orchid Club: San Francisco

Paris

- Paris Pleasure
- Paris Punishment
- Paris Promise
- *Complete trilogy:* Orchid Club: Paris

Vienna

- Vienna Betrayal
- Vienna Bargain
- Vienna Bliss
- *Complete trilogy:* Orchid Club: Vienna

Trinity Masters World: *Romantic Suspense Ménage Romance written with* New York Times *bestselling author Mari Carr*

Fall of the Grand Master

- Elemental Pleasure
- Primal Passion
- Scorching Desire
- After Burn (free short story)
- Forbidden Legacy

Secrets and Sins

- Hidden Devotion

- Elegant Seduction
- Secret Scandal
- Delicate Ties
- Beloved Sacrifice
- Masterful Truth
- Wildly Inappropriate
- World's Collide - Free short story. Crossover with Lexi Blake.

Masters' Admiralty

- Treachery's Devotion
- Loyalty's Betrayal
- Pleasure's Fury
- Honor's Revenge
- Bravery's Sin

The Hayden Brothers

- Fiery Surrender
- Necessary Pursuit
- Joyful Engagement
- Wrath's Storm

The Mafia

- Suspicion's Fire
- Desire's Addiction
- Danger's Heir

The Spaniard

- Power's Fall
- Control's Undoing

Undone Lovers: *Contemporary BDSM Erotic Romance with a rockabilly vibe*

- Undone Rebel
- Undone Dom
- Undone Diva
- Undone Toy

Monsters in Hollywood

- Monster without a Cause
- My Fair Monster

TAKE THE SUB AND RUN

Interpol agent Andrei Leonard doesn't believe in innocence. When a favor to a friend leads to him capturing a wold-famous forger, he knows her wide-eyed sincerity is a game.

He's proven right when he takes her to Interpol's newest safe-house--a BDSM club outside of Amsterdam—and Sofie knows exactly what all the toys and tools in the club are for.

While he waits to see if this off-the-books kidnapping is going to become an official Interpol arrest, Andrei decides to see if Sofie would like to have a little bit of fun. She readily agrees and, despite his misgivings at the unwelcome softer emotions he's starting to feel when he looks and her, they start to play.

Until Sofie's accomplice, a wold famous maybe-reformed cat burglar, run in, slaps Andrei, and announce that Sofie's a virgin.

A virgin?

After unstrapping her, Andrei vows to take her home and never see her, or touch her, again. Think about her? That he won't be able to stop doing…

But Sofie's sojourn at the BDSM club is the first time she's been out of her heavily protected studio in years, and someone noticed. Sofie's innocence isn't the act Andrei assumed it was, and she has no way to protect herself from the powerful people who want her, and will stop at nothing to get her.

TRIGGER WARNING

In addition to common BDSM elements, this story contains mentions of, or on-page scenes with:

- Graphic Violence
- Broken Bones
- Kidnapping
- Forced Labor/Human Trafficking
- Misuse of Religion/Religious Abuse
- Childhood Abuse
- Neglect

LETTER FROM THE AUTHOR

There's a saying in author circles: writing is easy, you just open up a vein and bleed.

Often that means the writer's own emotions bleed into the words. That definitely happened with me and this book.

I've been struggling with things in my own life recently, but didn't realize how trapped I felt until I was editing this book and realize that being trapped was a major theme for the heroine.

This story still has all the fun, improbable plot elements and delicious spice I normally write, but if the heroine at times seems like the walking wounded it's because I shifted a fraction of my own pain onto her.

Er, sorry Sofie.

As always, please suspend your disbelief, warn your partner you're about to read a sexy book, and enjoy.

~Lila

ONE

THIS MUSEUM HEIST wasn't going well.

Sofie didn't know for sure, since it was her first time robbing a museum, but her partner in crime had just been captured by Interpol.

That seemed bad.

Or maybe it was an opportunity. The perfect distraction. Her partner's arrest providing cover so Sofie could slide in and liberate the priceless pearl necklace they were here to steal.

Except, Sofie didn't actually know how to rob a museum.

Duplicate a painting until it was indistinguishable from the original? Sure.

Steal the original? No. That wasn't in her skill set, which is why she'd been so excited to participate in the theft tonight. Learning to be a thief was part of her long range plan, but more importantly, Sofie so rarely (never) got invited to go out on a girls' night, heist or no heist.

Sofie paused, glass halfway to her lips as she listened to her co-conspirator through the tiny earpiece. Colette Beaumont was a world-class thief and one of Sofie's closest friends. This job was supposed to be low risk and simple, which Sofie knew was the only reason she got invited. Interpol was not supposed to show up and catch them.

A smart person would run, but Sofie had no intention of leaving. She was plenty smart, but right now, she cared less about being smart than she did about having an adventure. Doing something.

For once, she was the one cat burgling and swashbuckling. No, wait. Swashbuckling was for piracy, and she wasn't robbing someone on the high seas. The point was, she was out of her studio, wearing a fancy dress, her blood sparkling with a mix of adrenaline and champagne.

All that was already wonderful in Sofie's estimation, but added to that, Colette was having a deliciously dramatic conversation, and Sofie got to listen to it all, live, via the earpiece she wore.

"Why do you assume I'm here to steal something?" Colette's voice was crystal clear in Sofie's ear.

The man's voice was fainter, but for Sofie to be able to hear him at all meant he was very, very close to Colette.

"Did you miss me?" Landon Malik asked. He was an Interpol agent. No, wait, he had been an Interpol agent. He'd just told Colette he quit.

"Yes, you did miss him!" Sofie said out loud in her excitement. She bounced on her toes, wobbling a little when her weight hit her heels. She was usually barefoot or in slip-on clogs, and rarely wore high heels like she had on now.

Colette made an odd sound, and Sofie frowned.

"What is he doing? What is that sound?" she demanded.

Colette hadn't yet responded to anything Sofie said—not that Sofie had expected her to. This was more like talking back to an audiobook, which Sofie did have a habit of doing.

Which is why when Colette did speak directly to her, Sofie was so startled she almost dropped her glass.

"Run, Sofie," Colette said.

Run?

Sofie looked around wildly, not really seeing anything as for a moment, panic gripped her.

It didn't last, especially once she slid around a corner and out of the crowds in the main gallery. She could, should, follow Colette's orders and run.

Or...

Maybe if she saved the day and completed the heist, Colette would bring her on more jobs.

Assuming Colette wasn't about to be arrested. Landon couldn't arrest her personally if he was no longer with Interpol, but the local authorities might be here. Or maybe Landon had come to find Colette, prove his love, and sweep her off her feet.

Sofie sighed wistfully at the idea, even if she was mildly embarrassed for herself. But art was romantic, so she excused herself for the flight of fancy.

The kind of love she was imagining was for art. Aspirational, but not real. Even the most accurate still life was a work of fiction, and paintings or artworks about love were even more unrealistic than an improbably pretty bowl of fruit.

But adventure? That was real. Sofie looked around again, considering and dismissing several options for how she could salvage this job and prove herself a worthy partner in crime.

Dramatically rescue Colette from Landon? Improbable. Sofie looked him up when Colette mentioned him, and he was a big man. Too large for her to take down without both a weapon and the element of surprise. She might manage surprise, but she didn't have a weapon.

Steal the necklace herself? That was her first idea, and

seemed like the best one. Sofie knew how it was supposed to happen. Colette had walked her through it. Ideally, Landon would bend Colette over his arm and dramatically kiss her like he just returned from war. Everyone around them would sigh and clap like it was a movie. The whole thing would be the perfect distraction.

But tonight's heist was a swap job. They weren't supposed to just take the one-of-a-kind priceless pearl necklace. They were supposed to replace it with a fake.

Just taking something was so…pedestrian. There was no art, no effort, to simply stealing something. Sofie knew she was biased, since her own livelihood depended on people like Colette needing forgery copies of the world's most valuable paintings.

There were several problems with that, first of which was that swaps were harder than straight thefts and, again, this was Sofie's first heist. Second, Colette had the replica. It was hidden in a brooch on her dress.

Rescue wasn't an option, nor was doing the heist herself. That left…what?

Create a distraction.

Yes, she could do that. Then Colette could either run or complete the job in the resulting chaos.

For a second, she hesitated, the sparkling, excited feeling that had filled her, now sharper with anxiety and fear.

Right now, no one was looking for her. No one knew she who she was.

No one was ever looking for her. She was a world-class forger, and for the handful of people who knew who she was, she was considered a rare talent.

Which is why those same handful of people worked so hard to protect her. To make sure no one ever came looking for her or knew who she was.

There was still time to be smart and run. Go back to her studio and wait. Wait for Colette to contact her and tell her what happened. Wait for a client to show up and demand a Rembrandt or Monet.

Wait.

Always waiting for something to happen. Waiting for life to come to her.

No.

Not tonight.

Not anymore.

Sofie was done waiting. She was ready for adventure.

TWO

INTERPOL AGENT ANDREI LEONARD watched as the beautiful woman in white slid behind the heavy black fabric curtain and disappeared from view. Her transition from wide-eyed excitement, her gaze unfocused to focused action would have been jarring to anyone watching her.

In fact, there had been several people watching her, but Andrei had stared at each of them long enough for their survival instincts to kick in. Whatever sense used to warn humans they were being watched by a predator activated, and one by one, they looked around, caught him staring at them, and moved on.

Meaning, no one but him saw her abrupt, not-at-all subtle, behavior shift.

With a sigh, he set his glass down and followed her, weaving through the elegantly dressed gala attendees. He needed to grab her before museum security did.

Her name was Sofie, and apparently, she was an accomplice to the infamous cat burglar Colette Beaumont. According to Andrei's former Interpol colleague Landon Malik, Colette was here to steal a nearly priceless rare pearl necklace that was on display at this gala.

And apparently, Sofie was her accomplice.

The pipe and drape sectioned off the wide hallway that branched from the main gallery of the Rijks Museum. It was now a staging area for the caterers. Silver catering carts were pushed up against the hall wall, and a man in a tux moved with brisk efficiency to fill a tray of champagne flutes.

He startled a little when he picked up the tray and saw Andrei standing just this side of the curtain. He opened his mouth to say something, but Andrei shook his head once. Something about Andrei's face or mannerism shut the server down, and he pushed through the curtain without a word.

Leaving Andrei alone with the woman…who apparently had no survival sense since she hadn't once looked over at Andrei, despite how intently he'd been watching her. Even now, she didn't turn.

She stood in the shadows, seeming to glow like an angel. He paused, struck by the image, though he knew it was just a trick of what little light there was bouncing off the fabric of her gown and the pale gold, almost white, wig she wore.

Andrei studied where she'd stopped, and smirked. There was a convenient doorway recess just to her right.

With quick, light steps, Andrei came up behind her as she peered at her phone screen. She stiffened a mere second before he grabbed her—those danger-sensing hindbrain instincts finally coming online.

It seemed…improbable that an associate of Colette's would be this unaware. Which meant, it might be a ruse.

Andrei spun her around and shoved her back into the recess all in one move, using more force than necessary in anticipation of this being a ruse and her counterattacking.

Her phone fell with a clatter as her back hit the door,

her eyes wide behind the white carnival mask. He pressed her wrists to the door on either side of her head.

That wasn't exactly a regulation hold, but then again, he wasn't technically on the job right now, and he didn't want to treat her like a suspect. He wanted to treat her like prey.

Their gazes met and something lurched inside him at that wide blue gaze.

"Hello, Sofie."

"I… How do you know my… Who are you?" She couldn't seem to settle on which question to ask.

How did he know her name?

Because Landon had warned him Colette had an accomplice. Andrei had gone looking for said accomplice, at first eyeing the security guards and catering staff…and then he'd seen her.

It had been rather easy to spot the woman muttering to herself. The odd behavior was explainable if you assumed she had an earpiece in to communicate with her accomplice, the same way Andrei could communicate with Landon. Except Andrei had turned his earpiece down so Landon's conversation with his runaway lover wouldn't distract him.

Sofie hadn't been hard to pinpoint, and now she looked so deliciously flustered, he couldn't help playing with her.

"Are you a bad girl who was planning on stealing something?"

He'd meant it as a taunt, and expected her to respond with outrage or a verbal jab of her own.

But Sofie made a soft, needy noise, her gaze first going wide, then dropping.

Ah. Interesting.

Maybe all high-end thieves were secretly subs. Colette certainly was, though she'd hidden her submissive needs well in the beginning.

Thievery, any crime really, was a high-stress job, and BDSM was a good outlet for stress relief. Many of the Doms he knew, including himself, were secretly video game nerds, so sure, why wouldn't most cat burglars be sexual submissives.

"I asked you a question." He sunk some warning into his tone.

"If I was, it would be foolish to tell you." Her accent said she was Dutch, and the pragmatic, quintessentially Dutch statement confirmed it.

She wasn't wrong. It would be foolish because despite the fact that he was out of his jurisdiction, he technically had a duty to report any crime he had direct knowledge of.

Then again, there were some things Interpol just didn't need to know. Like how he was about to treat this criminal like a naughty girl rather than following law enforcement protocols when interacting with a suspect.

"True. But when I ask a question, I expect you to answer." He slid her wrists over her head, holding them with one hand so he could pinch her chin with the other. He forced her face up with a quick jerk, wanting to shock her.

Her soft lips parted on a gasp, and he could see the tip of her pink tongue.

He nearly drowned in a flash flood of need. The need to possess her, to dominate her until she revealed every secret and shadowed corner of her soul.

"And if I don't?" Again, her words weren't a taunt, instead bluntly delivered.

"Then I'll take you someplace and…convince you…to answer."

"Like with a spanking?" she whispered.

God, he loved subs.

"Among other things." He released her chin to circle her delicate neck with his hand.

"But how would you get me there? I'll scream."

"Is that a challenge, Angel?" The endearment slipped out, that image of her seeming to glow imprinted on his brain.

"It's a statement. I will scream and tell them you're kidnapping me."

"All right, then. Let's see."

Andrei hauled her away from the door, bent, and planted his shoulder in her midsection. He stood, one arm wrapped over the backs of her knees. She made a little yelping sound, but he'd knocked the air out of her with that move, and it wasn't loud enough to draw attention over the low hum of conversation and string instruments coming from the gala on the other side of the curtain. Small hands dug into his back as she braced herself.

Andrei strode not back through the gala—too much attention—but down the hall toward the exit on to the gardens. Rijks Museum was large, but he'd committed the layout to memory in preparation for tonight.

"Sir," a security guard said as he approached the door. "You can't be here."

Sofie sucked in air.

Andrei bounced her on his shoulder, as if adjusting her weight. The air she'd taken in escaped as a whoosh as her midsection thudded against his hard shoulder.

"She's a little drunk, and my investors are here. They can't see my wife like this."

"Sir, you have to exit out the front."

"Fine, fine. Can you help me get there without anyone seeing?"

The guard frowned, then brought the mic on his shoulder to his mouth. He spoke Dutch now rather than the English they had been speaking, so Andrei couldn't follow it, but a second later, the guard nodded to him. "You may exit here. There are signs in the garden that will direct you back to the front."

"Thank you so much." Andrei adjusted Sofie again, and this time she grunted. Having his shoulder jammed into her midsection couldn't feel good, but he had no problem causing a sub a little discomfort.

A second later, they were outside, the night cold. Andrei strode toward where he'd parked the rented van. He'd gotten a larger vehicle specifically because he knew there was a possibility Landon would end up hauling a "less than fully willing" Colette out of the museum.

They hadn't anticipated an accomplice. Sofie was a fun little surprise.

Andrei let her slide off his shoulder when they reached the van. She tried to run, but he wrapped an arm around her middle and hauled her into the back of the van, climbing in with her.

"You're kidnapping me!" She sounded outraged more than scared. And maybe a little excited.

He really fucking loved subs.

"You would prefer I arrest you?"

She froze. "You can do that?"

"Yes." And technically, he could. He'd just have to turn her over to local law enforcement and then do a mountain of paperwork requesting they transfer custody to Interpol.

Kidnapping was simpler.

"Oh. You're Interpol. Like Landon."

Andrei paused, realizing he hadn't identified himself. As far as Sofie knew, he was a stranger who had, in fact, kidnapped her.

Given that, she was surprisingly calm.

Andrei pushed her into a seat, then forced her arms around the back of the chair, cuffing her wrists together.

He turned up the volume on his earpiece, but the crackling static meant he and Landon were too far apart for the devices to work.

"You…handcuffed me!" Sofie sounded shocked rather than scared.

"You prefer rope? Maybe leather?" Andrei took his phone from his pocket. He'd missed a text from Landon.

Have Colette. Don't want to wait. Getting a taxi.

Good. That meant he didn't have to wait either.

Andrei hesitated for a moment, but then reached out, sliding the mask off her face.

Fuck.

She was beautiful. And the wide-eyed, vulnerable way she stared back at him made her look not young but… innocent.

Andrei swallowed down the unwelcome soft feelings that were trying to take root and climbed into the front seat and started the vehicle. "Out of curiosity, what were you going to steal?"

He knew the answer—at least according to Landon—but wanted to see if she'd tell him.

"I shouldn't tell you that."

"Hypothetically, what were you going to steal?"

"Hypothetically?"

"You're not a fan of using that word the way Colette is?"

"You know Colette?"

He looked at her in the mirror. "Of course I know Colette."

The fact that they'd almost been too late to save her weeks ago when she'd been taken by the Bratva had exhumed memories Andrei wanted to stay buried.

"A painting," she said.

"Which one?"

"A Rembrandt. *The Night Watch.*"

"The wall-sized one so big the people are nearly life-sized?"

"Oh. You know that piece?"

"We were just in The Night Gallery, named after the painting which is prominently displayed."

"Oh."

Andrei turned, heading north out of Amsterdam. "Do you think I'm stupid?"

"No. I just didn't think you'd pay attention to the art."

"Insulting."

"I didn't mean to insult you. You asked."

"You must really enjoy spankings."

That was met with silence, and in the rearview mirror, he could see her throat work as she swallowed.

"I…do."

"Good to know that won't be an effective punishment."

"Are you going to punish me?"

He would never lay hands on a woman without her consent. And if Landon had Colette, they didn't actually need any information from Sofie. Bringing her in was still a good idea—best not to leave accomplices unaccounted for—but Andrei could pop Sofie into a locked room with a cup of tea and a book and then let Landon deal with it.

He could do that.

But teasing her was too much fun.

"Have you been a bad girl?"

"You mean, am I a criminal?"

"Are you?"

Her chin notched up. "I've never been arrested."

"You're a thief who's good at her job."

"I'm not a thief."

Oddly, that sounded true. Then again, truth was a fluid concept. Maybe she considered herself an art liberator or something equally ridiculous. "Then what kind of criminal are you?"

She didn't answer, piquing his curiosity.

"Maybe I'll spank you until you tell me." He would never do that, but it was a fun threat. He'd spank her, yes, but not as an interrogation technique for real information. The only kind of interrogation where spanking was appropriate was when he was getting a sub to confess every dirty thing she wanted and craved but was afraid to admit to.

"Torture isn't an effective interrogation technique."

Andrei laughed. "Are you trying to make me feel bad, Angel? Implying a spanking is torture when we both know you'd enjoy it?"

She shifted in her seat and licked her lips. He had to remind himself to focus on the road. He didn't know Amsterdam all that well, and if he missed a turn, that would just mean longer before he could get Sofie out of this van.

"Spankings hurt," she said, almost hesitantly.

"Of course they do. Not a masochist just submissive?"

"What?"

"I'm asking, do you like the pain from the spanking, or do you like the spanking because it makes you feel powerless and submissive?"

"I…don't know."

Odd that she didn't have an answer. Maybe she was one of those people who didn't analyze their desires, for fear of uncovering something dark and rotten at the root.

Andrei was one of those people. He accepted that he was both dominant and sadistic when it came to sex, and used the framework and rules of BDSM to control those impulses without having to analyze them.

The other option was that she knew but didn't want to tell him.

"Where are we going?" she asked, leaning forward as much as she could with her arms bound. The bodice of her dress gaped, giving him a lovely view of her breasts in the mirror.

He was going to crash this fucking van if he didn't stop watching her.

"Sit back, Angel."

"This isn't—"

"I said sit back."

She obeyed, back slapping against the seat in her haste to obey. Damn, he liked that. She was an odd mix of defiant and obedient that he'd never encountered before.

"Ask your question again," he prompted, finally turning off the main road.

"Where are we going?"

He wondered what it would sound like if they were properly in a scene, and he could make her tack "Sir" onto the end of each sentence.

First priority was finding out who exactly she was since according to Landon, Colette always worked alone. The presence of an accomplice meant Colette was changing up her methods, or this job needed a second person.

Then again, by the time they got there, Landon might already know everything he needed to about Sofie, thanks to Colette. Maybe Andrei wouldn't have to wait long before they could negotiate a scene, and then he'd strip off her dress and do terrible, delicious things to her.

He turned into the parking lot, a luxury the club in London didn't have.

He waited until he had her uncuffed and had helped her out of the van, before leaning down to whisper in Sofie's ear, "Welcome to Club Alibi."

THREE

A BDSM CLUB.

Sofie grinned in excitement as the man guided her into the large building on the banks of the river Zaan.

Sofie had a terrible sense of direction, but she was fairly sure that, given how long they'd spent driving, they were no longer in the city of Amsterdam.

For a moment, a shiver of unease worked its way down her back. She was far from home. Far from the places she knew and the paths she'd walked. She'd come here in a car, so if she tried to leave, she'd have to walk since she didn't know how to drive, even assuming she could find keys to one of the two cars in the parking lot.

Those worries were pushed aside by excitement as her kidnapper motioned for her to proceed him into the building.

She thought maybe this had once been an office building of some kind, given the size and the many windows. The stone floor of what had probably been a wide, shallow lobby was glossy, and Sofie slowed, nervous in her heels on the slick surface.

His hand came to rest on the small of her back and she sucked in a shocked breath. She was so rarely touched, that each time he'd put his hands on her had been startling. He touched her with confidence—as if he not only had every right to touch her whenever and however he wanted but also knew exactly how to handle her. There'd been no hesitancy when he pinned her wrists against the wall, tipped her face up, or thrown her over his shoulder.

But this...this was different. A hand on her back, guiding her, steadying her. It was a chivalrous touch, something a man would do when he took a woman out to dinner.

The heat of his palm seeped through the fabric of her dress and seemed to spread not just along her skin but sinking into her. Heat spread and pooled in her lower abdomen, and her sex throbbed.

She'd been mildly aroused but mostly alarmed when he kidnapped her from the museum. Their conversation in the car had tipped the scales all the way to arousal, and now, the gallant hand on her back was making everything worse. Her nipples were hard against the satin lining of her dress, and the fine hairs on the back of her neck and arms stood up as she shivered.

"Cold?" he asked. "Or scared."

"Neither of those is perfectly accurate," she stated, and it was true, though she was chilly, and now that some of the excitement was wearing off, fear was creeping in.

He leaned in, exhaling against her neck. The skin there was so sensitive that just the feel of his breath against her made her legs weak.

"Or are you just waiting for me to put you on your knees and treat you like the bad girl you are?"

It was utter madness the way he was talking to her. Not nearly as mad as the way she was responding though. Every single thing he'd said had arrowed straight into her, piercing and pressing on needs and desires she'd never had the opportunity to voice or explore.

Sofie wobbled, and the only thing that kept her upright was the firm press of his hand on her back.

"This is a BDSM club," she blurted out, and she wasn't sure even as she said it if she was trying to remind herself or if she was asking to confirm.

"Your friend Colette told you about Club Alibi."

Not as much as she wanted her to. Sofie had been hungry for details about the sex, but Colette's story had focused more on the emotional aspect of what had happened between her and Landon. And while it was a great story, Sofie really had wanted sex specifics.

"I thought Club Alibi was in London," she said.

"I shouldn't tell you this, but since you're here…there isn't, won't be, only one location."

"This is the Amsterdam branch?"

"Branch…" Andrei's chuckle was low and almost threatening. "Yes, you could say that."

"It looks very normal." Sofie looked around again, curiosity muting some of her arousal.

"You expect us to keep the spanking benches down here, where anyone can see them?" He gestured to the wall of windows that looked out onto the parking lot.

"No, I guess not. But it looks like an office."

"It was."

Directly in front of them was a curved counter that looked like a reception desk. Behind that was a break in the tall lobby wall. She could just make out two elevators and a door marked with the stairs symbol.

"This club isn't ready yet, but there's enough done that Landon decided this is where we'd bring Colette once he found her." He pressed on her back, and Sofie took a step forward.

Guided by the pressure of his hand, she skirted the

reception desk and slipped through an open security gate that blocked off access to the elevators.

"You came to help him? Or to arrest her since he can't do it anymore?"

Her kidnapper went still, hand moving from her back to her elbow as he turned her to face him. "What do you mean by that?"

"I mean, Landon is no longer with Interpol."

His eyes narrowed, and his expression made her swallow hard in fear. "And how do you know that, Angel?"

"I heard him say it."

His expression lightened, lips curved in a cruel smile as he looked her up and down. "That's right." He stepped closer, grabbing her hips as she tried to take a step back.

"Tip your head," he commanded.

"I...what?"

Rather than answer, he pinched her chin the way he had back in the museum, forcing her face up and to the side. His other hand brushed her hair—which had been carefully styled in an asymmetrical style—behind her ear.

A second later, he pulled the small earpiece from her ear. Sofie took shallow breaths, staring unseeing at the floor indicator above the closest elevator as he traced the curve of her ear with his fingertip before gently flicking the dangling diamond earring she wore.

"Are these stolen?" He flicked the earring again.

"No, they're Colette's."

"Which means yes, they probably are stolen." His fingers skimmed down the side of her neck, and Sofie sucked in a shocked breath. She felt that simple touch all over, and it made her nipples tighten further.

Need like she'd never known gripped her, making her feel reckless. She'd started the night out ready for excitement and adventure, and those desires required at least some recklessness. But this? This was something else. Something more, because the need growing inside her felt like it was bigger than anything else—her sense of reason, her self-preservation.

She swallowed hard, her eyes closed as he released her chin.

"I need to get you upstairs," he all but purred, and she loved the way everything he said sounded like a threat. It made her afraid and aroused at the same time.

But there was one thing she needed.

"What's your name?"

The startled silence had her opening her eyes, blinking up at him.

"My…"

"Your name. I can't keep mentally referring to you as my kidnapper."

That startled a laugh out of him, and oh, it was a wonderful sound. The corners of his eyes crinkled just a little, his lower lip—fuller than his upper lip—curving in a way that made her want to suck on it.

"Andrei," he said. "Agent Andrei Leonard."

"It's nice to meet you, Andrei."

"The pleasure is all mine, Miss…"

"Vermeer. Sofie Vermeer."

Andrei's smile disappeared, his gaze once more predatory. "I see, you want to play it this way?"

"Playing what way?" she asked in genuine confusion.

There was a flicker of uncertainty in his gaze, his brows drawing together in a frown. Then he turned, stabbing the up button for the elevator.

The doors opened immediately, and he gestured for her to step in. Sofie wanted his hands on her and considered not moving, forcing him to guide her.

Her curiosity and a renewed sense of being on an

adventure won out. The faster they got on that elevator, the faster she got to go upstairs and see a real BDSM club.

Smiling, Sofie stepped into the elevator.

THEY ONLY WENT UP one level, to the first floor, and when the doors opened, Sofie was disappointed.

Once again, it looked like what it had once been—an office building rather than a BDSM club.

At least at first glance.

The elevator shaft was in the middle of the building. Unlike the first floor where the elevator bank could be accessed from both sides, up here, they were forced to turn toward the back of the building upon exiting the elevator. The wide back wall of the building was solid windows, visible through the glass walls of the offices and conference rooms that lined it. The floor was concrete subfloor that bore marks from where carpet had once been glued down, and there was no furniture in the wide-open space between where they stood and the back wall.

A palette of wood and some neatly stacked tools and boxes made it clear this space was under construction, and that same pile was what partially obscured her view of the corner of the building.

Sofie took a few steps, her heels loud on the concrete floor, the sound bouncing off the glass walls to come back as an echo. She glanced around, shivering a little in the chill that was present here but hadn't been noticeable on the ground floor. Now, she could see the dark ribbon of the river through the windows, and off to the right, a few windmills that looked far too picturesque to be anything but decorative or a tourist draw.

She froze, nearly stumbling mid-step, when she saw the

playrooms that had been hidden by the construction materials until she got farther into the building.

The renovations and retrofitting had started in the far corner, with what had once been a large corner office, as well as a smaller office to one side, and a long room that was most likely a conference room in a previous life.

The smallest room had a hexagonal stage in the center, the stage made of black metal and what looked like white glass or high-shine plastic. A black dancers' pole rose from the center to touch the ceiling. The floor too had been stained black. Black metal frames were attached to the glass side walls. The frames were thin and rectangular, looking almost like oversized doorways mounted next to one another so there were three on each of the side walls for a total of six.

On the opposite side of the corner office, the conference room still looked a bit like a conference room, thanks to the long table-height solid block of concrete in the center of the room. It took Sofie a moment to identify why it looked oddly familiar—it looked like a sacrificial altar from a horror movie. It was large enough for a person to be laid out on. Padded benches and a few large steamer trunks lined the walls. A track lighting system mounted to the ceiling had a dozen small lights on it, ready to be positioned and angled to illuminate whatever, whoever, was on that stone slab.

It was the corner playroom that caused her to almost stumble.

The small angled wall that held the door into the corner space was glass, but the view was partially obstructed by a collection of paddles and floggers that hung from hooks mounted to the inside.

Two large X frames—St. Andrew's crosses—were positioned parallel to the exterior walls but not directly up against the glass. They were set back a meter from the walls. Metal supports jutted down from the ceiling to the top of each X, holding them in place.

To one side, a plush leather chair had a thick round floor cushion on the ground in front of it. In the center of the room was something that looked almost like a gymnastics' horse—a freestanding frame with a thick, padded top.

The floor was stained black, the St. Andrew's crosses glossy red.

"See something you like?" Andrei murmured in her ear.

Sofie jumped, not having realized how close he was, her attention entirely focused on what she was seeing and the dark, pulsing need that beat like a drum inside her.

"Yes," she answered honestly.

Andrei shifted so he was behind her, close enough she could feel the heat of his body in the chilly room.

"If you weren't a thief, we'd be negotiating right now, and in ten minutes, I'd have you on your knees at my feet."

A soft sound of need escaped her, and her sex pulsed in response to his words.

"I'm not a thief," she stammered out.

"I believe you believe that," he said after a pause.

Sofie wobbled on her heels, and with an aggravated noise stepped out of them. The cold cement floor was shocking against her soles and toes and she yelped.

Andrei reached down and yanked her skirt up to her knees, peering at her discarded shoes and bare feet. Slowly, he straightened, cocking a brow at her.

"I don't normally wear shoes," she explained.

His expression seemed to indicate that didn't actually explain much as far as he was concerned.

Sofie wasn't sure what else she could, or should, say. Yes, the floor was cold, but the heels were making her feet hurt, and she was so turned on, she was almost swaying—

Andrei bent and scooped her into his arms. Rather than throwing her over his shoulder, he held her in a bridal carry. Sofie went still, awkward for a moment, but then wrapped her arms around his neck, hooking one elbow over his shoulder.

A soft, romantic feeling slid over her, and now, her pretty white dress felt just right. She closed her eyes and saw the painting in her mind. Stroke by stroke, it came together in her imagination.

Painted in the Romanticism style—heavy details, especially in the central figures, and deep shadows. Artfully draped fabric for the female figure's white dress, maybe with a hint of Grecian style.

The in-progress image froze, like a sped-up video suddenly paused, as Andrei turned sideways pushing the door to the smaller playroom open with his shoulder.

Sofie stared at his profile in a delicious mix of anticipation and fear. This close, she could see the stubble along his jawline, the shallow lines at the corners of his eyes that would deepen as he aged.

And his full lower lip. It looked eminently kissable. Suckable.

Sofie drew in a surprised breath as he released her legs but kept a hold of her upper body. She ended up flush against him, clinging to his shoulders, her temple pressed to his jaw, her toes just skimming the cold floor.

She felt him swallow hard, and for a moment, he hugged her tighter against him. Sofie softened in his embrace, body molding to his, her face pressing against his neck. He smelled good.

Andrei's hand grabbed her ass, startling a yelp out of her as he used his hold on her butt to lift her. Her feet touched down on the top of the hexagonal stage, which was cool but not nearly as cold as the concrete floor. He gave her ass a pat that was almost, almost a spank.

Sofie looked over her shoulder at the glossy black pole, then back at Andrei. "I don't know how to pole dance."

"Pity." His gaze raked her up and down, lazy and self-assured. He reached into his back pocket. "But that's not actually why you're up on this stage. At least not right now." He pulled out a pair of handcuffs.

Sofie watched him fasten one cuff around her wrist, then pull her arm back as he circled around the stage.

"Back up, Angel," he said softly.

She did as he said, backing up and pressing her spine along the pole. He clicked the cuff into place around her other wrist, her hands behind her, the cuffs looped around the pole that stretched from floor to ceiling, ensuring that she couldn't go anywhere.

Sofie waited, needy and starting to feel impatient, for Andrei to do something more. To touch her.

Wait. First, they had to negotiate the scene. He'd mentioned it just moments ago.

But when Andrei faced her once more, it wasn't to discuss hard limits the way she anticipated—hoped.

"I'm going to find Landon."

"What?" She blinked in surprise.

"That was his rental car in the parking lot, so he and Colette are here. Probably in one of the private rooms upstairs. Once I find out what he wants to do with you, I'll be back."

"What do you mean 'do with me'?" Sofie demanded. "He can't arrest me."

"No, he can't." Andrei leaned in, gaze hard. "But I can. I haven't, because I can't arrest you without arresting Colette."

"You can't arrest me because I didn't do anything." She never did anything. That was why she'd jumped at Colette's invitation to go with her to steal the Bulgar pearl.

"I'm sure I can find something to charge you with."

"Ah, I see. You're one of those police who makes things up in order to arrest people."

Andrei's jaw muscle flexed, but then he smiled that cold, cynical smile. "I will admit that I consider the rules flexible. However, I would never fabricate charges. With you, I won't need to, will I? You're a thief just like your friend."

"I'm not a thief."

Andrei looked her up and down, and despite the fact that she was now taller than him, thanks to standing on the stage, she didn't feel as though she held the upper hand.

"We'll see."

Sofie was considering how to prove to him that she was not, technically, a criminal. She certainly wasn't a thief, and her father had made sure that she was not again technically, a criminal. But proving that something was not true, especially while handcuffed to a dancers' pole in a mostly abandoned building, seemed difficult.

Before she could find the right words, Andrei turned and walked out.

She was confident that Colette wouldn't implicate her, but Sofie was a little worried she might accidentally say something that countered whatever story it was Colette was currently spinning for Landon, and in turn, Andrei.

It would probably be safest not to attempt any sort of subterfuge on her own. She'd stick with the truth, whether or not Andrei believe her.

And while Sofie probably should care, and worry, about the possibility of being arrested, that wasn't her biggest concern.

No, the more pressing need was addressing this deep ache that had formed in her core. Being handcuffed to a pole was not exactly helping.

She wanted Andrei to make good on the threats, promises, he'd made so far. She wanted him to put her on her knees. Wanted him to strip off her dress and then put her back on the stage and use her body.

She wanted to feel something. She didn't care if it was pleasure or pain.

She watched as Andrei headed back for the elevator bank, detouring not to the elevator but to the stairs, the door swinging closed behind him.

Sighing, Sofie sank down to kneel on the stage, legs tucked to one side under her white skirts, and prepared to wait.

FOUR

COLETTE WAS GETTING PUNISHED for running away.

Andrei smirked, ear against the door of one of the only completed private playrooms on the third floor. Unlike the rooms downstairs, these had solid walls. Meaning, he couldn't see what was happening inside the room, but he could hear. The rhythmic thwack sound was distinctive and telling.

They needed this.

Andrei had seen how devastated Landon was when Colette left. The man had not only given up his career but started a new one for the sake of being with her. Andrei couldn't say he understood because he would never be such a fool as to convince himself he was so deeply in love with another person that giving up everything made sense. He was too practical, too aware of how the world really worked, to ever be that romantic.

However, it was fun to watch.

He'd happily taken a week of vacation in order to help Landon chase Colette down. He himself might be far too cynical for romance, but he wholeheartedly supported other people's delusions. And that support extended to not interrupting Colette's current punishment to ask what the hell to do about Sofie.

The presence of an accomplice had been a surprise because Colette always worked alone.

And now the accomplice was his to deal with. Given the hell that Landon, and particularly Colette, had gone through, Andrei anticipated both the scene and aftercare would take a while. That meant, he either needed to let Sofie go, stash her somewhere comfortable, or keep her here in the club.

And if they were already staying in the club anyway...

Grinning, Andrei turned and headed for the stairs.

Andrei indulged himself in putting together a few possibilities for what he and the lovely Sofie could do to pass the time. She was clearly an experienced submissive, so a quick little scene was a definite possibility.

Unethical, if he thought he were actually going to arrest her, but Andrei was sure that wouldn't be needed. She was right that she hadn't stolen anything tonight—they'd stopped her and Colette before it got that far.

And his instincts said she was telling the truth when she claimed she wasn't a thief. Maybe she was a driver. The image of the pretty, soft blonde gunning a car through the streets of Amsterdam made him smile as he jogged down the stairs.

Andrei pushed through the door into the first floor, slowing to a walk so she wouldn't see how eager he was to get back to her.

If she had been watching him, however, she would have seen him stumble when he caught sight of her.

Sofie looked like the angel he'd named her. An angel held captive in hell. She sat on the small stage, her skirts covering her legs and spilling over the side to drape the black floor. Behind her, the glossy red St. Andrew's cross seemed to loom over her pale form.

She looked vulnerable and soft, and fucked-up bastard that he was, he wanted to both abuse her and rescue her.

He wanted to deepen the imagery of her in hell by stripping her and binding her in ropes and chains, taking a whip to that pretty flesh.

He wanted to scoop her into his arms and take her away from here, then kneel at her feet to pledge himself to her.

Andrei shook himself to get rid of the fanciful ideas, abruptly irritated with himself. He was a fucking fool if he was still capable of imagining such ridiculous things, given what he'd seen and done in his life.

Sofie didn't look up until he pushed the door open, her pretty eyes going wide a second before she frowned in confusion.

"You're back."

"I am." He crouched in front of her, hands dangling between his knees. "Colette's getting her punishment."

Again, her eyes widened even as she wetted her lower lip with her tongue. "How?"

"Not going to ask why?"

"I assume she's being punished for attempting to rob the museum."

"That's not how we punish thieves."

"Interpol? I would hope it's not. I would assume it's prison."

"Correct," he said with a chuckle. "We don't punish thieves with spankings and whippings."

Sofie perked up. "Spanking?"

"That's what it sounded like. Possibly a nice heavy panel paddle." Andrei raised one brow at her.

Sofie tipped her head to the side considering. "I think I'd take paddle spanking over a whipping."

"Prefer thud over a sting."

She hesitated for a moment before saying, "Yes."

Andrei pushed to his feet, and he could feel Sofie watching him as he grabbed the heavy leather armchair and brought it over to face the stage.

Taking a seat, he crossed one ankle over the other, propped his elbow on the arm of the chair.

"The point I was making is that she isn't being punished for the theft." Andrei smirked. "Hypothetical theft."

Sofie frowned. "Why, then?"

Was she playing dumb? Or maybe while she, like Colette, was a sub, Colette hadn't told her much about the D/s relationship she had with Landon.

"You know that Colette and Landon…" He trailed off, brows raised.

"I know she loves him, but she thought staying with him would hurt him, so she left him and broke her own heart. Oh, and that she was his sexual submissive because she was hiding out in a BDSM club."

"Then you do know what's going on." He shifted to lean forward, elbows on his knees. "Yet you think she's being punished for attempting to steal some necklace only rich people care about?"

Sofie's mouth rounded in a soft O.

"He's punishing her for running away."

"Yes. And because she should have talked to him about what she was feeling, and her fears." Andrei tsked mockingly. "Your tops have let you get away with too much if you think lying to your Dom is okay."

"But it was romantic," Sofie insisted earnestly. "Leave him to protect him."

She couldn't really be that naive. Andrei opened his mouth, but the cutting words wouldn't come.

"It wasn't fair to Landon," Andrei said instead. "She should have trusted him enough to stay and work it out."

"No," Sofie said decisively. "This was better. More romantic, and more dramatic."

That startled a genuine laugh out of Andrei. "Running from him, getting caught in the act of doing the illegal thing that was the reason they couldn't be together, and then getting punished, is better."

"Well...yes." Sofie shifted, pulling her legs under her so she was kneeling and leaning forward slightly.

Andrei's attention dropped to the soft swell of her breasts. All it would take was a quick tug to free them. Expose the soft, sensitive nipples.

"You don't think it was romantic?"

Sofie's question jerked his attention back to their conversation.

"No, I think she ran out of self-preservation more than anything."

Sofie made an outraged noise. "No! Colette left to protect Landon—"

"I'm sure she thought of it that way. But what she really ran from was the possibility that he'd choose his career, and the law, over her."

Sofie looked heartbroken. "That's not romantic at all."

"I know."

She considered him, and for a ridiculous moment, as she looked at him, he was afraid he wasn't enough.

"You're a cynic," she accused.

"Maybe. Definitely a realist."

She made a disgusted noise, looking away from him and out at the dark river.

Oh, no no no. He didn't like that at all. Andrei rose slowly from the chair, and though she didn't look at him, he knew she was aware he was moving closer, based on the way her shoulders tensed.

"You like soft Doms?" he asked, and before she could answer, his hand was tangled in her hair. He gave a sharp tug, expecting the wig to come loose.

Instead, Sofie yelped in pain, gaze flying up to meet his.

Andrei slid his fingertips along her scalp, feeling for the bumps of her real hair coiled and braided under the wig. All he felt was the bone of her skull.

She really did have hair so pale it was almost white.

He massaged her scalp in silent apology, and her eyes slid closed in pleasure.

When she turned her face into his palm, he pulled his hand away, long strands of her hair sliding from between his fingers.

He turned, shoving that hand into his pocket.

"You didn't answer my question." He hardened his tone.

"What question?"

"Do you prefer soft Doms?" Though he knew there was nothing wrong with that, his question held an edge of accusation.

He wanted her to answer no, because he himself was a playful sadist, not a soft Dom.

He wanted her to answer yes, because it would make it easier—though not easy—to walk away.

"I prefer it harder," she said after a moment, and there was hesitation in her tone.

That wasn't exactly what he asked, but he chalked it up to a language issue. They were both speaking English, and while he was fluent, as she clearly was, there were subtilties of phrasing that would be lost, given English was most likely not her first language.

"We have a choice to make, Angel." The pet name slipped out once more. He needed to stop.

Maybe once he had her out of that white dress, it would be easier.

"And what's that?"

"What do we do while we wait for Landon to be done with Colette?"

"I assume we scene," she said bluntly.

Andrei barked out a laugh, returning to the chair.

"Straight to the point."

"You would prefer I wait for you to suggest it?" She shifted once more, legs crossed as she leaned back against the pole.

"Not at all. I demand blunt truth when planning a scene."

"So we're going to do it? We're going to scene?" The eagerness in her tone made him grin. He fucking loved eager submissives.

"Yes," he said, mentally striking the possibility that he would arrest her. If Landon came down here and declared he wanted Colette's accomplice in jail, the other man was going to be disappointed. Short of Sofie committing murder in his line of sight, she was safe from being arrested by him.

Sofie grinned, and Andrei felt his own smile widen.

"Alright, Angel," he said. "Let's negotiate our scene."

A REAL SUBMISSIVE probably wouldn't be smiling and almost giddy with happiness at this moment, but Sofie was. She hoped Andrei couldn't see the way she was jiggling one leg under her skirt in nervous excitement.

"No penetrative sex," Andrei said casually.

Sofie froze in disappointment.

Andrei barked out a laugh. "Your expression…"

Embarrassment curled in her belly, and Sofie dipped her head, knowing her face would be turning bright red. She couldn't stop herself from blushing when she was embarrassed or angry. Her father had always said it was one of the reasons she had to stay in the studio—her face gave away what she was feeling. Even if she controlled her expression, she couldn't control the way blood rushed to her cheeks.

Fabric rustled and then Andrei's hand was on her chin. She tried to jerk her head away, but he tightened his hold, pinching her chin and forcing her head up.

He studied her, his own expression at first closed before softening.

"You think I was laughing at you."

Sofie refused to answer. She wanted to close her eyes rather than look at him, childish as that may be, but she couldn't.

"I wasn't. I was laughing because I love it."

"Love what?" she demanded, words slightly warped because he hadn't let go, so she couldn't open her mouth all the way.

"Love how disappointed you looked at knowing I wasn't going to fuck you." He softened his hold, thumb sliding up to pull at her lower lip. "That will make it so much more fun to play with you. To deny you what you want. Make you come on my fingers no matter how much you beg for my cock."

Her nipples were almost painfully hard inside her bodice, and her pussy clenched in response to his words.

"You'll put your fingers inside me?" she asked hopefully. He hadn't moved his thumb, so as she spoke, her lips brushed against him.

"Ah. That is a fair point. When I said no sex, I was using an old-fashioned, narrow definition of the word." He shrugged. "I mean that I will not fuck your pussy or ass with my cock."

Her ass. The idea of taking his cock in her that way made a little whimper escape.

"Now that I know how much you want to be fucked, I don't think I'll use a dildo in either of those holes either." He smirked at her.

"That's…mean."

He laughed again, and this time she wasn't embarrassed, because this close, she could see the truth of it in his eyes—he wasn't laughing at her. He was laughing in pleasure.

"No, that's sadistic, Angel."

"You're a sadist," she said, with no small amount of trepidation.

"A sexual sadist, yes. Though I never give pain alone. The counterpoint of pleasure is necessary."

She nodded in agreement, pressing against the fingers still tucked under her chin as she did.

He released her, stepping back and sitting once more. "If you're not at least a little bit of a masochist, I fear our negotiation won't go far."

Her disappointment at the loss of his touch must have showed on her face because he shook his head. "No, I can't touch you while we negotiate. In fact…"

He stood, fishing something from his pocket as he came toward her. A second later, the cuffs clicked as he unlocked them.

Sofie rolled her shoulders, watching as Andrei tucked the keys into his pocket. Then, to her surprise, he sat, not in the chair but on the floor, back against one of the red St. Andrew's crosses. He pulled one knee up, forearm resting atop it, the other leg stretched out.

"Why are you on the floor?"

"Because if I sit in the chair while you're seated like that, we're already in the power exchange. Not appropriate during negotiations."

"You take this very seriously."

"I do." He leaned his head back, watching her from

under half-lowered lids. "Once we start the scene, I don't want there to be any doubt in your mind that you agreed to everything I do to you without any undue influence from me."

He all but purred the words, and they sounded like both a promise and a threat. Sofie pressed her forearms against her chest, fingers laced together in a single fist just under her chin. The pressure relieved some of the ache in her nipples, but not much.

He was far enough away that she couldn't make out details of his expression, but she was fairly certain his jaw muscles flexed. Had he guessed why she was so desperately holding herself in?

"You say no sex, but what if I say yes sex?" she asked.

He relaxed, corner of his lips clicking up in a smile. "Your arousal doesn't trump my hard limit."

"Oh."

"What are your limits?"

She wanted to say "nothing," but that was her arousal speaking. "No blood. No permanent damage." She forced herself to stop and really think. "I don't like real degradation."

"Real degradation?"

"I don't want you to mock me. Or tell me I'm ugly because my breasts are two different sizes."

He inclined his head in acknowledgment.

"But I...I liked it when you called me a bad girl," she rushed to add, knowing her cheeks were heating once more.

"Ah, I see why you clarified it as real degradation. I wouldn't even consider 'bad girl' degradation." He smirked. "Just a statement of fact for a pretty little thief."

"Not a thief," she shot back, though she wasn't able to stop the smile. She liked the teasing more than she anticipated, given she was used to blunt honesty.

"Other hard limits?"

Though this was the most aroused she'd ever been, the discussion was making everything feel very real, and trepidation crept in with it.

"You don't...don't want to actually hurt me, do you?" The question came out in a rush, and Sofie froze, sure she'd just ruined everything.

Andrei raised his head, meeting her gaze. "Yes."

Her stomach clenched in fear.

Andrei sighed. "And no."

She relaxed, but watched him carefully.

He took a moment before answering. "I enjoy giving pain, but only when I know it's wanted, needed, or ideally both. Without consent..." He made a disgusted face and shook his head.

"But also pleasure," she clarified.

"Yes. Though I must admit, I'm very good at mixing pleasure and pain." He grinned. "Especially edging."

Sofie shifted her weight from one butt cheek to the other and back, and though the movement was small, it was enough that she was aware of how wet she was, her labia sliding against one another.

"What about my mouth?" she asked, arousal making her bold in addition to blunt. "Will you fuck my mouth, or is that sex?"

"Technically it's oral sex, but..." He shrugged. "There are few things that make the power exchange as clearly felt as putting a submissive on her knees and forcing her to take my cock in her mouth."

Another pulse of need.

"It depends on if this room has been stocked with oral sex condoms."

"And what about the other way?" she asked.

Andrei let out another delighted laugh. "Hoping I'll return the favor and put my mouth on your pussy?"

Sofie kept her head up, even though her cheeks burned.

"I would enjoy strapping you down and tasting you. Exploring you with my tongue for my own pleasure while utterly ignoring yours. Except, of course, if you got too close to orgasm. Then I'd stop."

A full-body shiver wracked her and Sofie closed her eyes.

"Do you know why you like that idea so much, Angel?" His voice was getting closer, though she hadn't heard him move. Could barely hear his voice over the pounding of her own heartbeat in her ears. "Because you'll know, to the very deepest core of you, that you're not in control."

Not in control. She both hated and loved that idea. She had so very little control in her life that it should have been abhorrent, yet it wasn't because…

Because with Andrei, she was choosing to give up control.

"Are you ready to play, Angel?" He was right in front of her, and Sofie's lids fluttered as she considered and dismissed opening her eyes.

"Yes."

"We should negotiate more." He said it like a warning.

"I'll tell you if I get scared," she promised.

"If you get scared…" He repeated the words in a low voice, almost as if he were saying them to himself. "Your safe word?"

"Rembrandt," she said, The Night Watch still on her mind.

Andrei tsked her. "What a bad girl you are, my little thief."

"What do I… Do I call you, um…" She rarely stumbled over words, but right now, she was flailing.

"What do you usually use? It's fine if it's something in Dutch."

"Sir," she said.

"In English?"

"Yes."

He hesitated only a moment before saying, "Then you call me 'Sir.'"

Finally, Sofie opened her eyes.

Andrei was on his hands and knees in front of her. Had he crawled across the floor to her? Why did she find that idea so disturbing and arousing?

He was close enough that the reality of what it would mean to submit to him made an emotion approaching panic grip her chest. It was hard to take a full breath.

"You won't hurt me?" she whispered desperately.

Andrei looked away for a moment, and she was sure he would call it off. Was already trying to figure out how to fix it. How to undo what she'd done.

Instead, he smiled, a slow devil's smile that shouldn't have made her trust him more, yet it did.

"I will hurt you," he vowed, and his gaze dropped to her cleavage.

"You won't make me cry?" she asked, watching him watch her.

"Cry?" He tipped his head side to side to say maybe. "But beg? I will make you beg."

Need overwhelmed her. What had been slowly building, surging until she couldn't hold back. She would have agreed to anything, accepted anything he wanted to do to her, in that moment.

Sofie reached for him, wanting to feel his hair under her fingers, that plump lower lip against her skin.

Andrei sat back on his heels, grabbing her wrists before she could touch him.

Their gazes locked, her wrists captive in his grasp.

He gave her one small squeeze and released her. "I'm

going to leave. When I return, if you're naked on your knees, we start."

Sofie's breath caught, and she didn't exhale until he'd stood and walked out the door.

Then she rose and reached around behind her back for the zipper.

FIVE

ANDREI HESITATED, wanting to exist in a place of possibility for a little bit longer.

He wouldn't fault Sofie for backing out and remaining clothed. This was an odd night that seemed to exist outside of reality. A night where he kidnapped art thieves instead of arresting them and scening with a virtual stranger in a quarter-renovated BDSM club made perfect sense.

He wouldn't fault Sofie for deciding not to do this once the cuffs were off and he wasn't right there pushing and teasing her with wicked words.

But he would be disappointed.

So Andrei lingered in the stairwell, a few bottles of water in one hand, and oral sex condoms in his pocket. He'd torn through boxes of supplies in the storage room on the third floor. Most of the boxes had building supplies, but he'd found a box with the logo of a popular western-European adult store on it.

The image of his angel on her knees with his cock in her mouth had him rock hard. He could see her now—eyes wide and tears rimming them as he held her in place, the head of his cock pushed deep enough to make her gag.

Fuck it. Standing here for another minute wouldn't change her decision.

Andrei pushed out of the stairwell, craning his neck to see her around the pile of construction equipment.

She wasn't there.

Andrei let out a hard, cynical laugh.

He was a fucking fool.

Cursing himself, he started running across the stripped-down interior. He'd uncuffed her, left the room, gone to a whole different floor, and hadn't even considered the possibility that she'd take a third option: run.

Anger made his teeth clench. He was pissed at her but angrier with himself. He never made mistakes based on being too trusting. He didn't trust anyone, and yet Sofie—

Another dozen steps and he finally saw her. Some deep part of him hummed in pleasure, while a small voice at the back of his mind insisted that he'd known she wouldn't run, which was why it hadn't been stupid to trust her.

Sofie was on her knees in the center of the room. It wasn't the pile of construction stuff that had blocked his view but the armchair he'd been sitting in.

She wasn't fully naked—good girl, she was giving him an excuse for a spanking—but there was plenty of pale skin on display.

Andrei slowed to a walk, hoping she hadn't heard him running like an idiot, though given the echo, she probably had. He took a moment, hand on the door, to force the anger, and relief, down.

Looking at her made it easy to let go of the hot, jagged anger. She looked soft and vulnerable, and it made him want to be both gentle and unimaginably cruel.

Andrei pushed open the door.

Sofie twitched but didn't look up. She was on her knees on the thick floor cushion, her ass resting back against her heels, her thighs pressed together. She wore white panties, though given how thin the hip straps were, Andrei thought they were probably a G-string rather than full coverage. Either way, the virginal white seemed right.

Her hair was pulled forward over her shoulders. At first, he thought her breasts were bare, only her hair covering them, but as he got closer, he saw the bit of fabric a few shades darker than her skin tone between her breasts and wrapping around her ribs. A nude strapless bra.

The only off note in her posture was her arms, which hugged her middle. Otherwise, she was the picture of submission.

Andrei stopped in front of her, and even with her head bowed as low as it was, he knew that if her eyes were open, she would be able to see his shoes. Even if she somehow hadn't heard him coming, now, she'd see that he was right there in front of her. Still, she didn't react.

It wasn't until he reached out, sliding one finger along the silky strands of her hair that she shivered and let out a low moan. The intensity of that reaction gripped him tight and held on.

Andrei circled around her, internally at war over what to do first. From a distance, she looked like she needed a soft introduction. Maybe sit and use only his voice to dominate her—commands to stand, strip, take up various submissive postures.

The other side of that battle advocated for more. To take her, use her, make her feel in the most visceral ways possible that she was now his. To rip the remaining fabric from her body until she hid nothing from him and then put her over his knee and mercilessly spank her until she vowed to never hide her lovely body from him again.

Catching her hair in his hand, he brushed first one side and then the other, back over her shoulders. He'd been right. She was wearing a strapless nude-colored bra. She hugged herself a little tighter, her upper arms pressing in on the sides of her breasts to deepen her cleavage.

Andrei gathered her hair in one hand, sliding his fist far enough down the tail that he could then loop it around his hand once, getting a good grip right at the base of her skull.

Sofie's needy little moan when he tightened his hold on her hair made the decision for him as to what would come next.

"Up," he commanded in a hard voice.

Sofie immediately started to rise. She first tried to lean forward and brace her hands near her knees to push herself up, but he didn't let go of her hair. She hissed out a breath when she yanked on her own hair, apparently thinking he would move with her. It took only a moment to course correct, though she surprised him when she reached out and back to grab his leg, using that as a handhold to roll up onto her feet. This time, he moved with her, careful not to pull on her hair.

Once she was standing, she again hugged her middle with her arms, and while he appreciated what it did for her breasts, she was hiding herself from him, and that he would not allow.

"Arms down."

She hesitated, and her body language made it clear it was uncertainty, not deliberate disobedience to further the scene at the root.

Andrei spread the fingers of the hand he had wrapped in her hair, massaging her head for a moment with the pads of his forefingers while his thumb kept her hair securely wrapped around his palm. She leaned back into the gentle scalp massage, a quiet acknowledgment of his equally quiet praise.

He wanted to be harsh but found himself needing to be gentle, which is why he leaned in, lips nearly against her ear. "I see you chose to be a bad girl right from the start."

"What?" The alarm in her voice made him smile and he was glad she couldn't see the way his lips twitched.

"I told you to be naked. And here you are wearing clothes."

"This is underwear, not clothes."

"Are you naked?"

"Technically perhaps not," she hedged.

Andrei chuckled, splaying his free hand over her belly to pull her back against him so she could feel the way his body rumbled with amusement. It was insanely gratifying to feel her instantly melt back against him, and he used his hold on her hair to pull her head to one side and rest it against his shoulder.

"You should know better than to play semantics with a Dom."

"I was nervous."

The soft honesty gutted him. Andrei's stomach muscles clenched as if he'd taken a blow to the middle. It was insane how everything she said or did elicited overtly intense responses.

Andrei closed his eyes and seriously considered stepping back and taking a break. Just to get himself under control.

But that wouldn't be fair to her. This early in the scene, especially with a new partner, submissives were intensely emotionally vulnerable. He was certain that would be even more true for his angel. If he walked away now to gather himself, he doubted she would be this soft and trusting the next time he took her in his arms.

"Nervous, or were you trying to get that spanking I know you want?"

"No. No, I know that topping from the bottom is bad. That's what that would be, right?"

Andrei rubbed his hand side to side across her waist,

enjoying the way her abdominal muscles fluttered and tensed under the touch.

"If a sub feels the need to top from the bottom, it means the pre-scene negotiation didn't go well. If a sub has very specific needs she knows have to happen in the scene for her to feel satisfied, then those should be listed out during negotiation. So as I said, if she feels the need to top and bottom during the scene, it means that negotiation didn't go the way it needed to."

"We can negotiate again if you want..." Sofie sounded unsure.

"If I thought you were trying to top from the bottom, that is what we would do right now. But you aren't, are you?"

The tension that had crept into her muscles eased away. "No, Sir."

Andrei slid his hands down until the tips of two fingers brushed the waistband of her panties. Then he forced her hips back against him, until his rock-hard cock was digging in to the top of her ass. Hearing that "Sir" from her lips made him ravenous.

Sofie gasped when he wiggled his hips so his cock was firmly wedged in the top crease between her pretty ass cheeks, his pants an unwelcome barrier.

"I think being a bad girl was your way of being a very good girl, and giving me an easy reason to spank you."

"Do you need a reason?" she asked in a low husky voice.

"No. I don't." He gave in to the urge that had been riding him and pressed his lips to the soft spot under her ear. A whole-body shiver wracked her. If she was that sensitive, this was going to be so much fun.

"But," he went on, "it's fun, isn't it? When I tell you that you're going to get a spanking because you're a bad girl who tried to hide this pretty body for me."

"Am I?" she asked, sounding genuinely inquisitive rather than mocking. "Am I going to get a spanking, I mean."

"Is this your way of telling me I'm going too slow?"

"No. If you were going slow, I'd tell you."

"Angel, you are always welcome to tell me anything. In fact, I want to know everything. I want to know how the things I do to you make you feel."

He inched his hand lower, the pads of several fingers now firmly on fabric. Sofie pressed her hips forward against his hand, which meant her ass was no longer nestled against his cock.

Andrei slammed her hips back against him, squeezing her between the vice of his hips and his hand. She sucked in air then surprised him by reaching down and back to grip the fabric of his pants and holding tight. As if anchoring them together.

He really fucking loved submissives. Completely illogical that she would cling to him even as he was the greatest threat to her person. Illogical and wonderful.

Andrei held her there for a moment, her body molded to his, her neck arched as he pulled slightly on her hair, forcing her head both back and to the side. Then he released her all at once, taking a step back.

Sofie wobbled, having to take a half step to catch her balance. She hesitantly looked back at him, worry and the question stamped on her features.

Andrei smirked at her, one brow raised in an unnamed question, and she relaxed.

Good.

Impatience riding him, Andrei went to the corner of the room where a large, low black trunk sat. The trunk was mounted on hidden wheels, and a flick with the toe of his shoe unlocked them, allowing him to easily move the trunk away from the wall. The top of the trunk looked like hard leather but was actually padded so it could be used as a seat. Except this was a BDSM club, so it was never going to be a seat; it was always going to be a platform for displaying or playing with a submissive.

When he was satisfied with the placement, he made a show of getting ready, unbuttoning his cuffs and rolling them up, undoing the top button of his shirt, and finally removing his belt.

Sofie had turned to watch him, and when he pulled his belt free of the pant loops with that distinctive snick sound, she tensed. Clearly, she'd taken a belt before.

The idea of his angel with red stripes across her ass and upper thighs was lovely in his mind.

But the thought of another person being the one to do that? To hurt her when she was his to both please and abuse? That made him nearly homicidal.

For only a moment, he gave in to the internal alarm that was sounding. He was far too possessive of this woman, given he'd known her for a matter of hours, and they had yet to actually do any intense play. It was one thing to feel not just responsible for but possessive of a submissive in the midst of an intense scene. And the feeling usually faded during aftercare. And even in those odd instances where he had felt possessive of a submissive, it had never happened this early, or been this strong.

Andrei took that worry, balled it up, and chucked it into a dark corner of his mind.

It was time to play.

SIX

SOFIE WAS TREMBLING. It wasn't cold—though she wasn't exactly warm standing here in her underwear. It wasn't fear. She knew what it was like to be so terrified that her body shook with it, and this wasn't that.

No, this trembling was anticipation. Nervousness too, but mostly anticipation. The hot, dark excitement that rolled in her, mixing with the desperate arousal and the reality of the forbidden made her feel like a different person. The next evolution of the person she'd chosen to be when she agreed to the heist with Colette.

And now she was going to get a spanking.

Andrei rolled up his shirt sleeves, and Sofie had to swallow hard to hide her reaction to the precise calculated tug and fold of him slowly revealing some skin. She'd seen plenty of women talking on the Internet about a man's forearms in a rolled-up dress shirt, and while she'd intellectually appreciated that beauty could be found in the most unexpected places, she hadn't herself seen the appeal.

Now she understood. Or maybe it was that she only understood when it was Andrei's forearms.

His belt snapped as he pulled it free from his pants and

her shaking increased as she watched him fold the belt, the tip and buckle and in one hand, the looped dangling from his fingers. But then, with that smirk she now recognized meant so many different things, he instead rolled the belt up and set it to the side. Finally, he took a seat on the long, low steam trunk he'd wheeled away from the wall. She was surprised to see the top give a little. It had looked like solid wood wrapped in leather but was clearly padded.

Andrei sat not in the middle but toward one end, and shifted so that he was sitting at a slight angle. There was something very deliberate about it, and she wished she knew why. She had a feeling it was important, but all her research and the hours she'd spent living vicariously through other people, were failing her.

"Angel?"

"Yes, Sir?" Saying sir came almost too easily.

"Come here."

She obeyed the command easily though the trembling didn't stop.

When she was close enough to touch him, Andrei raised one hand and twirled his finger in a circular motion. Slowly, Sofie started to turn a circle, only to have Andrei stop her with his hands on her hips when her back was to him. Sofie tensed, ready for him to touch her intimately, given that the height of the low trunk meant her ass was almost in his face.

Instead, he brushed her hair out of the way and undid the back snap of her bra.

Sofie gasped more in surprise than anything, and instinctively reached up to cover her breasts with her palms, holding the cups of the bra in place.

"Hands down." Now, there was bite in the command, a hint of disapproval or disappointment.

Sofie swallowed a sound of distress. She wasn't

distressed because she was worried; she realized she was upset because he was disappointed.

"I'm sorry, Sir." Sofie dropped her arms and the strapless bra tumbled to the floor. She stared down at it, remembering when she'd bought it online, paying slightly more to get the one with pretty lace overlay, even though she knew no one would ever see it.

"That's all right," he murmured. "I already have plans to remind you not to hide what's mine."

Andrei's hands slid from her hips up her naked sides. When the backs of his fingers rubbed along the insides of her upper arms, Sofie instinctively raised them to get her arms out of his way. Not sure what to do with her hands, she awkwardly stacked her palms on top of her own head.

"Fingers laced together behind your neck," he commanded. "Under your hair so I still have access to that."

It was a relief to be given instructions, and Sofie readily obeyed, sliding her hands under her hair and lacing her fingers together so she was cupping the back of her neck.

Andrei's hands continued up, his fingers finally brushing the outer curves of her breasts.

Then his hands slid forward cupping her breasts as his thumbs stroked once over her nipples.

Sofie sucked in air between her clenched teeth and arched her back pressing harder into his palms as pleasure gripped her and refused to let go. It felt as if her nipples were connected to every nerve ending in her body and every pleasure center in her brain.

"Did that hurt?" Andrei sounded genuinely concerned, and Sofie closed her eyes as her cheeks heated embarrassment.

"No, Sir. I didn't expect it to feel that good. I won't overreact again." She was already embarrassed, so she might as well be honest. Plus, she was no good at lying anyway.

"No." He gently squeezed her tits to emphasize the command. "Never hide or mute a reaction. I told you I want to know what you're thinking and feeling."

"Okay," she whispered in a smaller voice.

The lingering embarrassment vanished when he did it again, thumbs bumping over her nipples. This time, it wasn't as intense, but she did let out a happy little moan.

"Face me." Andrei released her only long enough for her to turn, and then he gripped her breasts once more, palms cradling the undersides.

Sofie didn't realize she'd closed her eyes until he said, "Watch."

She opened her eyes, gaze locked on her own breasts.

Andrei delicately placed the pad of each thumb directly on the tip of each nipple and then rolled them. He worked her nipples like they were tiny toggles of a delicate machine, the movements precise and small but exquisitely acute.

"Closer," he commanded.

Sofie inched forward, until she was between his spread thighs.

"Watch."

She had been watching, but now her gaze jumped to his face, and the naked desire in his expression made her breath catch. She'd read that the greatest aphrodisiac was knowing your partner desired you.

She'd found that idea odd, that being wanted in turn made one want, until now. Andrei looked at her, as if he would come apart, and she in turn felt nearly desperate in her arousal. For a moment, she felt the power shift from him to her as she stood all but naked before him, looking down on him as he worshiped her breasts.

"Now bend down and give me a taste."

The power slid back to him as she obeyed, hesitantly bending at the hips until her breasts were near his face. He didn't let go of her tits as she moved, though his thumbs shifted off her nipples.

With a soft tug to one tit, he had her twisting just enough that her nipple brushed first his cheek, and then his lips.

She saw that full lower lip curve up in a smile before he captured the tip of her breast in the warm heat of his mouth.

Sofie closed her eyes and moaned as he sucked gently at her nipple before tonguing it. When he held her nipple with his teeth, she stilled, and when he bit down enough to cause soft pain, she whimpered.

He tugged on her nipple, the vice of his teeth inescapable, before releasing her and soothing the hurt with his tongue.

Then, "You have very sensitive nipples." He covered her breasts with his hands, her nipples now nestled against the warmth of his palms. "And before you say anything, I am not looking for you to apologize or explain. I'm merely getting to know my new plaything."

"I'm your plaything?"

"Yes. But you're also my bad girl, aren't you?"

Sofie nodded eagerly.

His low chuckle of appreciation made her feel soft and warm.

Then his tone took on a harder note. "But you have been bad, Sofie."

"I'm sorry, Sir."

"Sorry for what?"

"Sorry for not being naked."

"That's right, because when you're with me, I want you naked. I won't order you to follow high protocol and keep those pretty thighs spread, but I do expect that when I reach for your pussy if it's not easily accessible, you move to make sure I can touch you. If that means spreading your legs, then you do that. If that means bending over, I expect you to do that too."

Sofie's vagina clenched in response to his words. And she felt fresh arousal fluid soak in to the small gusset of the thong she wore.

The white thong. That had probably turned dark as she saturated the fabric. He once more used his grip on her breasts to turn her the other way, bringing her tit to his mouth rather than moving his head.

The issue of the wet thong was dealt with almost as soon as she thought of it, and before she could blush.

Andrei released her breasts, hooked a finger over the thin hip straps, and yanked her panties down around her knees.

Sofie gasped at the rough, quick removal.

Andrei once more splayed his hand across her belly, but this time, his thumb rested at the very top of her slit.

"What did I just tell you, Sofie?"

There was a threat and a warning in his voice, and she realized she loved it when he sounded like that. When that little hint of fear crept in.

Sofie stepped back so she was no longer in the cage of his knees, and spread her feet. The thong pulled tight in the space between her knees, and the cool air against her hot flesh made her shiver.

With a casualness that made her feel like his plaything, Andrei slid his thumb along the seam of her sex. With his palm cupping her mons, his thumb pressed up, parting her labia. She moaned in the guttural need, hips thrusting toward him. The tip of his thumb nudged her entrance and she wanted him in there. Whatever part of him he was willing to thrust into her, she would take. His thumb, his fingers, his tongue, his cock. She knew she wouldn't get his cock, but it didn't stop her from wanting it.

Instead, his thumb slid up the warm, wet valley of her sex to gently press against her clit.

Sofie's knees went weak and she nearly buckled. She had to drop her hands and brace them against her shoulders, their foreheads nearly touching as pleasure washed over her in soft shallow waves.

"Did you just orgasm?"

Sofie shook her head, wishing she knew how to interpret the tone he'd used when asking that question. "No. No, I don't think so. That felt really good but it wasn't the same as when I touch myself."

"All right, Angel. Even if you did, I wouldn't blame you. I'm still getting to know the best ways to touch you."

"If I orgasm without permission, you won't punish me?"

"I didn't say that…"

Sofie leaned far enough away that she could look at him, and the devil's own smirk that curved his lips made her smile in return.

"That doesn't make any sense," she insisted. "If I come without permission, you won't blame me, but you will punish me?"

"Makes perfect sense to me."

This whole time, his hand had stayed on her, his arm twisted oddly so that his palm remained pressed against the fleshy top of her sex, his thumb still buried between her labia. But he was no longer directly touching her clit, thanks to the way she'd moved in reaction to the first touch.

Now, he slowly dragged the pad of his thumb up, only to veer just before he touched her clit.

"That's mean, Sir," she insisted.

"No, Angel, that's sadistic. And now that I know exactly

how sensitive you are, it's time for my bad girl to get her punishment."

Andrei removed his hand from her sex and gripped her hips, forcing her back another step. When he released her, she could feel the wet mark his thumb had left.

"Naked," he barked.

Sofie wiggled her legs so the thong dropped around her ankles then stepped out of it and kicked it to the side.

Andrei nodded once in approval then repositioned himself on the trunk. He was sitting so that his right side was in line with one end of the trunk, though he'd turned slightly to the left. His right knee was bent, foot firmly planted.

He patted his thigh. "Over my knee for your spanking, Sofie."

Sofie shifted to stand beside him and hesitated, not sure how to actually go about this. Did she put her stomach on his leg? Her hips? And where should she put her hands?

Sofie looked at him rather helplessly, but his face had turned into a stern mask. They stood there for an awkward moment, her unwilling to make a move when it might be the wrong one and derail the spanking she so desperately wanted.

She'd been hoping he'd give her specific instructions but got something even better.

Andrei grabbed her and yanked her down over his lap. An arm under her ribs just below her breasts helped guide her fall. She landed with her upper body on the padded top of the trunk beside his left hip, her upper thighs on his leg, her feet sticking out awkwardly.

Andrei grabbed her hips and yanked her back until her hips rested on his thigh. She yelped as her tits dragged across the leather, scrambling to help shift back, once she realized what he was doing.

The new position allowed her legs to bend, and she

braced her toes on the cold floor. Now, the way he'd positioned himself half turned made sense, as it allowed most of her upper body to rest on the trunk beside where he sat. She was relatively comfortable, though her leg muscles were tense in an effort to keep herself in place on his thigh.

Andrei's hand slid along her bare back, over her ass, down the back of her thigh to touch the crease of her knee.

His hand felt far bigger and harder now than it had when he was cupping her breasts and touching her softly.

Nervous anticipation brought back the fine trembling. He must had felt it.

"Cold or scared?"

"Neither. Nervous."

"This will hurt," he said resolutely, and perverse arousal flooded her.

"I know, Sir."

"You need it, don't you, bad girl?"

"Yes, Sir."

"And you're going take your bad girl punishment like a good girl, aren't you?"

Sofie closed her eyes and concentrated on breathing as his words washed over her.

"You're going to stay right here on my lap while I spank this pretty ass. You can cry, tell me it hurts, and wiggle all you want, because that won't stop me."

His hand continued the long, firm strokes over her naked body.

"If the pain is too much, or if you get truly scared, you tell me immediately. And when I ask you how you're doing or what you're feeling, you answer me honestly. Understand?"

He pinched her butt when she didn't response fast enough.

"Yes, Sir!"

"Good girl." Another long stroke of his hand. "And

when I tell you to spread your legs so I can play with your pussy—"

Sofie had her thighs spread, toes once more braced on the floor, before he was done talking.

"See? You are my good girl, aren't you, Angel?" He reached between her legs and stroked her labia with two fingers.

Sofie pressed backward in frustration, wanting his fingers deeper. Wanting the fingers between her pussy lips on her clit, or thrust up inside her.

"Sir, please…"

"Punishment first. Then pleasure."

He gripped her thigh, pulling her legs closed and making a few small adjustments to her posture.

He stroked her a few more times, and she mentally settled in for more soft touches and talking.

The first swat to her left ass cheek took her by surprise. Sofie shrieked in pain as heat flared across her skin. The second swat to the other cheek was just as hard.

Sofie went still as Andrei started to spank her in earnest. Spankings hurt.

Her shock at the pain held her in place as his hand moved around her ass and upper thighs, until every inch had experienced that stinging pain.

Then he started hitting previously spanked spots, and she couldn't hold still any longer.

"Ouch, ouch!" Sofie's feet kicked up as he continued to spank her. The quickly faded sting turned into a burning sensation that lingered.

"No," Andrei commanded sharply when one particularly hard swat along the lower curve of her ass had her reaching back in a desperate attempt to cover her bottom with her hand.

Gripping her wrist, he forced her hand to the small of her back, holding it there.

"These next six are for trying to hide from your punishment."

Sofie stopped breathing as he hit her ass.

Hard.

He left behind heat and pain that sunk deeper into her than any of the spankings before it had. This then was a real punishment spanking.

It hurt, and she wanted it to stop, yet...

Yet she didn't.

Sofie pressed her forehead hard against the cushion and whimpered as he spanked her with that same ruthless force five more times. The sound of each blow echoed off the glass walls, yet the sound was muffled.

A soft, floaty feeling had slid over Sofie. She no longer tensed and jumped with each spank, even after he praised her and went back to the gentler but not gentle spanks of before.

Heat spread from her ass to the rest of her body. She felt warm and soft all over. Well, everywhere but her butt, which felt raw and hot.

A soft muffled feeling muted everything except the feel of his hands and the sound of his voice.

In all the world, it was only them. Two figures on a canvas where the background hadn't yet been sketched in. They were alone in a vast, soft whiteness, with no place or time to anchor them down or pull them apart.

He released her wrist, and she tensed her arm muscles to keep her arm across her back the way he wanted it.

"Turn your head."

She did, blinking open watery eyes as he brushed her hair away from her face.

"How do you feel, Sofie?"

"Floaty," she said on a sigh as the backs of his fingers brushed her cheek.

His fingers went still, and maybe if she hadn't felt so soft and floaty, she would have worried about that.

"And your pretty ass?"

"Hurts."

His chuckle made her smile.

"I need more than that, Angel."

"It feels hot and achy. It's not stinging anymore though."

"Good girl," he murmured, and she felt the praise all the way down to her toes.

"You slipped into subspace beautifully," he murmured. "But I don't want you to go quiet on me."

"I won't, Sir."

"Okay." He stroked her ass once more. "Then get on your knees so I can fuck your mouth."

SEVEN

ANDREI GUIDED Sofie as she slid off his lap to kneel on the floor between his feet.

Under different circumstances, he would have gotten a cushion for her rather than letting her kneel on cold, unforgiving concrete, but right now, he didn't bother.

He was so fucking aroused he might only last two thrusts, and then he'd have her back in his arms.

Andrei slid a hand into her hair, cradling the curve of her skull as he remained sitting, knees spread on either side of her kneeling form.

She tipped her head back into his palm, looking up at him with veiled eyes, her mouth parted, lips full and pink.

His angel on her knees, needy and submissive and ready to take his cock.

Later, he promised himself. Later, he would savor this. There would be subtilties and tone shifts in the way he took her mouth. Now wasn't the time for it. Now, it was time to connect with her, to possess her, in a primal way.

Andrei leaned back, fishing a condom out of his pocket, then held it out to her.

Sofie took it with a delightfully confused expression, bowing her head over the foil packet.

Andrei's lips twitched as he watched her. "Are you reading the instructions?"

She stilled. "Should I not?"

"No, by all means."

His lips twitched again when she carefully ripped the package open right along the dotted line printed on the foil.

Her head jerked up at the sound of his zipper, and he watched her first look at his face, then his crotch, then away, her cheeks pink with a blush.

She was a wonderful, surprising mix of innocent and wanton. He'd never before played with someone who was both an experienced submissive yet reacted so innocently, seemingly not jaded or cynical about the power dynamic.

Andrei stood, and she had to lean back so he didn't knock into her. Reaching into his pants, he freed his cock.

The air felt cold, especially given that the tip of his dick was wet from leaking pre-come. Teeth gritted against the cold, he shoved his pants halfway down his ass and then sat once more, his cock nearly touching his stomach he was so erect.

Sofie was looking at his cock.

She looked nervous.

It was probably an act, but fuck, he loved it.

"Nervous?" he asked, but his voice was husky with desire, so it didn't sound faux mocking the way he wanted.

"Yes," she answered with simple honesty.

"You're still going to take my cock in that pretty mouth," he commanded. "Put the condom on."

Sofie raised the condom, carefully placing it on the head of his dick without any skin-to-skin contact. Andrei gripped the edge of the trunk to keep himself from grabbing her hand and wrapping it around his dick.

She started to roll the condom on, but it didn't get far.

Now, there was an occasional light brush of her fingers against his shaft, and that was enough to distract him from figuring out what was wrong.

Finally realizing there was a problem, he looked down to see she'd put the condom on upside down.

With a frustrated noise, he moved her hands away from his cock, flipped the condom over, and rolled it on with quick, sure movements. Now wondering if she was stalling on purpose hoping for another punishment, he once more gripped her hair, this time sliding his hands through the strands and making a fist.

She made a needy sound when he tightened his fingers, her head tipping up.

"No, no, Angel. That's not where your head goes."

Andrei gripped his dick with his free hand, angling it away from his stomach even as he drew her toward him. Sofie's hands briefly landed on his thighs, bracing herself, but fell away as he drew her closer.

Andrei had to close his eyes when he felt her exhaled breath wash over the tip of his cock. She was too close, too perfect.

A sound of near pain was torn from him as her lips pressed against the head of his cock. She kissed his dick, almost chastely, before parting her lips and taking him in her mouth.

Abruptly, she pulled back. "Oh. It's flavored."

"Pineapple," he said with a knowing smirk, giving her hair a gentle tug.

She kissed the tip of his dick again, this time quicker to take him into the warm wetness of her mouth, but then she stilled.

Her tongue tapped against his glans with teasing, tentative motions, and he used his hold on her hair to force her head down, and more of his cock into her mouth.

Her teeth grazed the vein on the underside of his cock and he hissed his displeasure. "No teeth, Sofie."

She made an apologetic noise, then started working her tongue along his shaft.

When he pushed in a little deeper, she gagged slightly. He wasn't that deep, so it must have been the angle.

Sofie's hand came up between them to grip the base of his dick. He wished he'd taken off his pants—they were in the way. He wished he weren't already so close to the edge that he could savor this. Tease both of them.

She made a needy sound, and it spiked his desire to the point his teeth clenched.

"Move," he growled. "Work my cock until I come."

He heard her noisy inhale through her nose, and then she took more of him. The sensitive head of his cock bumped the back of her mouth, then slid along the soft, slick skin of her throat.

She gagged again, harder, and pulled back sharply. He gave her a second, then pressed on the back of her head. Gentle, not insistent. A patient command.

Suck my cock, but take all the time you need.

She took him deep again, again gagging. This time, he frowned. Did she not normally do oral? She'd specifically mentioned it, but what she was doing felt tentative and chaotic.

"Angel..."

She looked up at him, head of his cock in her mouth, and the sight nearly undid him.

"If you can't do this right now, we can stop." Maybe she was having trouble transitioning from submitting to a spanking, to offering submission in a more active way.

Her eyes widened, and she shook her head, his cock head making her cheeks bulge out momentarily in a way that shouldn't have been adorable but was.

Adorable.

He was momentarily dumbstruck at realizing he'd used that word, when he was definitely not the one who called things adorable unless he was mocking.

His distraction was short-lived when she popped her head up for a minute, licked her lips, and then took him deep in one swift movement.

Slowly Sofie built herself into a steady rhythm, her head bobbing up and down. Every so often, she'd gag slightly but didn't stop. His concern for her muted some of his pleasure, but he couldn't deny he enjoyed the feeling of her throat clenching the tip of his cock when she took him deep.

The pressure and heat, the wet sound, and best of all, the sight of her on her knees with his cock in her mouth had him breathing unevenly, his hips working in small movements to match the motion of her head.

"I need to be deeper." He was balanced on the edge of orgasm, needing something to push him over. "Take a breath."

She stilled, then inhaled through her nose. The head of his cock still in her mouth, the inner edge of her teeth barely nudging the crown.

Andrei thrust up as he pulled her head down, his cock hitting the back of her throat and sliding down. He felt her gag but held her there, pushing past. Her throat worked around the head of his dick, the parts of his shaft that had yet to feel her warm lips finally passing into the softness of her mouth.

The orgasm jerked through him and he pumped once as he felt the first spurts fill the condom, the tightness of her throat around him what he'd needed. But Andrei wasn't an animal, and when he felt the pressure and push as she once more gagged, he pulled back so only the head of his dick was inside her. Reaching down, he worked his own shaft with hard strokes to finish out the orgasm.

He let out one final guttural sound, head tipped back, teeth clenched.

The ferocity of the orgasm surprised him. This was far from the most skilled blowjob he'd ever experienced, but it still rocked him.

Andrei looked down, kneading her scalp with the hand still tangled in her hair. He gently eased her head back, and when she hesitated, tightening her lips around the crown, he grinned.

"Greedy girl."

Drool coated her chin, and there were damp trails down her chest too. He stopped her, gripping her wrist, when she went to wipe it away.

"Sir?"

"Not yet. We're almost done, but there's one more thing I want."

She looked both expectant and patient, as if she'd wait for him forever.

Andrei stood and side-stepped, leaving her on her knees. With quick movements, he first removed the condom, taking it to the garbage can. Then he repositioned the trunk against the glass and relocked the wheels. He crooked a finger at her.

His angel started to rise, but he made a warning sound.

"No. Crawl to me."

She shivered, then bent forward. Her hair was more gold than white in this lighting as she crawled toward him.

Andrei sat, scooting back as far as he could on the seat while still keeping his feet on floor.

She knelt between his spread feet, but he patted his thigh. Gripping one of his legs for balance, she rolled to her feet, then bent forward, clearly preparing to go face down over his lap once more.

He stopped her, instead turning her to face away from

him before pulling her down onto his thighs. She whimpered when her abused bottom made contact with his lap.

Banding an arm around her waist, he gripped her right leg, hooking it over the outside of his own. Then he repeated the motion with the other leg, spreading her wide and keeping her that way with his own legs.

Finally, Andrei leaned back, shoulders and the back of his head against the glass. His upper body was reclined, and at least partially supported.

His left arm around her meant that she came with him as he moved, resting against his chest, her head tucked under his chin.

He adjusted his left arm, hand cradling one breast so he could tease her nipple.

"Comfortable, Angel?"

"Yes, Sir."

"Good." He nudged her head to the side with his chin, which allowed him to dip his chin and get a nice view down the length of her naked body. Ideally, he'd have a mirror in front of them so he could see her pretty pussy, which he hadn't gotten to look at and visually explore. There was probably a mirror in one of the set-up playrooms, or among the boxes of supplies one floor up, but he wasn't going to waste time going to look.

Andrei kissed her temple, a tender counterpoint to what he did next.

Andrei's right hand darted between her thighs, gripping her pussy, his fingers pressing hard against soft, wet flesh. She gasped, back starting to arch until he applied pressure with the forearm braced diagonally on her torso.

He rubbed her pussy hard with the whole of his hand, giving her physical sensation but without the precision he knew she needed.

"Andrei," she whimpered, and he didn't give a fuck that she was using his name. A different sub, he might have used that as an excuse to throw in a little pain, but with her, all he wanted was to see her come apart in his arms.

He tugged her nipple with one hand, while two fingers of the other hand slid between her pussy lips. She was soft, slick, and hot. Reaching down, he pushed just one finger into her. She was just as tight as she had been before, and tensed, only to relax when he curled his finger, finding and pressing on her G-spot.

"Oh, that... Oh!"

He played until he found out exactly how she liked her G-spot touched—hard pressure with little back and forth rubs.

Sofie moaned, turning her head toward him and tipping her face up so her nose was pressed against his neck and he felt her hot, panting exhales.

The way she sought what almost seemed like comfort from him, even as he was the one who both hurt and pleasured her made him smile.

Sliding his finger out of her, he trailed it up the smooth valley of her sex to her clit. He stroked her once, twice, then settled in, his finger circling her clit in soft, steady rotations.

"Sir, please," she whimpered.

"Please what, Angel? What do you want?"

"I want..."

He couldn't see her well enough to detect a blush, but he could hear it in her voice.

"No, Angel, you won't get away with that." He spread his legs, opening hers farther, then slapped her pussy in gentle punishment. With her labia spread open by the position of her legs, his middle finger had landed directly on her clit.

Sofie cried out, trying to twist away as he held her down.

"You're going to tell me how you want to come. How

you want to come all over my fingers and then watch me lick your taste off my hand."

"Yes, yes," she panted. "I want that. I want to come. I want to come while you touch me."

He rewarded her obedience by resuming the steady circling of her clit.

He knew she was close when she went statue-still, the small rolling motion of her hips stopped and her breath held in her chest.

He rolled her nipple in sync with the stimulation of her clit, slow and steady.

"Breathe," he commanded when she'd been still too long.

Her breath puffed against his neck as she exhaled.

"Keep breathing." He shifted the hand on her breast, instead pressing it over her lower abdomen, just above her mound. "I want you to breath deep, pull the air down into your body. Pull the air toward my hand."

He felt the shift in her muscles as she obeyed, felt the rise and fall as she inhaled and exhaled.

"Does it feel like you aren't as close to coming now?"

She hesitated, then nodded, bumping her face against his neck.

"Tensing, tightening those pussy muscles, that makes the orgasm come faster, doesn't it?"

"I… I don't know."

He smirked, though she couldn't see it. "By tightening your muscles, you're bringing yourself closer to orgasm. You're choosing." Hot dark need—need for control, need to pleasure her—swept over him. "You don't choose when you come. I do." Andrei knew his voice was too low, tone almost angry. Subs before had told him that they thought he was mad at them based on his voice when things got really intense.

"I come only when you let me," Sofie breathed out, and

her acceptance, the fact that his sweet angel hadn't been afraid of his sudden intensity made him want to hold her even tighter, dominate and touch her in every depraved way he could think of.

He pressed harder on her lower belly and fractionally increased the pace of the clit manipulation.

Her breathing became uneven, occasionally catching and stuttering.

"Sir, I'm close. I have to tell you that. I have to tell you I'm close."

Though she'd addressed him, it felt like the second half of what she said was her talking to herself. Reminding herself.

"You don't need my permission to come, because you have it. If you come, it's always, always, because I chose it. I used this sweet, soft body in all the ways it needs to be touched, in pleasure or pain." He shifted his hand from her belly to her nipple, pinching hard.

"Please, please," she pleaded. Her legs were shaking, the muscles twitching. He could both see the slight tremor and feel it from where her limbs were hooked over his.

The urge to order her to come, to come now, rode him. It was something he hadn't felt in a long time, because he'd learned that sometimes the order actually had the opposite effect as the sub worried about being obedient, and got in their own head about it. What was it about this woman that seemed to strip away all his strategies? His angel was reducing him to his raw, base form.

She inhaled sharply, perfectly still, her knees pressing against the outside of his own, so he had to actively tighten his own thigh muscles to keep their legs spread. He slipped his finger down her entrance, gathering more of her arousal fluid, and she whimpered piteously.

"Close, Angel?"

Her answer was a soft guttural sound as she exhaled,

only to inhale slowly. Her hips rolled, working in small, gentle thrusts. He pressed hard on her mound with the heel of his hand, holding her in place as he kept up the steady, soft circling of her clit.

The only sound was her breathing and the slick, wet sound of flesh moving over flesh.

Then she was there, her body tensed and tight, her head pressing hard into his neck and shoulder.

She was utterly silent as her body bowed up, pretty breasts thrust high, her legs shaking so hard they made his vibrate.

Like the string of a drawn bow, she was a tense, tight curve, until the pinnacle of release allowed her to relax.

Sofie went limp, her body thumping down on top of his. He pressed his fingertips on either side of her clit, grounding her through the final ripples of her release.

Then she started to cry.

EIGHT

SOFIE SLAPPED a hand over her mouth to muffle the sound of her crying. The sobs had come on unexpectedly, their ferocity shocking, though pale in comparison to the power of the orgasm she'd just had.

What was she doing? This was so embarrassing…

Sofie snapped her legs closed, trapping Andrei's hand against her sex. She tried to turn to the side, both so his hand would move and so she could curl up into a ball of pathetic embarrassment, but all that did was cause his fingers to rub against her orgasm-sensitive clit.

A strange sound—half sob, half moan of pleasure—escaped her, only partially muffled by her hand.

The world spun as Andrei took control, turning her so she was sideways on his lap, her ass in space between his spread thighs. That meant moving his hand away from her sex, and she made a small sound of protest without meaning to.

That same hand gripped her wrist, forcing her hand down from her mouth.

"Don't hide from me," he scolded softly.

"I don't know why I'm c-crying."

"Don't you?"

Once more, the world spun, this time as he stood. Sofie wrapped her arms around his shoulders, holding on as he carried her.

"Grab a blanket for us," he said as he crouched by a set of low wooden drawers.

With one hand, she pulled a drawer open, grabbing out a soft, fluffy blanket. She held it in her lap as he stood with a grunt of effort.

She'd never been carried before, and wondered if she was too heavy. She should tell him to put her down but... but she didn't want to be put down. She wanted him to hold her in his arms. Wanted to feel safe and protected.

It was madness that he was the one she felt safe with, when he was the reason she felt naked far beyond lack of clothes.

He returned to the wide padded bench he'd pushed up against the glass and set her down on her feet, but only for a moment. To her surprise, he sat cross-legged, back against the glass, then pulled her into his lap before spreading the blanket over her.

"Wait," she said, sitting up. She shook out the blanket then tugged his shoulders so he leaned forward.

"The glass is cold," she said as she slid the blanket around him.

Darting a glance at his face, she saw his eyes widen in surprise as she finished protecting him from the cold glass. Settling back into his lap, she pulled the edges of the blanket around herself. It was just barely big enough.

"Taking care of me, Angel?" he murmured against her hair as she wiggled until she was comfortable, head tucked into his neck.

"Yes. As long as the blanket stays over my toes."

He immediately grabbed the bottom edge of the blanket and tucked it under her feet, his hand staying there, his fingers holding the blanket against the ball of one foot, his thumb smoothing over the top in slow sweeps.

The logistics of getting the blanket had dried her tears, but now the feel of that simple, almost absent-minded touch on her foot brought tears to her eyes once more.

Quiet, quiet, quiet, she chanted silently.

"Cry if you need to," Andrei murmured, proving she wasn't fooling him.

"I was trying to be quiet," she sobbed. "It didn't work."

His low laugh rumbled through her, and fresh arousal stirred in her gut.

"I don't know why I'm crying." She rubbed her cheeks against his shirt to dry them. "I'm not sad. And I almost never cry, anyway."

"Well that explains it, doesn't it? If you never cry, never relinquish control and give in to your emotions, then when you finally give control to me…" He paused. "Control to a Dom, I mean. Then you can cry."

"Oh," she said softly, then quickly added, "of course."

They were quiet for a moment, her tears dried, a soft, warm lethargy all that remained.

"Did you try the shrimp?" he asked unexpectedly.

"The shrimp?"

"At the museum party."

"Oh! No, I was too excited." She sat up enough to look at him. "Were they good?"

"Delicious. I ate four and would have had four more."

"Why didn't you?"

"Well you see, I was hanging back, enjoying myself with food and drink while Landon went and got his girl."

Sofie's stomach clenched with jealousy. Not that she wanted to be Landon's girl. But to be someone's girl, to have someone care enough to follow her, try and find her…

"I was pretty sure I wasn't going to have to do anything except maybe follow Landon here in his car if he ended up needing the van. Otherwise, I was going to spend a day or two in Amsterdam before heading home."

"Why would he need the van?" Sofie propped her elbow on his shoulder, cheek in her palm. The posture made his lips twitch.

"If Colette didn't come willingly." Andrei arched an eyebrow. "The van was set up to have an unwilling woman step in it."

"That's…not good." Sofie tried to keep her face straight, but her lips twitched. "You shouldn't know how to set up a kidnapping van."

Andrei grinned. "It's even a white van."

"Like in the TV shows!" Sofie couldn't help but do a little excited wiggle.

The blanket would have fallen off if Andrei hadn't wrapped his other arm around her and used that hand to hold the blankets together.

"People always do crime and kidnapping in those vans," she finished.

"Do crime…" Again, his brow arched. "That's why you were too excited to eat at the museum. Do a little crime."

"I didn't steal anything," she pointed out.

"Then you should have had some of the shrimp."

Sofie laughed, snuggling back into his lap. Once her head was safely tucked under his chin, she let her smile widen into a foolish grin.

She'd just done witty banter with a sexy man.

The bubbly happy feelings mellowed to a lethargy. Time passed, though she wasn't sure how much. So much of her life was quiet unless she actively filled it with noise, but this quiet was different. It wasn't still and solemn. This quiet was warm and soft.

She realized she still felt floaty, though not as intensely as she had after the spanking and while he used her mouth.

Sofie licked her lips, remembering the feel and taste of him.

Her pussy pulsed with fresh need, her nipples hardening.

A terrible thought occurred to her and she sat up abruptly, knocking his chin with her head as she did.

Andrei grunted in pain, a grimace marking his features.

"Did that hurt? I'm sorry."

"It's fine, I didn't need the tip of my tongue."

Sofie's eyes widened. "Let me see." She grabbed his chin, trying to pull his mouth open.

It had worked when he did it to her, but Andrei's mouth didn't open. His brow rose, his eyes sparkled with amusement, but his mouth remained closed.

Sofie pulled down his lip, but all that got her was a view of his bottom teeth. It was only when he started to laugh that she got a look in his mouth.

"No blood and your tongue looks fine."

"Thank you, Doctor," he murmured.

Sofie had never really seen the appeal of medical fetish until that moment. Her nipples tightened as she imagined Andrei with a stethoscope around his neck as he told her to spread her legs so he could examine her.

"I don't want aftercare," she blurted out. Realizing this was aftercare was what had made her sit up so precipitously.

The amusement dropped from his face. "Aftercare is a nonnegotiable."

"But I don't want to be done!"

His expression softened. "I see."

"Colette and Landon aren't done yet, so we have time, right?"

"We do."

"Good." Sofie tried to shrug off the blanket, but Andrei tightened the arm around her, holding her against his chest.

"You're still coming down off the scene. We'll wait."

"I don't want to wait," she grumbled. "I should have realized when you talked about the shrimp." He'd been easing her out of the scene by having a normal conversation.

The thought had her trying to slip away so she could kneel at his feet once more. Show him she was still ready, or maybe ready again, to submit to him.

This time when he clamped her against his chest, her nipple rubbed against his shirt. Now, all she could think about was getting him to touch and play with her nipples again.

"Do you want to hear about the time Landon was an asshole to Colette and didn't do her aftercare so I had to?"

Sofie froze, thoughts of nipple play vanishing. "You and Colette… You scened?"

"No, but Landon questioned Colette during one of their scenes."

"And that's…bad?"

"Of course."

The frown in his voice made her wince, realizing that was the wrong thing to say.

"Mid-scene, he switched from being Master Landon to Agent Malik, questioning her while she was in subspace. She, rightly, stopped the scene, but here is the best part. They ended up fighting in the hall, which means I got to watch her throw a butt plug at his head."

Sofie laughed, but the mention of the butt plug didn't help her arousal levels.

"Wait." She peered at him. "You questioned me about crime."

"Did I? What question did I ask?"

She opened her mouth, then closed it again. He was right. He hadn't actually asked a question.

"Tell me the rest of the story about you and Colette," she demanded, stomach tight.

Andrei leaned his head back against the glass, looking at her with half-lidded eyes. "Later that night, she was wandering the hall. I thought it was delayed sub drop, but she admitted Landon hadn't done aftercare with her—and to be fair, she'd used her safe word and told him to never touch her again."

"So you did…this? With her?" Sofie would have motioned to their current position if her arms hadn't been trapped in the cocoon of the blanket.

"Yes, I gave her the physical comfort she needed—"

There was no denying it, Sofie was jealous. And felt very small. Colette was bold, beautiful, and fearless. She lived a big, wonderful life.

Sofie's life before tonight was quiet and small. And once Colette and Landon appeared, it would go back to being quiet and small. Maybe she should be worried about getting arrested, but she wasn't. Everything she did was a gray area, and thanks to Andrei's intervention, she hadn't actually managed to steal anything tonight.

"—and then helped her find straps so she could tie Landon to the bed."

Sofie jerked her head up. This time, Andrei moved in time to avoid her cracking her head against her chin.

"What?"

Andrei's grin was wicked, his eyes bright as he explained how Colette hadn't known what to do because in the heat of their argument, she'd told Landon to never touch her again. So Andrei had suggested she touch him, then helped her find the straps she needed.

"To tie him to the bed," Sofie said slowly.

"Yes."

"And fuck him."

"Yes."

Sofie licked her lips, eyeing Andrei as she pictured doing that to him. Having him naked and at her mercy. Her breath quickened with arousal, except... Except she had no idea what she'd actually do with him if she had him like that.

Andrei released her foot, his hand traveling up her leg to her knee. Then it skipped over to her breasts, cupping one and lazily rubbing his thumb over her nipple.

Sofie arched back, offering herself.

"Are you a switch?" he asked as he tugged her nipple.

"No?"

"Not sure?"

"I've never tried," she said honestly.

"I see. So you're not sure if the idea of having a partner at your mercy is because you want control, or because..." He leaned in, lips brushing her cheek, her ear. "That first orgasm wasn't enough. You need more. Need to come again. And you think you can get what you need if you could ride my cock."

She nodded frantically, paused, shook her head, then nodded again.

"No, tell me," he scolded, pulling hard on her nipple.

She yelped. "Yes, I want to come again. No, I don't think I'd get what I need if I were in charge of riding your cock. I wouldn't know what to do."

"Wouldn't know what to do if you had to top?"

That wasn't exactly what she meant, but she nodded.

"If you need to ride...then you'll ride."

NINE

COOL AIR HIT HER WARM, naked body as Andrei released the edges of the soft blanket and she shivered, instinctively tucking into him. This time, Andrei didn't let her cuddle against him. Leaning forward, he forced her to lean back against his arm as his head bent, his lips fastening on her nipple. She sucked in a breath as he sucked hard on first one, then the other. When his mouth lifted, the air against her wet nipples made her shiver once more, the areola ruching tight around the hard, pink tip.

Andrei shifted her off his lap and stood.

Not sure what to do, Sofie got to her knees, legs slightly spread, and watched him. Replaying his words, nerves twisted her gut, because she didn't really know what he'd been implying when he said, "If you need to ride, then you'll ride."

If he expected her to know what to do if he just lay on a bed, cock out, they would both be disappointed.

She half expected him to make a bed magically appear, so frowned when he brought over what looked like a modified, heavy-duty sawhorse. She had a few collapsable sawhorses in her studio she used to set up large work tables when needed, but this one was both taller, wider, and sturdier.

The wide top piece was covered in a matte fabric, though not padded like the trunk. The rungs on the sides were mounted horizontally, like little platforms rather than in line with the black wood legs. It wasn't a spanking bench she didn't think, because didn't those have two different platforms—one for legs, one for chest? And usually the leg parts stuck off the back.

Her confusion deepened when he brought over a heavy black case. Setting it down, he undid latches on all four sides, then lifted the top half off. The first thing he removed was a long extension cord. After that, a heavy black item that looked like half of a cylinder, the side profile a half circle.

He set the half cylinder on the top of the sawhorse, which was just barely wide enough to accommodate it. He spent some time fiddling with the underside, presumably attaching the half circle item to the sawhorse. Once he was satisfied, he plugged the extension cord into what must have been a piece of machinery, then unwound the cord as he walked it to the wall and plugged it in.

Sofie leaned forward, trying to see more details as she wracked her memory for something that looked like this.

The final piece of preparation was for Andrei to adjust the height of the side rungs, raising them up until they were just below the top piece.

"Come here, Angel." The command wasn't hard, but it was resolute. There was no question that she would obey.

Submission swept down her body, an almost physical sensation. She closed her eyes swaying for a moment as she let herself feel it. Sink into it.

Sofie shifted so she was sitting on the edge of the trunk, toes braced on the cold floor. "Do you want me to crawl, Sir?"

"Yes."

Obediently she slid to her hands and knees, crawling across the floor to him. She stopped with her fingertips only centimeters from his shoe and rubbed her cheek against his leg. His hand tangled in her hair, massaging her scalp before making a fist. Her scalp prickled and she exhaled slowly.

"Up."

This time, she rose smoothly, moving with his hand as he tugged her up.

"Up," he said again.

Sofie stared at the curved machine mounted to the top. Slowly, she raised her knee, bracing it on the platform piece and then hiking herself up, so both knees rested there. He placed them a little too high because as she bent to face down over the curve, she almost tipped over the other side.

"What are you…" Andrei's hands caught her waist, tugging her up.

"Trying for another spanking?"

"No, Sir." She hid her wince of embarrassment that she'd guessed wrong.

"Oh, you don't know what this is?" He patted the machine.

Slowly, she shook her head, since there was a very poor likelihood that she'd get away with lying.

"I'll be the first Dom to strap you to a Sybian?"

The name rang a bell, like she'd read about it in one of the erotic stories she liked, but she didn't remember what it did.

"Sofie," he barked, and she realized she hadn't answered him.

"Yes, Sir. You'll be the first."

"Good. Straddle it."

He liked that he was the first to do something to her. Maybe that meant…

Sofie lost her train of thought as Andrei helped to guide her into position so she was kneeling astride the Sybian, legs spread wide. With the kneeling platforms raised almost to the height of the top of the sawhorse, there were several centimeters of space between her sex and the Sybian.

Andrei reached beneath her and casually spread her pussy lips with one hand. He gave her clit a quick stroke, and she tipped her face to the ceiling and moaned in pleasure.

"Sit down on it. Good. Now up."

She obeyed, watching curiously as he went to the case, though his body blocked her view. He came back with a long rectangular silicone piece. A hump ran down the center of it. There was a patch of small rounded studs, and a slight rise just behind that point.

"Lean back."

She reached behind herself, bracing her hands behind her ass as Andrei bent to attach the panel to the top of the Sybian, his hands brushing her pussy as he worked it into place.

"Sit forward."

When she did, the bumpy bit pressed against her clit, while that slight rise was now nestled against her entrance. Not enough to penetrate but enough to make her desperately aware of how much she wanted to be penetrated.

She rocked her hips, working herself against the new piece...

Until he gently slapped her breast and gave her a stern look.

"You don't have permission to play yet."

"Yes, Sir," she whispered.

He slowly walked around her. "I want to see what you look like when you're coming endlessly, but still frustrated because your pussy is empty. I want to watch yourself grinding down trying to get the penetration. Once you've come enough..." He stopped at her side, looking up at her as he casually stroked and tugged her pussy lips. "And begged enough...then maybe I'll switch to the dildo piece."

He pointed to the box and from this height, she could see down into the case. Several other rectangular silicon skins rested inside. One had a curved dildo set on an angle, another had an oval bulk atop of short stock—probably a plug, and the last had two dildos for double penetration.

Now she understood what he meant by ride. She was going to ride this machine first without penetration, and then with it. She swallowed the urge to protest. To tell him that she wanted him inside her. His cock, his fingers. As long as it was him, and not some unfeeling toy.

Then he turned the machine on, and all protests and worries were forgotten. The Sybian vibrated far stronger than anything in her toy box. The nubs pressing against her still-sensitive clit were almost painful.

With a gasp, she sat up, putting space between herself and the machine. She just needed a moment.

A sharp sting to her breast had her opening eyes she closed only moments ago.

Andrei watched her with hard glittering eyes, a riding crop in one hand. She looked down at the faint pink spot on her breast where he'd struck her.

"You can wiggle and lean forward and back all you want, but you stay on. Your pussy stays in contact with the toy at all times. Next time you disobey and try and escape the scene, I'll strike your nipple."

Sofie whimpered low in her throat, though her pussy clenched at the idea. She wanted that. Wanted him to hurt her nipples.

"No, Angel. I won't be gentle, it will hurt and pull you out of the orgasm unless you're a very committed masochist."

She nodded more in acknowledgment than agreement.

He studied her for a moment. "Arms up. Hands behind your head."

She obeyed, only to curl forward with a cry when the crop landed hard on her left nipple. She had to dig her fingers into her own hair, pulling hard, to stop herself from reaching down to cover her now-throbbing nipple.

"Sit up," he said gently. "So I can punish your other nipple."

With a whimper, she straightened. "I didn't try and get away. I'm still on it."

"I know, but I could see that the thought of having your nipples cropped wasn't a deterrent. I want to make sure you understand that when I intend to punish you, I will use more pain than is comfortable. True pain, not pleasure pain."

Their gaze locked, held, and then she lowered hers. "I understand, Sir."

"Good. Take a breath."

She inhaled, held it, only to release the air as a scream when he cropped her right nipple even harder than he had the left.

This time, she didn't fold forward, instead keeping her position, her elbows up and spread wide, her breast entirely vulnerable. Fine trembles ran up and down her arms and legs, and her panting exhales contained soft pained noises.

"Well done," he murmured, the praise helping dull some of the stinging pain. "Now you're going to be my good girl, aren't you?"

"Yes, Sir." She swallowed and looked at him. "You're not disappointed, are you?"

"Never," he said fervently. "You're beautiful. Perfect. Even if you lift that pretty pussy up again and again, until your nipples are red and raw from punishments earned, I won't be disappointed."

She relaxed at that, sinking down even harder onto the Sybian.

Andrei slid one hand into his pocket, and the machine turned on.

This time, she gritted her teeth, bracing herself for that first shock of pleasure. The nubs against her clit were perfectly spaced, one on either side. She wiggled until a third nudged the underside of her clit.

The sensation was so strong—a bone-deep rumble—she actually thought she wouldn't be able to come from it, though this was pleasurable in and of itself.

Only a few minutes in, her body proved her wrong. The orgasm slammed through her, hard and sudden. There was no slow buildup, just a constant pleasure that turn into a muscle-clenching pleasure.

Sofie nearly tumbled off as the orgasm quaked through her. Andrei lunged to grab her just as she managed to reach down and grab the top piece of the horse. Now, she was leaning forward, which only pressed her clit harder against the vibrating panel. She felt the vibration not just on her skin, not just on the glans of her clit but all through her lower body. The deep parts of the clit, her vagina, her muscles low in her body—they were all rumbling with the vibration.

Mad, nonsensical words tumbled out of her mouth. Pleas and curses in a mix of languages, as a second orgasm came on the heels of the first.

"Andrei, help," she finally managed between pants.

He was there, helping her to sit up, though once she was upright, his hands gripped her hips, holding her down.

She whimpered, tipping her pelvis to give her clit a break.

"My good girl," he murmured, eyes fixed on her pussy. "My beautiful angel." His hand went into his pocket and the vibration eased just enough that after a few moments she perversely wanted more.

"I want to restrain you," he said half to himself as she started to rock herself forward and back.

"Oh, yes please." She didn't know what to do with her hands, and the idea of having something to pull against was a relief.

A moment later, padded straps were buckled around her wrists, short chains leading to matching cuffs on her ankles so each hand was held down close to her foot.

It was the restraints going on, the relief of not having to think about what to do with her arms, that pushed her into the third orgasm.

"Open," he said when she bowed her head at the end of that one.

It took her a moment to lift her face to see what he meant, her hair sliding against her cheek.

He held a bit-style gag in one hand.

"You're clenching your teeth."

Sofie didn't even think. She opened her mouth, and he placed the rubbery stick between her teeth, buckling it in place behind her head.

"You can still make noise. Still make yourself understood. Tell me your safe word."

"Rembrandt," she mumbled awkwardly.

"Good." Then that devilish glint was back in his eye… and he turned up the vibrations.

Her clit felt huge and raw, but needy, her sex so terribly empty. She would beg as he'd told her to. Beg him to fill her, and no longer care if it was a dildo or his flesh. She was a being of need and physical sensation, totally and willingly at another's mercy.

Sofie closed her eyes and let go. No worry. No fear. She was safe in his care. Trusted him completely.

The gag, the restraints…she sank deep into that place

she'd found when he spanked her, except now it was more than a disconnected place of peace. Now the space she sank into was awash in pleasure and sensation. Not just peacefully floating but floating in blissful, pleasure-filled surrender.

She was constantly moving now, rocking her hips against the machine in a way she was fairly certain meant that if there had been a dildo, it would be sliding in and out of her. She wanted that desperately.

There was a low-level buzzing in her ears that meant she didn't hear anything. Didn't realize there was a problem until Andrei took a step back, brows raised in surprise and concern.

Sofie was facing the glass walls, looking out at the river, her back to the door. If she'd been thinking straight and not consumed by the deep, constant pleasure, she would have turned to look over her shoulder and see what had caused Andrei to react that like.

But she was too deep in being his obedient, needy sub.

She didn't see what had caused him to fall back in surprise until Colette was far enough into the room to move past her.

Her friend was wearing a short robe, her hair rumpled, her expression murderous. Colette shot Sofie a glance, her expression shifting from rage to guilt and then back again as she looked at Andrei.

Oh.

Oh no.

"You bastard!" Colette raised her hand, clearly to slap Andrei. Landon appeared, confusion marking his expression as he lunged for Colette.

"What the fuck?" Andrei caught Colette's wrist as she swung, stopping her hand centimeters from his cheek.

Sofie yanked at her wrists, desperately needing to get

the gag out so she could stop Colette. But she couldn't. Her hands were bound, the gag mangling her pleas…

And her traitorous body chose that moment to launch into another orgasm.

She watched though half-lidded eyes, whimpering in pleasure, as her friend yanked her wrist out of Andrei's hold.

"How dare you," Colette raged as Landon gripped her waist, pulling her away from Andrei.

Distance might prevent her from hitting Andrei, but it wouldn't stop her words.

"What the fuck is this?" Andrei snarled. "Landon, control your woman."

"Andrei…" Landon's voice rumbled in warning.

Sofie was looking at Colette, willing her to stop. To not say anything that would reveal the lies Sofie had told to get where she currently was.

Which was panting through the downhill side of a bone-rattling orgasm, her entire body thrumming in time with her heartbeat.

"I knew you were an asshole, but not this much of an asshole," Colette snarled at Andrei. "I can't believe you'd scene with her!"

"Why the fuck wouldn't I?" Andrei snapped back, but there was a wariness to the set of his jaw.

Don't say it don't say it don't say it, Sofie willed her friend.

But there was no stopping Colette. She stabbed one finger toward Sofie, as she said, "She's a virgin!"

TEN

MOVEMENT CAUGHT ANDREI'S ATTENTION, and he watched through the glass as Landon and Colette strolled across the empty center of this floor. Colette was leaning into Landon, looking soft and well-used.

A surge of affection filled Andrei. Colette and Landon deserved to be happy, especially Colette, who'd been through hell and back.

The affection turned to confusion when Colette abruptly stopped as she caught sight of him and Sofie, then started running toward him.

Landon stared at her, clearly as confused as Andrei, before following her at a quick walk, but not a run.

Colette burst into the playroom, and Andrei took a step away from Sofie, not wanting to risk Colette knocking into the horse.

He opened his mouth to say something, but Colette came at him fast, one hand raised to slap him.

What the fuck?

"You bastard!" Colette's hand swung toward his face, even as Landon lunged for her.

"What the fuck?" Andrei repeated, out loud this time, catching Colette's wrist before she made contact.

Andrei glanced quickly at Sofie to make sure she was okay. It was unacceptable that Colette was interrupting a scene, pulling his attention away from his sub. Not just because she deserved his attention but because she was physically vulnerable due to the bondage and her position atop the Sybian.

Sofie was tugging at her restraints, and he couldn't tell if her mangled pleas were about the relentless sensation he was forcing her to endure or Colette's interference.

Then she froze, going perfectly still, as her eyes half closed. Another orgasm. He watched her body begin to shiver and shake, and satisfaction slid down his spine.

Colette yanked her wrist out of Andrei's grip, forcing his attention away from his angel.

"How dare you." Colette didn't resist as Landon gripped her waist, yanking her back against him.

"What the fuck is this?" Andrei snarled as anger finally overtook his shock. "Landon, control your woman."

"Andrei…" Landon warned.

But Andrei only raised a brow. Colette was interfering with a scene. She was experienced enough to know better. After this was over, he'd tell Landon what he expected for Colette's punishment, though Andrei was fairly certain she'd just gone through an intense punishment for running away.

"I knew you were an asshole, but not this much of an asshole," Colette snarled.

Andrei jerked, unexpectedly stung by her words. This is why he didn't have friends, because then he gave a shit when they called him an asshole. Strangers could call him an asshole all they wanted.

"I can't believe you'd scene with her!"

Abruptly, Andrei's emotions shifted from hurt to unease.

"Why the fuck wouldn't I?" Andrei snapped defensively.

He had a bad feeling that question wasn't going to be rhetorical. He was going to get an answer, and one he didn't like.

The rumbling sound of the Sybian's motor was a constant presence. Atop the sex saddle, Sofie was pleading…with Colette. His angel was looking at her friend, her expression desperate.

Colette's eyes blazed bright with anger…and panic, he realized. She pointed back toward Sofie. "She's a virgin!"

Andrei froze in shock.

Nothing surprised him. He was cynical and jaded. He always expected the worst from people. Of the possibilities that had started to float through his head, the top of the list had been that maybe Sofie was ill, or had a hidden medical issue, and Colette was panicking that he was being too rough with her.

One time, he'd had a sub who didn't tell him she had a heart condition until after he'd been teasing her breasts with a violet wand for several minutes.

He'd even briefly considered that she might be pregnant —though that was just a different kind of medical condition.

Married was a possibility, though marital status didn't mean a person wasn't also an active player.

"A virgin?" he croaked out.

That had never even crossed his mind.

"Give me the remote." Colette yanked away from Landon, then stuffed her hand into Andrei's pocket, fishing for it.

Andrei backed away, reaching into the other pocket and flicking off the Sybian.

The silence was loud once the machine went quiet, the only sound Sofie's panting breaths.

Andrei looked at her, held her gaze. There was panic and apology in her eyes.

It was true. She was a fucking BDSM virgin.

It was Landon who went to Sofie, quietly asking her permission to touch her before undoing the restraints and draping the blanket they'd used for aftercare over her shoulders.

Andrei wanted to rip Landon's arms off for touching Sofie, even as he wanted to stalk out of the room and never think about, let alone see, his angel again.

Andrei was aware of Colette staring at him, as he stared at Sofie.

"You didn't know," Colette said quietly. "Oh no. Andrei, I'm so sorry. And virginity is, of course, a bullshit patriarchal construction…" Colette started, clearly trying to backpedal.

Andrei shot her a look.

Colette winced and said no more.

Landon had removed Sofie's gag, but she had yet to say anything. She still sat astride the sex toy, and even with the blanket held tight around her body, Andrei could see the fine tremors that ran up and down her body. Her emotions were probably a mess—she'd been deep in the scene and this abrupt halt and emotional shift would have been hard on even the most experienced player.

Of which she was not, because she was a fucking virgin.

But of course, it wasn't her experience or lack thereof that was the real issue.

"You lied to me." Andrei's voice was cold with rage.

"I-I'm sorry," Sofie said, but then she straightened, meeting his gaze. "I didn't actually lie."

Andrei barked out an incredulous laugh. "Every time I

asked you how you like to scene, or what you preferred, you lied."

"I didn't. I...guessed."

"You guessed." Andrei let out a bitter laugh. "You're a fucking BDSM virgin."

Colette and Sofie both winced. Then the women exchanged a look, Sofie shaking her head, eyes wide, while Colette grimaced.

Andrei's stomach sank further. "You're a BDSM virgin."

"Yes," Sofie said, though it hadn't really been a question.

"But you're not a virgin in the vanilla sense. You've had sex before. Whatever definition you want to use. Penetrative, intimacy. You've had sex."

Andrei knew he sounded desperate—his words a plea rather than a question. Landon snort-laughed at his tone. Colette glared at her lover, slapping a hand over his mouth, which only made Landon's eyes sparkle in mirth.

It would have been so easy to take his roiling emotions and channel them into beating Landon's ass, but Andrei kept his attention on his sub.

No. Not his.

And apparently, not a sub.

Not in the way he was used to thinking of subs, as knowledgeable, experienced players.

Sofie held his gaze, her chin high, though her chin and lower lip were quivering. She was scared or upset, and trying to pretend she wasn't.

"No," she said firmly. "I've never had any kind of sex before."

Andrei staggered as if those words had been a physical blow. Fuck. Fuck. All the things he'd done to her. Worse, the way he'd done them.

"I haven't ever had a romantic or sexual partner." Her

words were bold and matter-of-fact, but her expression was raw and pleading.

It made him want to scoop her into his arms, hold her close, and tell her everything would be okay. And that was ridiculous. That wasn't who he was.

"No romantic partner?" Andrei closed his eyes. "Tell me you've at least been kissed."

The silence that followed was deafening.

"Fuck," Landon said quietly, all amusement gone as the magnitude of how completely fucked up this whole situation was became apparent.

"Sir, please," Sofie whispered.

Sir.

He winced. Sofie may not be a sub, but she was sexually submissive, and still in that headspace.

"I'll take care of her," Landon said. "I owe you."

Landon stepped forward, reaching for Sofie, but she shied away from him, almost falling.

Andrei lunged grabbing her by the upper arms. They stared at one another, and the mix of desperation and defiance in her gaze made him want to…

Made him want to put her over his knee.

"That was your first spanking?" he asked roughly.

She nodded.

"It was too hard. Your first time should have been different."

"It wasn't."

"And how would you know?" Anger took over, and he wrapped his arms around her, yanking her off the Sybian gently but not slowly.

He set her feet down, but Sofie clung to him, arms around his shoulders, head tucked under his chin. The part of him that was cold and cruel wanted to push her away. Push her into Landon's arms and wash his hands of the lying virgin.

"Please don't be angry with me," she whispered.

"You lied. No matter what you said or didn't say, you lied and we both know it. If you were really a sub, you'd know how unacceptable that is."

He felt her flinch at his words, and had to ball his hands into fists at his side to keep himself from wrapping his arms around her.

"I didn't think you'd touch me if I told you I hadn't done, uh…anything…before."

"And you'd be right. You let me think you were like Colette, an experienced player."

"I read a lot," she said defensively.

Landon let out another snort-laugh. Andrei yanked the remote out of his pocket and threw it at his friend.

Landon caught it out of the air. "Colette had better aim than that with a plug."

Against his chest, Sofie shivered at the word plug.

Fuck.

At least he hadn't fucked her pussy or ass. Everyone deserved to have a first time that was careful and deliberate. An exploration of what they liked and needed. Andrei's first time hadn't been like that, and look how he'd fucking turned out.

"Let us do her aftercare," Colette urged. "You're upset with her."

Sofie burrowed harder against his chest.

"No." Sofie flinched as he snarled the word, and he both regretted causing it and was darkly satisfied.

"Andrei, please, let us—"

"No, Colette." Landon tugged her against him, wrapping his arms around her in either a hug or restraints, depending on the point of view. "She lied to him, and they need to have a conversation about it. And if this is her first scene, she needs to get the aftercare from her scene partner."

"You were happy enough to let him do my aftercare," Colette said absently, her worried attention on Sofie.

"No. I wasn't. But you told me never to touch you again and threw a butt plug at my head."

Andrei cleared his throat before their banter ramped up any more. "Landon?"

"Yea?"

"Leave."

Landon's face was solemn as he nodded before sweeping Colette into his arms and carrying her out of the playroom.

They didn't go far—just into the playroom next door. The glass between them wasn't a visual barrier but would keep them from hearing his and Sofie's conversation.

Now that they were nominally alone, Andrei wasn't sure what to do. How to handle this.

Anger and guilt both burned low in his gut. He was in shock but looking back, there were signs, which in turn made him feel stupid.

But first, aftercare.

Again.

Andrei led Sofie back to the trunk against the exterior wall with a hand on the small of her back. Some cruel part of him wanted to sit her down and then take care of her without touching her.

But that would hurt Sofie, and as pissed as he was, he didn't want to hurt her.

He wasn't a man who gave second chances. Being lied to should have burned away any tender feelings, but when he glanced down at her tear-stained face, a lock of hair stuck to her wet cheek, and a soft emotion he refused to label slid through him.

Andrei took a seat, pulling her into his lap once more.

This time, he made sure the blanket was securely wrapped around her. Only her head and toes weren't covered by the blanket, and the moment he saw her soft little toes poking out, he grabbed the edge of the blanket and tucked it around her feet.

"Why," he said after a moment.

"Why?"

"Why did you lie?"

"I didn't."

"Don't," he snarled. "Don't try and use semantics. You knew I thought you were an experienced sub."

It wasn't a question, but she nodded.

"Why?" he said again.

"Would you have scened with me if I told you I'd never done it before?"

"No."

She raised her head, meeting his gaze. "That's why. I told you. I read a lot."

He shook his head. "No. The fictional version of BDSM as presented in romance novels with ridiculous premises has nothing to do with real-life BDSM play."

"I mean, surely there's some factually accurate..."

She trailed off as he just stared at her.

"I read a lot...and Colette," she finally confessed. "Not that Colette told me everything. She knows I've never had a romantic or sexual partner before, so she censored. But with the things she did say, I went on forums and message loops of real people."

"Were you interested in BDSM before Colette told you about all this?"

"Yes. I even went to a club."

Andrei's jaw clenched. "I thought you said you hadn't played."

"A public club. A bar." She seemed to be working through the correct English words. "Where people put on scenes, but you can just sit and have a drink."

"Ah."

"I only went once."

"Scared?"

"No. I just…don't get out much."

"A little hard to be a thief if you don't get out much."

"I told you I'm not a thief." She frowned at him as if he were being deliberately stupid.

"You were at that museum to steal a pearl necklace."

"First time."

Andrei wanted to shake her until information that made sense fell out of her pretty mouth. Thinking of her mouth brought him another horrible realization.

"Sofie?"

"Yes?"

"First of all, is your name really Sofie?"

She looked offended. "Of course it is."

His lips twitched. "So lying about being a sub, about having had sex at all, is reasonable. But lying about your name is ridiculous?"

"Yes," she said matter-of-factly.

Andrei couldn't help it; he started to laugh.

"In all that reading, did you ever see that people take on club names, so actually changing your name would be entirely reasonable."

She blushed. Even with her head tucked, he could see the pink of her cheeks.

A virginal blush.

Fuck.

Abruptly he was back to guilty and angry.

"Answer my question. Truthfully."

She flinched at his barking command, but his own emotions were roiling and barely contained.

"I will," she said in a small voice, and he hated it. Hated that she sounded not exactly scared but as if she were trying to curl into herself and disappear.

"Have you even been kissed?"

Sofie froze on his lap, her head ducked. Andrei notched a finger under her chin, forcing her head up.

He'd thought this was her first BDSM experience, learned this was her first sexual encounter of any form.

And she'd repeatedly said she'd never had any romantic or sexual partners.

The sinking feeling from a few moments ago had led him to wonder if maybe, just maybe, there was another first she'd never experienced.

Sofie's gaze met his as he forced her chin up, and he saw the answer to his question in her too-wide eyes, and the blush on her cheeks.

"Fuck." He leaned his head back, eyes closed.

She'd never even been kissed and he'd spanked her. Fucked her mouth. Made her crawl to him.

He was an asshole of the highest order. Not new information—he had cultivated his assholery—but this was a whole different level.

He wasn't solely to blame. He would have never done anything if he'd known she was innocent in a way he'd never been. But still, he'd ignored those odd moments and signs that should have made him stop and ask more questions.

"Fuck," he said again on a sigh.

Sofie slid off his lap. Instinctively he reached out to stop her, to grab her, and pull her back onto his lap. But he halted, fingers curling into the palm of his outstretched hand.

"I'd like to go home now," Sofie said quietly.

Out of the corner of his eye, Andrei saw movement as Colette and Landon both got to their feet, watching Sofie.

"Yes." Andrei rose too, not looking at her as he went and picked her dress up off the floor. "I think it's time for you to go."

ELEVEN

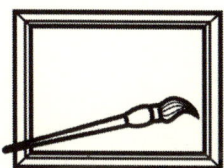

THE DRIVE to the Jordaan District was quiet and tense. Sofie held perfectly still in the passenger seat, despite her throbbing backside. Beside her, Andrei was like an angry cat—quiet, seemingly calm, but there was tension in him that would have been a lashing tail had he actually been a cat.

Sofie had assumed—hoped—that Landon or Colette would drive her home.

But Landon refused to leave Colette to drive Sofie by himself, and Colette was "in no condition" to sit in a car.

Sofie sympathized with that.

But that meant there was no one to drive her but Andrei. Colette had argued and proposed alternatives until Landon quieted her with a kiss and whispered words.

Leaving Sofie and Andrei to head down to Landon's rental car in tense silence. A silence that hadn't changed since.

Time had ceased to exist, or maybe ceased to have meaning, in the club. She'd seen the way the sky lightened over the course of her time with Andrei, but hadn't really processed the meaning.

Now, they were stuck in Amsterdam's famous traffic, the city not really meant for cars.

"Is this the best route?" Andrei said, startling her.

She glanced at him, and he motioned to the map on the screen in the car.

"Oh…I think so?"

His hands tightened on the wheel. "Is driving another thing you've never done?"

Her face burned with embarrassment so deep it was bordering on shame.

"That's not unusual," she said through a tight throat. "There's no need for a car."

Some of the tension faded from his arm muscles. "I suppose there isn't."

Andrei had gone upstairs to the top floor of the club and returned in a soft sweater and casual pants. Sofie was back in her dress, feeling rumpled and overdressed. She'd forgotten her mask back at Club Alibi, but at this point didn't care. Before, she'd planned to keep both the dress and mask a memento of her first theft.

Now, she would burn the dress, despite the hours she'd spent on it. The idea of destroying her own art hurt, but there was some comfort in knowing Colette would keep her dress and mask, so at least some of the things she'd created for this ill-fated plan would survive.

They inched through the city, over narrow bridges and cutting down narrower roads.

Andrei made a cold sound of amusement as they passed a sign.

"Isn't De Wallen the red-light district?"

She raised her chin, hoping she wasn't blushing. "It's the medieval part of the city. It's where Oude Kerk, the oldest building, is."

They were stopped, so Andrei glanced over, brow raised.

"And it's the largest of our prostitution district."

"And you live there."

"No, I live in the Jordaan District. It's close, but not the same."

It looked like he might ask another question, but instead, a muscle in his jaw flexed and he faced forward, hands tightening on the wheel.

Sofie swallowed hard, looking out the passenger window.

Another fifteen minutes, and they were on the road that bordered the Prinsengracht canal, turning away from the water onto a narrow, one-lane road. Tall, narrow row houses crowded close to the street, and several bikes swerved around them, almost scraping the car as they navigated the too-small space left between the vehicle and wall. They didn't even slow down, navigating the street with the fearless confidence of Dutch bike riders.

Andrei cursed in a language she didn't know, and she couldn't stop a smile. He was just…perfect.

What a stupid thought, though the stupidity didn't make it less true.

Andrei was cunning and quick, devilish and yet caring. Part of her wanted to tell him that. To say that she was glad so many of her firsts had been with him. But he didn't want to hear that. He was here to drop her off, drive away, and never see her again.

"I'll get out here." She reached for the door handle.

"No. Where is your house?"

She wanted to argue, but it wasn't like he could back up or turn around. He had to keep going until the end of the street.

"Do you see the break between the buildings? Just up there?" She pointed.

Andrei inched farther down the street. Most of the narrow houses that the Jordaan District were famous for shared walls, the entire street a single solid front. But here, there was a break between two buildings, just wide enough to walk down.

One of the buildings stuck out farther than the other, which is what had concealed the break when viewed from their direction.

"Here," she said, then the little path was clearly visible, and Andrei stopped the car.

She glanced over, even as she put a hand on the handle.

Thank you?

I'm sorry?

Sofie raised her chin, met Andrei's gaze, and said simply, "Goodbye."

The locks clicked just as she tried to open the door.

"I'm not just letting you out," he said, bending a little to look out her window.

He pulled in to the narrow bit of space created by the building that was set back farther from the road. It left enough space on the road for a bike, though not another car.

"You can't park here," she said as he got out.

"I can."

She waited until he'd opened her door to say, "You can't."

"They're welcome to give me a ticket. I'm here on official Interpol business."

Sofie paused, half out of the car, and looked up at him, abruptly reminded that her lies of omission weren't the only reason she'd never see him again.

Andrei cocked a brow, and she climbed the rest of the way out of the car, wobbling a little in her heels. He didn't touch her to steady her, and Sofie told herself she was glad. Andrei did close her car door, but kept distance between them as he followed her down the meter-and-a-half-wide path between the buildings.

It was dark and cool in the shadows, making the light seem startlingly bright when they emerged into the green space at the center of the long narrow block.

Mature trees, fat shrubs, and creeping vines filled the space, the backs of the buildings the walls of the hidden garden. Her path continued for several more meters, the low iron fence that bordered it obscured by greenery, a tree just in front of them concealing her house.

"This is beautiful," Andrei said, pausing to look around.

She glanced back over his shoulder in time to see him close his eyes and take a deep breath.

"I'm there," she said, pointing at the building just visible through the branches of the tree. "Goodbye."

Andrei cocked a brow, shoving a hand into his pocket.

Fine. He could walk her to her door.

Sofie turned and followed the path to her door. Her home was a freestanding building in the middle of all the green. Three stories tall with picture windows on all sides, the footprint of the building was small, though it was more than enough space for her to live and work. Her front door was painted forest green, and the security keypad had been specially made with a brass housing so it matched the hardware.

Sofie typed in the code on the brass-buttoned keypad. The panel slid up, and she bent to the hidden camera so the facial recognition software would work.

Andrei let out a huffing laugh. "Now I need to see inside."

She ignored him and typed in a second code on a six-button keypad just under the camera—this time, the buttons showed symbols rather than numbers—and the lock clicked.

Sofie grabbed the round knob and pushed the door open, preparing to slip in.

She wasn't going to look back. Now that she was almost

home, her emotions were swelling to the point that she couldn't take a deep breath. She was going to take off this dress, curl up, and cry out all the embarrassment and sadness.

Andrei caught the door before she could push it closed.

Sofie turned to look at him through the narrow gap. Both his foot and the hand he had wrapped around the edge of the door would stop it from closing.

She gave it a try. First shoving the door then leaning her whole body weight against it.

The door didn't move. Andrei merely raised a brow.

"Back up so I don't hurt your toes, Angel."

It was his use of the nickname that had her falling back in surprise. The instant she did, he pushed his way inside. Sofie backed up as he entered.

"You can't be in here."

"Why not."

"You don't have…paperwork. You need paperwork to enter my home."

"I'm not here on official business." He started to walk around the ground-floor studio space.

"You said you were." Sofie stepped into his path to stop him. "When you parked the car."

"I lied."

Sofie crossed her arms. "I thought you didn't like lying."

"I lie all the time. Unless I'm topping." His gaze finally shifted from the room to her, a line between his brows showing the start of a frown. "This is…"

Sofie didn't answer, but there was clearly no way to stop him, so she stepped out of the way, turning to glance at her studio, trying to see what he would see.

Windows on all four walls let in light tinted faintly green as it filtered through the vegetation outside.

The center of the large room was open, her easel in a

place of honor in the center. When she was working, there would be a drop cloth under her easel, but now, she was between projects, so the wood floor was bare. Given that she usually went without shoes, there was under-floor heating beneath the wood, which itself covered the original stone floors.

Wood shelving in one corner held sketchbooks, art reference books, and jars of pigment supplies. Some were glass, the exposure to light necessary, while others were brown glass or metal to keep out the light. A long metal counter ran the length of an entire wall, the lower shelf holding jugs of turpentine and linseed oil, along with varnish and less obscure supplies like tallow.

An apothecary cabinet held her brushes, organized by materials. When she first received them, her father had organized them by time period so she wouldn't accidentally use a material unfit for the period of the painting. But now, she knew by heart when hog hair versus badger hair brushes were to be used.

The stairs hugged one wall, the windows in that wall a series of smaller square windows that paralleled the stairs themselves.

Tucked under the stairs was her technology station, with a large monitor, computer, professional scanner, overhead camera, and a small X-ray machine. Everything was set on steel tables or carts with wheels so she could pull them out into the center of the room when needed.

Andrei made a slow loop of the room, stopping to peer at the jar of lupus lazuli chunks, then again to study the soldering iron and bits of metal strewn across the long work counter, leftover from creating the pearl necklace.

Finally he studied her computer setup, and Sofie hid a wince. It was, perhaps, the most incriminating part of her studio, though everything could be explained away if necessary. Her father had made sure of that.

When Andrei didn't move or speak, she took several steps toward him, though she wasn't sure what she was going to do or say.

Her monitor caught her eye, because there was a message displayed on the screen, white text on black.

SOFIE,

Je stelt me teleur. Je weet dat het niet veilig is om je studio te verlaten. Ik had beter verwacht. Er zullen consequenties zijn.

- Vader

SOFIE'S STOMACH KNOTTED, and she pressed a hand to it. She checked Andrei's face, but he seemed to be studying the portable X-ray. The message was in Dutch, not English, so Andrei probably wouldn't understand it. And even if he did, the message, like so many things in Sofie's life, could be explained away. Made to seem like something other than what it was.

The silence stretched, and though she was used to silence, she was used to silence when she was alone. This silence with another person was unbearable.

"Andrei—"

"You're a forger." Andrei turned to face her, and he was smiling. "You're Colette's forger."

"No."

"Yes."

"No."

"You have an X-ray machine."

Sofie shrugged. "I do."

"No one but forgers need to X-ray paintings."

"That's not true. Auction houses, museums—"

"You are neither of those."

"—restorationists," she said louder.

"And are you? A restorationist?"

"I have done restoration work."

Andrei let out a hard laugh. "I knew I should have arrested you."

"For what?" Sofie spread her hands. "You have nothing."

Andrei's gaze hardened and then slid down her body. It wasn't until he licked his lower lip that she felt the shift, and her body started to heat.

"I had something," he said, but it was almost to himself. "Or at least I thought I did."

Sofie didn't know how to answer that, but she understood it. The sense of loss was there, buried under her embarrassment. Loss of what could have been, had she been truthful.

But it never would have been, because he would never have touched her if he knew how innocent she was.

"Painting is not a crime." Tired of wearing the heels, she slipped out of them, toes wiggling happily on the warm wood floor. "Even attempting to recreate a masterpiece is not a crime. It's how art is taught in many schools."

"And the fact that you're friends with a world-class thief?"

"What is it you said Colette says? Allegedly?"

"And that your friend the thief was eyeing a pearl necklace, and you just happen to have jewelry-making supplies?" He gestured back to where the soldering iron rested in its spiral mount, and small pieces of precious metals were laid out on a soft leather mat.

"I'm an artist, but not confined to one medium." She gestured at her dress. "I made this too. My sewing studio is upstairs. Does that make me a forger?"

Andrei stalked toward her, a slow, focused prowl. Sofie held her ground until he was an arm's-length away, and then her instincts took over and she backed up. He backed her all the way up to the wall, slapping his hands on either side of her shoulders to cage her in.

Andrei leaned in close, and some stupid, romantic part of her thought maybe he was going to kiss her. She stared at his lower lip, aching with the need to be kissed.

"I wish you weren't such a liar, Sofie."

Her gaze jerked up to his, and there was hunger and regret in his eyes.

"If I'd told you the truth?"

He caught of piece of her hair, sliding his fingers along it. "Maybe I would have taken you. Maybe the chance to touch an innocent angel would have been too tempting."

Touch me, touch me, touch me.

His gaze hardened as his jaw clenched. "But my soul is not that black. Not yet."

He pushed away from the wall and backed up.

Sofie stayed where she was, mouth parted, breathing deep but too fast.

"Goodbye, Angel."

Andrei raked her with one last look before quietly opening the door and slipping out of her life.

ANDREI LEANED against the driver's door of the rental car, which now sported a large scratch. He both was and wasn't surprised to find out that Sofie was a criminal like her friend.

He'd known she was at the museum for nefarious reasons. He'd thought perhaps she was new to the game. Colette's apprentice. She'd clearly be inexperienced, given that she hadn't blended in well at all.

If only he'd stopped to ask exactly how inexperienced she was.

Once he got back to Club Alibi, he was going to ask

Colette what the fuck she'd been thinking bringing her forger with her on a job.

But first…

Andrei brought up a translation app, and letter by letter typed in the message he'd memorized from her large monitor.

SOFIE,

You disappointment me. You know it isn't safe for you to leave your studio. I expected better. There will be consequences.

- Father

ANDREI'S JAW CLENCHED. This was none of his business. He needed to leave it alone.

But as he got into his car, a stone of worry formed in his gut.

TWELVE

THEY CAME IN THE NIGHT.

Sofie half woke to the faint beep of her alarm system being disabled, but after her sleepless night the evening before and her difficulty falling asleep tonight, she merely rolled over in bed, pulling her pillow over her head.

She didn't realize the danger until the covers were ripped from her body and she was dragged from the bed by one ankle.

She screamed, but it was a high thin sound that cut off when she hit the floor with a thud.

Adrenaline flooded her system as she stared up at three entirely black figures—black clothes, black hood, black full-face masks without eyeholes. One still held her ankle, his fingers tight and hard.

She opened her mouth to scream again, but another of them leaned down and slapped her. It wasn't the first time she'd been slapped, but every time, she was surprised by how much it hurt. Her cheek stung, her neck twinged from being jerked, and her ear was ringing.

"You want to come out and play?" One of them snarled in Dutch.

Sofie shook her head, hair whipping around her face. She hated that she was flat on her back with them above her. She braced herself on her elbows, only for the man holding her ankle to yank, forcing her to fall flat again.

The man who'd slapped her put a booted foot on her stomach, holding her down.

"Our boss wants you. If you'd stayed at the museum even an hour longer, we'd have taken you."

"Is that why you're here? To kidnap me?" She was proud of herself for speaking, but the words trembled.

Two laughed at her fear, while the third merely stared at her, the featureless mask terrifying.

"I want to." He leaned into the foot on her stomach, until it was hard to breathe. "Our boss is pissed at us for not taking you when we had the chance."

Sofie knew she shouldn't have gone with Colette. She knew the rules. The danger.

"But we can't take you if you're here."

He removed his boot and leaned down, hauling her up. At the same time, the man holding her ankle let go, and her heel cracked against the floor. She yelped in pain, but the man now holding her by the upper arm slapped his gloved hand over her mouth.

He leaned in, and her eyes had adjusted enough to see the mesh eyepieces in the mask.

"The next time you leave, you're ours," he whispered.

Sofie could only stare into those mesh panels, trying to see the man behind the mask, and hopefully the humanity within the man.

"You could make it easy for us. You could come to the Tulip Museum tomorrow at noon. You do that, we'll let you ride in a seat in the car, instead of the boot."

Sofie closed her eyes, vowing to be good. To never, ever leave her house except to go to the market at the corner, or the Basilica of Saint Nicolas. Her father had made sure those three places were safe—her house, the store, and a church so beautiful that she almost believed in the power of the divine when she walked inside. As long as she kept to those places, kept her life small, she was safe.

"We'll see you tomorrow." The man shoved her back, her calves hitting the edge of the low bed before she fell back onto it. For a moment, a different kind of fear gripped her, but the men merely turned and jogged down the stairs, leaving her sprawled on top of her rumpled duvet, heart racing as tears of fear started to slip down her cheeks.

RAGE like he'd never known gripped Andrei as he watched three masked men abuse his angel.

Rage and fear.

The message from her father had bugged Andrei all day. He'd tried to shake it off but ended up going in to the Interpol offices in Amsterdam, despite being on vacation. He'd had no luck looking up a forger named Sofie, so her name might be another thing she'd lied about. He should have gone back to the club to talk with the construction crew about the progress, or to help Landon install some of the more unique pieces they didn't trust the construction crew with.

Instead, he'd stayed in the city, and as night fell, he made his way back to the Jordaan District. The buildings on the exterior of the block were a mix of businesses and residential. One building had a café on the top floor with a tiny rooftop patio. There was a nice view of the canals, and the tops of several church spires, but what he cared about was the view of the lone building on the interior of the block.

Given the lush trees that filled the space, Sofie's home wasn't really visible. Luckily he'd picked up a few things at the office, including a wall-crawling camera that wasn't illegal for law enforcement use only because it was too new for laws to have been passed about it. He'd been able to stick the remote-control device to the exterior wall of the café and then pilot it along the back of the buildings until he had an only partially obstructed view of Sofie's home.

The camera on the crawler was advanced enough to zoom in and use AI to fill in blanks in the image where the tree blocked the shot. He'd watched on his phone as Sofie climbed into bed, only to toss and turn for hours before finally falling asleep.

A flash of his badge and some money had convinced the café to let him stay up here after they closed, and he'd called himself ten kinds of fool as he sat, shivering, in a cold metal chair in the middle of the night.

Until the video feed flashed up a warning and automatically switched to thermal imaging, which revealed four figures instead of one.

Andrei had sat up, shocked and half thinking he was imagining things.

In nonthermal mode, only Sofie was visible, but the feed kept flashing to thermal imagining, and though the vaguely humanoid blobs of color sometimes merged together, he watched them pull her out of bed. Hit her.

He raced down the café stairs, slapping open doors until he hit the ground floor. Rather than going out onto the street, he turned in the narrow hallway and headed for the rear exist.

The fucking thing was locked.

Andrei glanced down at the video, which had switched to regular camera, and the clouds must have shifted because now, there was enough light for him to see three figures in all black. Sofie wasn't visible, except for one leg. They had her on the floor.

With a grunt, Andrei forced open the back door

emerging into the verdant garden. There was a small patio here with tables—probably a break area for the people who worked at the international aid organization on the ground floor.

Andrei scaled the wall and hit the ground, taking out a bush on his way. He should call the National Police Corp. He should call Interpol. Hell, he should call Landon.

To do any of those things would mean stopping, if only for a moment. Every bit of training he'd ever had, told him the smart thing to do was to stop and call for backup.

But Sofie was in danger, and nothing else mattered unless she was safe.

Andrei shoved through overgrown bushes, skirting the fences and walls that delineated the back property line of the buildings. All the while, he held his phone, glancing at the feed every few steps.

He watched them shove her down onto the bed, and his stomach sank with different, sick fear.

No, no, no. Don't do that to my angel.

The feed switched to thermal. The three figures… retreated?

Andrei cursed when he realized how far he still was from her house. If the assailants were leaving, he wasn't going to get there in time to beat them to death for touching his angel.

It took him nearly five minutes to reach her house. Crouching low, he slid along the side of the building. Using his phone's camera, he checked around the corner.

Her front door was closed, and there was no sign of the men outside.

Switching back to the video feed, he could see her heat signature. It looked like she was curled up in bed. The men could be on one of the lower floors. He'd tried positioning the crawler lower, but there was too much vegetation. He'd been happy enough with only having a view of the upper floor when he realized it was her living area.

Now he cursed not having a way to find out if the assailants were on the lower floors. If he tried to go in through the front door and they were still inside, more than likely they'd hear him, and this could too easily become a hostage situation.

He needed to get to Sofie.

Andrei backed up to the rear corner, then swiveled on the balls of his feet and looped up at the tree that obscured the back of Sofie's house.

SOFIE WAS SCARED TO MOVE. She thought she'd heard the door close, the security system beep, but what if that was a trick? What if they were still here and waiting for her to move or make a noise?

No, her father wouldn't have allowed that. They respected his word. The way he'd protected her home.

Her home was safe, and what had just happened proved it.

Chest stuttering as she continued to cry, Sofie forced herself to move. To go to the panel on the wall. It unlocked with her palm print. Her finger shook as she tapped the security program controls, but she calmed a little when she watched the footage of the three men leaving. She didn't go back far enough to see them entering.

Sofie swiped at her cheeks with her palms, wishing for dawn. Maybe she would go paint. Or sew. Colette had bought more than enough fabric. She could make another dress with the pale lavender satin.

No. What would be the point? She'd would never have anywhere to wear it.

She'd make it for Colette, and next time Colette came to commission a painting…

Except, would she? Colette was now going to steal things only to help museums improve their security. Would she need copies of the works she stole to do that?

A sense of loss swept over her, and Sofie pressed her back to the wall, sliding down until she was sitting on the floor. Colette wasn't the only person she worked for, but Colette was the only one she considered a friend. Now who did she have? No one.

No one except her father, who'd warned her again and again. She'd finally decided to ignore those warnings, to break the rules, leave her sanctuary, and look what had happened.

The tap at her window caused her to freeze. Terror choking her, she slowly turned to look at the back window. A branch tapped in a steady rhythm against her window.

Someone was out there…in the tree?

A strangely detached feeling came over her. Maybe she'd simply felt too much in the past forty-eight hours, and there was no more room for any emotion, even fear.

Curious and oddly fearless, she climbed to her feet and peered out the window, slapping her hand over her mouth to muffle a shriek when she finally spotted the figure balanced on a large branch just below her window.

Fumbling for the latch, she swung the window up, ducking under the double-glazed pane to stick her head out. She stared at the man in the tree, and he stared back.

Andrei was in the tree.

"Andrei?"

She felt stupid even saying it out loud, because there was no way the man who walked out of her life earlier was now in the tree, tapping her window with a branch.

"Shhh," he said, barely audible. "Are they still inside?"

Sofie blinked. "What?"

"Are they still inside?"

"How did you… Are you watching me?"

He dropped the branch he'd been using to tap on her window and climbed higher in the tree.

"You're going to fall."

"No, I'm not."

"You are."

"Angel, if I were you, I wouldn't argue with me right now."

The cool, smooth tone of his voice didn't negate the hard warning. She responded to that threat in an unexpected way. The tension born of fear that made her shoulders and arms tight relaxed.

Now, they were eye to eye, though he was several meters back, having to stay close to the trunk for the limbs to support his weight.

"Sofie, are they still inside?"

"No. They left."

"Are you sure?"

"Yes, I saw it on the security video."

"I don't think you can trust your system. They must have overridden it to get in."

Oh. He was right. She remembered hearing it beep the way it did when it was disarmed, so they must have hacked it.

"So they could still be inside?" she whispered.

"Probably not, given that we're not being all that quiet," Andrei said, "so… What are you doing?"

Sofie had already thrown one leg over the windowsill. "Escaping."

"Fuck. Sofie, stop. The branches close to the building aren't—"

Sofie didn't care. The fear that had retreated only moments ago returned like a high tide, washing away everything else. Those men might still be in her house.

Waiting. For one wild moment, she considered simply jumping. Maybe the tree and bushes would break her fall. Maybe she'd break her legs. But she wouldn't be trapped in her house with men who swore the next time they'd take her away from the place she should have been safe, but now knew she wasn't.

"Do. Not. Jump."

She froze at the command.

"You're going to reach out with your left hand and grab this branch." Andrei jiggled a thick branch, the end of which was just within reach.

"Then you're going to put your foot on this one." He indicated a second branch.

Sofie nodded, watching his face, shadowed by the tree and the night itself.

"Keep your weight on the windowsill until you have a good grip with your hand and firm placement with your foot. Understand?"

"Yes."

"Once you do, you're going to move fast. You're going to push off the wall, get both feet on the branch, but don't stand there, keep moving. Come toward me." Andrei held out his hand.

Sofie glanced from his hand to his face. "I don't want to fall."

"Why don't you climb back in, and use the front door."

Fear gripped her, and Sofie couldn't stop the whimper that rose up her throat.

"Okay, okay. No door. Climb out the window into a tree in the middle of the night."

His exasperated tone made her laugh. The laugh shifted this from terrifying escape to wonderful adventure.

Ignoring the fact that it was a request for adventure and excitement that had gotten her in this very situation, Sofie followed Andrei's instructions, getting one hand and one foot firmly in place on the branches.

"Ready, Rapunzel?"

"Rapunzel? She was locked in a tower and…" Now that she said it out loud, that comparison was perhaps a little too apt. "I could make a rope out of sheets."

"You could use the door," Andrei grumbled.

No, because if she used the door, there would be no reason for Andrei to take her hand.

Shaking with a different kind of fear, Sofie swung her other leg out but balanced on the windowsill, one hand gripping the frame.

"Sofie, look at me."

She'd been looking down, but at the command, her gaze met Andrei's.

"Come to me, Angel."

Sofie pushed off. For one terrifying moment, all her weight was on the too-thin branch below her. She felt it start to bend under her weight.

"Sofie," Andrei barked.

Holding her breath, Sofie took three desperate, quick steps along the branch, hands moving one over the other on the branch above her. Then Andrei was there, and because she was too scared to let go and take his hand, he leaned out, wrapping an arm around her middle and hauling her into his arms.

Sofie curled into him, gasping as adrenaline once more pumped through her body.

"I did it."

"You did."

"That was fun."

He squeezed her. "No it was not."

"How do you know, you didn't do it?"

"I meant, it wasn't fun for me."

The bark was scratchy against her bare feet, and Sofie

was fairly certain her lower legs were scratched up, thanks to the smaller branches she'd scraped past in her mad scramble.

Andrei rested his chin on her head. "We can't stay in this tree."

"Why not."

"Either your assailants are still in your house, or they're not. Either way, we need to get away from here."

"Away?"

"Yes. We'll go to… Shit." He paused to think. "I'll get a hotel and we'll work this out. I can't take you to the Interpol offices. Too many questions."

"No." She jerked back, remembered they were in a tree, and reversed course, slamming herself against his chest hard enough he grunted.

"What exactly are you saying 'no' to?" His question was dangerously mild.

"I can't leave."

"Why not?"

"Because this is the only place I'm safe." She pointed back over her shoulder at her house.

Andrei chuckled.

Why was he laughing?

"Angel, you can't be serious."

"I am."

"Three men just pulled you out of bed."

"You saw that?"

Instead of answering, he gently gripped her chin, forcing her head away from his chest. "Did they hit you?"

"Just once."

He turned her face to the moonlight. She wasn't sure if there was something visible, but when he released her, his jaw was tight.

"The point is, your home clearly isn't safe."

"It is. It's the only place. There and the store."

Andrei stared at her, then firmly pushed her body away from his. Not far, and he guided her hand to grip the thick branch above them.

"What are you doing?" she demanded.

"We are getting out of this tree."

"Oh."

Andrei climbed down one branch, then reached up and guided her down with him.

That's how they made their way down, step by step, him going first, then guiding her down beside him.

There were a few more scrapes on her arms and legs by the time they reached the ground, and Sofie was shivering. The soft shorts-and-shirt sleep set she had on was one of her favorites, but not meant for tree climbing.

Andrei looked around. "What's the best way out of here that's not the path to your front door? We can try going back the way I came, but I probably set off an alarm when I broke the back door."

"I told you, I can't leave."

Andrei stared at her. "Are you deliberately trying to make me crazy?"

"No?"

"Sofie, we're leaving."

"I can't! I have to stay here where it's safe."

"It's not safe. You were attacked in your bedroom. You know it's not safe, that's why you climbed out the window."

Sofie was starting to shake and it had nothing to do with the cold. "I know, but I was…I was scared the men were still there, and you were in the tree, and for a minute, I wasn't scared and it felt like an adventure but I can't. I can't leave. If I do, something bad will happen."

Andrei's expression shifted from frustrated to something softer as she rambled on. Sofie forced herself to shut up, her cheeks the only part of her that were warm. She hoped he couldn't see her blush of embarrassment.

"You're in shock," he said gently. "We're going to go, and I won't let anything happen to you."

"No! I can't leave."

She couldn't breathe, couldn't think. Sofie tried to pull away from Andrei, but he wouldn't let go.

"Sofie, stop. I'm not letting you run back in there when you're not thinking straight."

"I have to stay!" She twisted and turned, but his arms were like a steel band around her. "That's the rule. I shouldn't have left before. That's why they came."

"Fuck, that's a lot to unpack... Sofie, stop fighting me."

She sagged in his arm, resting her cheek on his chest.

"It's okay, Angel. It's just the shock. The adrenaline."

"I wish it was," she whispered. Then Sofie dropped, sliding out of his hold. She winced as she hit the ground on hands and knees, but scrambled away, racing along the side of her house.

Andrei's footsteps pounded behind her. Strangely, she wasn't afraid of him chasing her. The desperate panic to get back inside overrode any other feeling.

She never made it to her door.

Andrei grabbed her, yanking her back against his chest, but only for a moment.

He spun, pushing her face-first against the wall and yanking her arms up behind her back.

"Fine, Angel. We can play it like that." He leaned back, until the only point of contact was his hand holding her wrists at the small of her back. "You're under arrest."

THIRTEEN

"I THOUGHT YOU WERE ON VACATION." Rolf Pederson stared at Andrei through the video feed. It wasn't as intimidating as it would have been in person, given that the video couldn't capture Rolf's sheer physical size.

Andrei cocked a brow and lounged back in his chair. "I can do two things at once."

"I know. It's how you can be a good agent and a pain in my ass at the same time."

That got a genuine laugh from Andrei, who sat forward, elbows braced on the desk. "I am multitalented. But you signed off on it?"

"Yes, but only because not signing off would raise more questions. You're on thin ice, Agent Leonard."

"I usually am."

Rolf shook his head and ended the video call.

Andrei sat for a moment in the silence, needing to gather himself. It had been a bad mix of desperation and frustration that drove him to arrest Sofie. He'd dragged her back through the tangled garden to the door he'd burst through. As expected, there had been police there investigating the back door being forced open. They'd opened an overgrown gate in the patio wall that he hadn't notice in his panic to get to Sofie to let them in to the patio.

They'd looked ready to arrest both of them until Andrei flashed his badge.

Then he'd had them arrest Sofie.

He didn't have the authority to arrest a Dutch citizen, but he could ask the local authorities to arrest someone and then have them transferred to Interpol's custody, which is precisely what he'd done. Sofie had spent less than ten minutes sitting in the back of a warm police car before the rush paperwork was authorized. Andrei had parked nearly a kilometer away, since parking was scarce, so an officer had dropped him and Sofie off at his car.

He'd brought her back to Club Alibi.

The paperwork he'd filed to authorize her arrest and transfer had been coded to the Club Alibi project, which had a high security clearance. Given that, the transfers had gone through automatically, though clearly someone had woken Rolf, the lead agent, to let him know an arrest had been made in Amsterdam.

Twenty minutes ago, Andrei had stopped being able to ignore messages from Rolf, and after removing the cuffs and passing Sofie off to a very confused Colette and Landon, Andrei headed for the mini office suite they'd built on the private playroom floor to make this call.

Now, it was time to go find Sofie and get his questions answered.

Sofie's desperate panic to get back into her house had disappeared in favor of other emotions when he arrested her. She'd looked scared when she was shoved into the back seat of the police vehicle, but he'd made sure to always stay in her line of sight. Once she'd been transferred to his car —and he redid her cuffs with her hands in front of her rather than behind her back—she'd gone quiet.

That silence had hurt, because her expression hadn't

given him any hints about the reason for her silence. Did she feel betrayed? Scared? Angry?

By the time they reached Club Alibi, she'd nearly been asleep. If not for the buzzing excitement of having an excuse to spend more time with her, he would have been exhausted.

And acknowledging, even in his own thoughts, that his handling of the situation was driven by a desperate need to spend more time with her was a bit too much honest self-reflection.

The upper floor of Club Alibi Amsterdam was all private playrooms, many of which were complete. Unlike in London, there weren't any overnight rooms, but there were several playrooms with beds.

The door to one of those rooms was slightly ajar. Andrei nudged it open, then stopped to blink at what he was seeing.

Landon was seated on one side of the bed, back against the ornate tufted headboard. His long legs were stretched out and crossed at the ankles.

Colette was half reclined against his chest. He had one arm hooked around her, casually possessive with his hand cupping one breast.

And curled up in the middle of the bed under a soft white blanket was Sofie. Her cheek was pillowed on Colette's thigh, and Colette had one hand protectively on Sofie's head.

Both Colette and Sofie were asleep.

As Andrei opened the door, Landon's eyes opened. He raised his brows in silent question.

Andrei tipped his head toward the door.

Landon leaned in to whisper to Colette as his hand shifted, thumb gently stroking her nipple. Colette woke with a needy sound, and Andrei looked away.

This moment felt too intimate for voyeurism. And

besides, it made him jealous. Not that Andrei wanted a full-time lover or sub, but the closeness was enviable.

He jerked his attention back to the bed when he heard Landon's and Colette's quiet voices. Colette slid a pillow under Sofie's head as she slipped off the bed. Sofie burrowed into the pillow, pulling the blanket up over her face. Her pale hair blended with the fabric, until only the person-shaped nature of the lump in the middle of the bed indicated there was anyone there.

Landon led Colette toward the door as she yawned. Andrei stepped to the side to let them pass, his attention on Sofie.

Then nearly fell on his ass when Colette reached back, grabbed his arm, and yanked him out into the hall.

"What the hell?" Andrei snarled.

"Colette…" Landon rubbed the back of his neck.

"Why did you arrest her?"

"Why do you think I owe you answers?" Andrei countered.

"Don't you think she's been through enough?"

Guilt and regret gnawed at him, which only pissed Andrei off more.

"I'm not the one who should feel guilty. You dragged her into this."

"She wanted to go with me," Colette hissed, keeping her voice low.

"But she's not a thief, is she?"

"No, she's not, which is why you shouldn't have arrested her."

"But she is your forger."

Colette didn't so much as twitch. The woman was an excellent actress. "Forger? She's not a forger."

"I was inside her studio."

"She's an artist."

"She had an X-ray machine."

"She does some restoration work."

For a moment, Andrei doubted himself. Maybe she was just an artist who did some restoration work.

An artist who was friends with a thief.

Andrei leaned back against the wall, eyeing Colette. Landon loomed at her back, clearly ready to back up his woman, even if she was a damned liar.

"I have questions," Andrei said after a moment. "I think you can answer them, but I prefer to hear it from her."

"No," Colette said quickly. "Let me answer for her."

"I wasn't offering you a choice." Andrei straightened. "Don't forget, he's not Interpol anymore, which means you're guests here. Don't make me ask you to leave."

Colette opened her mouth to argue, but Andrei slipped back into the playroom and closed the door.

NOT ONLY WAS she warm and comfortable, there was a delicious weight against her lower back.

Colette rolled onto her slide, and a hard, warm, weight pressed against her back.

Oh, that was nice. That felt good. Safe.

But she wasn't safe.

She'd been attacked and then arrested.

Sofie's eyes popped open.

She stared at the arm draped over her hip—masculine, with a very sexy forearm.

Slowly, she turned her head until she could see him out of the corner of her eye and confirm that Andrei was pressed against her back.

She was in bed with Andrei.

She remembered sitting on the bed with Colette. Her friend had asked questions, but Sofie had just shook her head, so Colette had started telling stories of some of her more daring and dangerous heists. Sofie had laughed watching Landon's expression as Colette talked. Clearly he hadn't heard some of the stories.

There was familiarity in Colette's voice and the rhythm of her storytelling. That familiarity had led her to first recline on one elbow, and finally lie down on the bed.

She didn't remember anything else until now.

Andrei was at her back, protecting her even as they slept.

No, that was wishful thinking. Her romanticism at work. Actually, it was quite problematic that he was in bed with her. He'd arrested her.

Sofie looked around, dread slowly working its way through her. Where was she?

She knew where she wasn't. She wasn't at home where she should be.

None of this would have happened if she'd done what she should have and stayed home.

"Breathe, Angel."

His voice rumbled against her back, slow and sleepy.

Sofie hadn't realized she was breathing fast and uneven until he said something. She forced herself to take several measured breaths before speaking.

"Where are we?"

"Back at Club Alibi."

At that, she sat bolt upright.

Andrei grunted, flopping onto his back, one hand pressed to his midsection, eyes closed with a grimace.

Unlike the room they'd been in before, this one had only one glass wall—floor-to-ceiling windows that looked out over the river. The walls were painted a deep matte navy. The bed was massive, with a royal blue leather tufted headboard. Black leather wingback chairs flanked a round ottoman in one corner, while the other had a brass and glass bar cart. The only overtly sexual item in the room was what at first looked like a lounge chair, but it was too tall. Instead, it looked like a narrow version of the adjustable exam table found in doctors' offices, positioned with the back up and feet down so it looked like a chair.

She saw herself there, in the chair, waiting to be examined. Played with.

Sofie jerked her attention away as she scooted away from Andrei. Back against the headboard, she wrapped her arms around her knees, making sure to bring the blanket with her.

Andrei was still lying on his back, grimacing.

Sofie pursed her lips as she studied him. "What's wrong with you?"

"You elbowed me in the stomach."

Sofie shook her head. "You're fine."

Andrei opened one eye. "I can't decide if it's better or worse that you're accidentally violent."

"I'm not violent."

"My tongue and stomach both beg to differ." Andrei sat up and scooted back to sit with his back against the headboard, legs stretched out. Sofie shifted so she was facing him.

"You arrested me."

He studied her, and the seriousness of his expression was unfamiliar. For the first time, she could see him as an Interpol agent—cold, calm, implacable. "You were attacked in your own home, and first tried to escape by jumping out the window, but then refused to leave."

"Are you saying you arrested me to protect me?"

He shrugged, looking almost uncomfortable. "I'm saying that your story doesn't add up, Sofie Vermeer."

Hearing him say her full name made her jump.

"Though that's clearly an alias."

"It's not."

Andrei arched a brow, his expression back to the lazily

amused and devilish one she was used to. "Your last name is Vermeer."

"Yes."

"And you're an artist."

"Yes."

"But not a forger," he mocked.

"Replicating existing paintings isn't a crime."

"Selling them as the originals is."

"I don't pretend they're the originals."

Andrei laughed. "Clever. Because you're right. If someone asks you to paint a copy of The Night Watch—"

"I wouldn't, it's too big."

"—you do it, and sell it to them as a reproduction. What they do with it afterward..." He raised his brows.

"None of my business."

"Clever, Angel, clever." There was genuine appreciation in his gaze, and that made her shoulders hunch.

"It's not me," she said quickly. "I'm not clever. My father is."

Andrei's expression sobered. "Your father. I saw the message he left you."

Sofie blinked. "You read Dutch?"

"No, but I know how to memorize and use translation software."

"Is that..." Sofie stared at nothing, thoughts whirring. "You were watching me. That's how you saw the men. And you were watching me because you saw the message from my father?"

"It's not just your father who's clever."

"But...why? I mean, why would that message make you watch me?"

Andrei frowned at her, his gaze tracing her features. "Because it was a threat."

"No it wasn't."

"Tell me, in English, what it said."

"I disappointed him because I'm not supposed to leave my studio, and there would be consequences for breaking the rules."

Andrei's frown deepened. "That's a threat. Saying there will be consequences."

"But there were! I left, and our enemies found me."

"That's who attacked you, your enemies?" Andrei's frown was deepening.

"Yes."

"And who are they?"

"Men who don't like my father's business."

"So they attacked you, but didn't really hurt you." His gaze shifted to her cheek, and Sofie raised her hand to touch the side of her face. It was a little tender, but nothing bad.

"Sofie...surely you see that your father sent them."

She flinched, not meeting his gaze.

"Sofie, who is your father?"

She didn't answer.

"Sofie, do you have a passport?"

At that, she looked up. "I assume so."

"Do you have possession of it? Is it somewhere in your house?"

She knew where this was going, and in a way, she was... relieved. Maybe it was time. "No, I don't have it."

"Fuck." Andrei leaned back against the headboard, and she watched his throat work. "Sofie, how long have you been painting, as a job?"

"As long as I can remember."

"Since you were...a child?"

She nodded. "It's why my father adopted me. Even when I was small, I loved art and he saw that."

Andrei didn't say anything, but his eyes had widened at the word "adopted."

"Andrei, why are you...why are you looking like that?"

Andrei opened his eyes and sat forward, twisting to face her. His expression was serious, with a soft edge she'd never seen before.

For a moment, she considered leaning forward and clamping a hand over his mouth, because she was sure that she didn't want to hear what he'd say next.

"Sofie, do you know the definition of human trafficking?"

FOURTEEN

"I JUST WANT to confirm again that you're comfortable talking here." The dark-haired older woman smiled gently at Sofie.

Sofie, now wearing a tracksuit Colette had gone out and purchased, nodded.

"And you want Agent Leonard here?"

Sofie twisted in her seat to look over her shoulder at him, where he sat in a chair against the wall. "Yes."

Andrei offered her a reassuring smile. At least, he hoped it was reassuring.

The dark-haired woman—Agent Baas, a Dutch Europol agent currently on rotation in Interpol—glanced at him. She was an expert interviewer, holding both specialized certificates and degrees in therapy and victim interaction.

"Unless he doesn't want to be here," Sofie said slowly.

Fuck. Clearly his reassuring smile wasn't reassuring.

"I want to be here if you want me here, Angel."

Agent Baas's eye twitched at the pet name. She'd asked for a briefing on Andrei's relationship to Sofie, and he'd been a coward and said it was classified as it related to the

Alibi initiative. That was also why they were on the ground floor of the building, in what had probably once been the security office but now served as a cozy meeting space. He and Landon had hauled down chairs, the decadent things looking entirely out of place with the industrial carpeting and beige walls.

Sofie studied him for a moment, then turned back to the woman who'd driven out to conduct the interview.

"I want him here."

The question was why. Why did she want him here. If it was just a matter of someone familiar, it would make much more sense for Colette to be here.

Maybe it was because he'd shown up right after she was attacked, which slotted him into "rescuer" in her head. Except he'd then arrested her.

And maybe it was because of the connection they forged that first night. He'd been the first person to ever touch her intimately. Had he known that, he would have done every damn thing differently, but he hadn't. He'd put her through intense situations, then given her emotional whiplash. It made sense that she would feel some kind of attachment to him, given everything that had happened.

What made less sense was his attachment to her. Because he did feel something for this woman.

He felt protective even before seeing that message from her father.

The rage and fear that he had gripped him when he saw those men standing over her in her bedroom was unlike anything Andrei had ever experienced before. The acuity of the emotion was terrifying.

And beyond any of that, he just wanted to spend time with her. He loved the seeming contradiction of her. She was both blunt and shy. She blushed easily, and yet spoke her mind. She was funny, smart...

And deeply sexually submissive.

Andrei's teeth ached as he clenched his jaw, fighting to push away that thought.

"I'm going to start the recording." Agent Baas leaned over and clicked on the small video camera she'd set up on the counter still mounted to one wall.

The agent went through the standard start of interview protocols, getting all the necessary consents on the record.

Sofie answered each question while showing no visible emotion.

"Do you understand why we're conducting this interview, Ms. Vermeer?"

"You think my father is forcing me to work, and that's illegal."

"Forcing anyone to work is illegal. But tell me about your father. What's his name?"

Sofie shook her head, her expression flickering. "No. I won't talk about him."

"That's fine. You mentioned to Agent Leonard that you were adopted. Do you remember your birth family?"

"No. I was adopted when I was young."

"How young?"

"Maybe six or seven."

"And you have no memories before that?" Agent Baas asked gently.

Sofie shook her head and Andrei winced. Lack of memories was rarely a sign of a happy childhood.

"Do you remember where you were born?"

Sofie shook her head.

"After you were adopted, where did you live?"

"My house."

"The house you were at earlier?"

"Yes."

"And who did you live with. You mentioned your father. Did you have a second parent?"

"I had a nanny. Father traveled for work, so he hired nannies to live with me full time."

"And where did you go to school?"

"At home."

Agent Baas's brows rose. "That is not very common. Exceptions that allow homeschooling are rare. Do you know why you were homeschooled?"

Sofie hesitated. "My nannies acted as my teachers."

"There's more to going to school than just the academics. School when we are young is how we learn to make friends, to interact with other people, and the world around us. Did you have any friends?"

"A few. I attended art classes, painting classes. My father got special permission for me to attend classes at the university when I was still young."

"I saw that in your file. You were only eleven and in an art residency with artists three and four times your age."

"Some of my first classes were with other children."

Agent Baas clasped her hands and leaned forward. "You were a child prodigy in art. Based on some articles published about you during that two-year residency, it sounds like you see the world just a little differently from the rest of us, and that makes you a, quite literally, world-class painter."

"Thank you." Sofie sounded fine, but Andrei was looking at her feet. Colette had gotten her slippers, and from the way the soft toes of those slippers were bunched, he was sure she was nervously curling her toes.

"So why is it that I couldn't find any mention of gallery shows or auctions of your work?"

"I only sell to private collectors."

"And why is that?"

"It's better that way."

"And who decided that?"

"My father handles the business side."

Agent Baas shot Andrei a grim look. He knew what she was thinking. She was thinking that Sofie was entirely unaware she was a victim of a very serious crime, and that, even if they explained, she might not understand.

But Andrei's thoughts were leaning a different direction. He studied Sofie's profile, turning over every piece of information he had about her.

Agent Baas asked several more questions, and Sofie answered each of them without really giving any information.

"Sofie," he barked. "Enough."

She looked back over her shoulder. "Enough what?"

He arched a brow…and she blushed.

Agent Baas sat back, brows raised as she glanced between them.

Andrei rose from his chair in the corner. He very deliberately turned off the camera, stopping the recording, then leaned against the counter.

"Agent Leonard, we—"

He ignored the other agent. "Who is he?"

"Who?"

"Your father. He's someone powerful enough that you don't dare leave."

She shook her head. "It's not safe to leave."

"Because your father has you creating forgeries for dangerous people. And he's one of them. I'm betting you could make yourself a passport if you wanted to, because we know Colette had several."

Sofie only smiled.

He wanted to kiss her and then put her over his knee and then kiss her again.

"Sofie," he barked.

"Yes?" She seemed entirely unruffled.

"You know that what you've experienced is human trafficking. You were adopted, relocated, and forced to work. That's a crime."

Sofie merely gazed back at him, but there was a faint blush of shame on her cheeks.

"You clearly had access to the internet, and read all sorts of things."

Now the blush was something else. That's what he'd wanted, to shift her attention away from the feeling of shame so many victims felt.

"The man you call father adopted you because of your artistic talent and put you to work forging paintings."

She raised her chin and held his gaze but didn't speak.

"You're smart enough and skilled enough to leave if you wanted to. But you haven't, and I know why."

"I would be very surprised if you do."

"Your father is a member of law enforcement, isn't he?"

Agent Baas sucked in a shocked breath, but didn't say anything.

"Someone who handles art crimes," Andrei went on. "Is he with Carabinieri Art Squad, Europol cultural crime?"

Andrei watched Sofie as he spoke. He wasn't looking for confirmation he was right—he was sure he was right. He was watching for fear, because fear and a certainty that she could never get away was the only thing that made how she'd behaved back at her house make sense.

But a small line appeared between her brows—a frown of confusion.

"No. He isn't with any agency or police."

Andrei blinked. He'd been so sure...

"Then why do you stay?" He dropped into a crouch in front of her. "Angel, given the timing and what happened, I think your father is the person who sent those men into your house to scare you."

She shook her head vehemently. "No. He wouldn't risk hurting me."

"Wouldn't risk it because you're a valuable asset?"

She nodded, but didn't meet his gaze.

"Maybe I am wrong. What did the men say?"

"They said that they would have taken me at the museum if you hadn't kidnapped me first."

"Excuse me?" Agent Baas interjected.

"No, it's fine, we had sex afterward," Sofie said bluntly.

Andrei closed his eyes with a wince.

"Agent Leonard..."

"I know," he said to the older woman. "It's...messy. And getting messier."

Andrei looked back at Sofie and saw the glint in her eye. She'd done that on purpose.

Kiss her. Spank her. Kiss her again.

It was a good plan.

One he couldn't act on, for so many, many reasons.

"Sofie," he growled. "What did the men who came into your bedroom say?"

She quickly recounted their threats, and what she said only confirmed his theory.

"Sofie, based on what you're saying, I don't think you were in any real danger of being a kidnapped the way they implied. They were just there to scare you into compliance."

He swallowed his anger and held out a hand to her. Sofie's eyes widened as she placed her fingers in his. They were cold and trembling a little.

"Your father clearly monitors your security system, realized that you not only left but were gone overnight, and decided to bring you back in line by sending in men to hurt you. Scare you."

"No. That's not it." For the first time, she seemed unsure.

"If they could come into your home, right into your bedroom, why wouldn't they just kidnap you?"

"Because it's not allowed."

"Yes," he said slow slowly. "Kidnapping is not allowed. Anywhere or at any time."

Her lips twitched with a smile and she opened her mouth, no doubt to say something about the way he hauled her out of the museum, so he shot her a hard look. Her mouth closed, sadness touching her features, and he felt like even more of an asshole than usual.

"The point is that there's no magical barrier around your house. If there was, they wouldn't have been able to get in there."

"Not a magical barrier, but it is…" Sofie looked away, brows drawn together. "It is…sanctus."

Her eyes widened as she jerked her head around and met his gaze while yanking her hand out of his.

"I don't speak Dutch," Andrei said slowly.

"That wasn't Dutch." Agent Baas leaned in, studying Sofie. "That was Latin."

Sofie winced, looking down at her hands.

"Sofie, are you saying that your house is holy ground? Like a church?" Agent Baas asked.

Her utter stillness was confirmation.

Holy ground…

Andrei was so rarely surprised, but again and again, Sofie surprised him.

He pushed to stand, taking a step back as he processed. Maybe she was in a religious cult of some kind. Often cults used drugs and smuggling to finance their operations…

Then an entirely different, and somehow worse, idea came to him.

"Sofie…who is your father?"

She sighed, shoulders slumping a little. "I can't tell you."

"I'll protect you," he vowed, meaning every word.

She looked at Agent Baas, and he could tell from the set of her jaw she wasn't going to say anything.

"Agent Baas, give us the room."

The other agent hesitated only a moment before getting up and leaving.

Andrei waited, hoping that being alone was enough, but after the click of the door closing behind the other agent, Sofie was silent.

But then she looked up and their gazes met.

His angel's eyes were a beautiful blue, but not one shade. Her eyes were the sea at sunset or dawn when the water, sky, and horizon were all distinct shades of blue.

Her lips parted as she let out a soft breath. He saw the tension leave her neck as if she finally let go of a heavy weight.

She was going to tell him who her father was. Not because he was an Interpol agent. Not because he'd been in that tree to catch her as she made her ridiculous escape attempt.

She was going to tell him because she trusted him.

"My father is the prefect of the Vatican Secret Archive."

FIFTEEN

SOFIE FELT ODDLY LIGHT.

There was a not inconsiderable part of her that was in a blind panic over what she'd just done.

She'd never before told anyone who her father was.

It wasn't that it was a secret. Certainly some people knew, because the only way his declaration that her home was holy ground held any weight was if they knew his connection to the Vatican. Her father's enemies, or perhaps it was more accurate to say rivals, respected the church enough to honor his declaration.

The men who'd invaded her home at least knew that her home had been declared holy ground, even if they didn't know specifically who her father was. That's why they hadn't done more than scare and slap her.

Yes, her father's identity was known to some, her home's status known to an even wider circle than that.

But she'd never told anyone.

She'd never had anyone she trusted enough to tell.

And now that she had told someone, her body felt lighter than it had before.

"Wait, wait, wait." Colette held up her hand, clicking

her tongue in a very French way. "What you're saying…it's all too disconnected. Sofie, just tell us everything from the beginning to now."

Sofie wiggled into a slightly more comfortable position and thought about where to start.

She, Andrei, Colette, and Landon were in a partially completed bar and lounge area on the glass floor, as she'd decided to call it.

She hadn't been able to see this room previously, given that it was on the opposite corner of the building from the playroom she and Andrei had used, with the elevator bank blocking direct line of site. This space had a view not only of the river which curved in just past the building, but also the skyline and lights of Amsterdam. If this area once had small glass offices, they'd been removed, leaving a large open space.

And unlike the other spaces on this floor, here there was no visible BDSM equipment, or hints as to the purpose of this place.

A bar was being built against the back of the elevator bank—the bar itself was in place, as was the plumbing for the sinks and the under counter dishwasher, but the glasses were still in their boxes. A bank of small refrigerators was installed and plugged in under the back counter, which is where Colette had gotten the cold bottle of mineral water Sofie now held as she sat on a long, low leather couch.

Andrei was beside her, slumped on the couch with his eyes closed, a Belgian beer in one hand. The other arm was laid out along the back of the couch. His hand almost brushed Sofie's shoulder.

She kept waiting for him to touch her again, but so far, he hadn't. Even when he'd led her upstairs after saying goodbye to Agent Baas.

Colette clicked her tongue. "Sofie. Pay attention and start talking."

Landon, seated with Colette on the couch across from Sofie and Andrei, chuckled as he took a sip from his bottle.

Sofie opened her mouth, closed it, then took a sip of her water. "I've never told anyone my story before. I guess I've never had anyone to tell."

Colette's face twisted. "I'm so sorry that I wasn't a good enough friend to you."

"You're my best friend," Sofie said simply.

"Exactly. That's why I should have known. I should have realized that there was more going on."

Sofie dipped her head, embarrassed, though she couldn't say why.

After another sip of water, she'd gathered her thoughts enough to begin.

"I was adopted when I was either six or seven. They weren't sure when I was born, so they had to guess."

Landon raised his brows in question, though didn't actually ask a question.

"Oh, you're wondering where I'm from? I used to think in French. Sometimes even now, I will hear something in French and have this almost memory moment. But I don't remember enough about the French to help narrow down where I learned it. I was left at an orphanage outside Maastricht as a toddler."

"A toddler? Not an infant?" Colette asked.

"A toddler." Sofie had spent more time than she cared to think about imagining what had been happening in her parents' life that leaving her on the steps of a church was the solution. Paintings of mother and child were hard for her because of it.

Unless of course it was a medieval piece with a homuncular Jesus.

"I could walk, but not talk well enough to tell them my name. At least that's what I was told."

It was almost unnerving, having the attention of three

such intense people. Landon and Colette were both looking at her, but Andrei was still reclined, head on the back of the couch, eyes closed. Despite that, she knew he was listening. Focused not just on her words but on her.

Had he sat up and turned to face her, she might not have been able to go on, and part of her wondered if he knew that.

"I told the agent downstairs I don't remember anything from my childhood, but I do remember some. I remember getting in trouble because I would leave the orphanage, go across the graveyard behind the new church to the old church. It was nothing grand. Not a cathedral. But there was beautiful stained glass, and the altarpiece was…"

To this day, she found it hard to describe the feeling she got when she saw beautiful art.

"It was the light. Not just the light from the windows in the church but the light that the artist depicted in the altarpiece. I didn't understand who the sad people were, but I understood the light in the sky, and the way the light made some colors bright, and some dark. I remember getting yelled at for climbing up on the altar to try and look behind the altarpiece. To see if there was a window or a lamp behind that illuminated it."

Sofie looked out at the landscape before her. It was dusk once more, the setting sun painting one half of the skyline a hazy color somewhere between yellow and blue. People rarely thought of the light of sunset as having green in it, but there was green in gold. The tones were there, if one looked closely enough.

Her mind's eye flashed up image after image. This view. This moment in time, unique unto itself, never having happened before or to happen again, rendered in a dozen different styles. The stark realism and luminosity of the Dutch Masters, the saturated colors of the Renaissance, the thick strokes of impressionism.

"One of the nuns gave me a sketchbook, and this little briefcase of art supplies—she figured out what I loved about the old church. There were colored pencils, charcoal, pastels, and even a little row of oil paints."

"They gave you that as a child?" Colette asked softly.

"I don't think it was a children's art set, and I've never been able to figure out if that was on purpose. If she deliberately gave me something more than crayons." She'd turned to Colette to answer the question, but now looked back at the window. "I never stopped getting in trouble for going over to the church, but once they brought me back and slapped my hands, they'd say no dinner for me, but sit me down with paper and my supplies and I'd try and do what I saw in that altarpiece."

The view shifted as she tried to render the paintings she was imagining with more detail, colors brightening and darkening, shifting and changing.

"Try to capture the very soul of darkness and light."

Sofie felt herself blushing. She was an artist, but words weren't her medium, and she felt deeply embarrassed by having waxed poetic.

"I understand," Colette said softly.

She shot her friend a grateful smile. Looking over at Andrei, she expected to see him with his eyes still closed, but he was looking at her with something akin to wonder.

Sofie jerked her attention back to the view, cheeks hot.

"I think my father first came to visit the orphanage when I was five, because I remember sitting at a desk, so I was school-aged. I remember the grown-ups pointing and looking at something on the wall, and then they came over to me. He handed me a piece of paper and a single pencil and asked me if I could draw God."

"What did you draw?" Landon asked.

"The night sky, but in reverse." She had to stop and think about the word in English. "Inverted. So the stars were black in the white, and the swirls of the galaxy looked like wings. Then I told them to take a picture of it, and use the filter—I don't know why or how I knew about camera filters—to invert the colors.

"He came back again, at least twice that I remember. One of those times he called me Vermeer—a forgotten Dutch artist. He must have asked them to encourage my art even more, because when the other children had to do math, I got to paint. When the other children learned their sounds, I watched a video on color theory."

"That's a unique kind of neglect," Landon said dryly.

Sofie laughed, and it felt good to have her story acknowledged but not pitied. "Then when I was six or seven, they told me I was adopted. That's when my name became Sofie Vermeer.

"My father brought me here, to Amsterdam. To my house. I had nannies who stayed with me—one for day, one for night. And art tutors. Every type of visual art. Every medium."

"But surely those people knew who adopted you? Your father's identity can't be a secret," Colette said.

Sofie waited for Andrei to speak. When he'd had the police officially arrest her, she'd given them her name, which meant they'd have looked her up. No doubt as an Interpol agent, Andrei also got that information.

But he didn't say anything, leaving it to her.

"Legally, I was never adopted—Catholic priests are discouraged from full legal adoptions. I guess you would say that he is my foster father. The church was my legal guardian. Everything was paid for by the church, though I don't know exactly how."

She took a minute, letting herself breath before continuing. "I didn't go to school. I know that's not common, and I don't know what exception was used to allow it, but I was taught by my nannies at home."

"Did you get to...leave the house?" Colette's expression was worried.

"Of course. We went to museums. That's where the art is."

Beside her, Andrei started to laugh, though it was an oddly humorless sound.

"My childhood was not bad. One of my nannies was too strict, and her punishments would not have been allowed if I'd had anyone to tell." She shrugged. "But they let me do what I love. Had I had a normal life I would never have been able to spend most of my day creating."

"That might be true, but it doesn't make the childhood you did have any less problematic," Colette said gently.

Sofie shifted uncomfortably, and Andrei sat up. She could feel him watching her.

"Get to the good part," Colette said with forced brightness, clearly seeing Sofie's discomfort. "When did you start..." Colette grinned. "...allegedly...creating forgeries."

"If I just say allegedly, he can't arrest me again?"

"Yep," Landon said with a grin.

"No. That is not how it works," Andrei grumped.

"You're going to start following both the letter and spirit of the law?" Landon raised his brows at Andrei.

Andrei ignored him. "Technically," he told Sofie, "you're still in custody."

"I'm still arrested?"

"Technically."

"Okay, then I'm not going to tell you."

Andrei's head thumped back onto the couch. "Just tell us. I arrested you for your own protection, not because you committed a crime."

"But if I confess to a crime, the arrest will be real."

"No. I don't actually care that much," Andrei sighed.

"How the hell did you ever get hired?" Landon muttered.

"I knew I liked you." Colette beamed at Andrei, who couldn't see it because his eyes were once more closed.

"Confess all you want," Andrei said. "Unless you killed someone. Don't tell me that. Then I'd actually have to do something."

Sofie trusted Andrei, but saying more would be risking more than herself.

Sofie raised her brows at her friend, who nodded and said, "Tell the story of how you became one of the world's greatest forgers. Allegedly."

Landon growled, his eyes predatory as he looked at Colette.

Sofie rolled the still-cool glass bottle between her palms and watched the sky darken as she started talking.

"One day, my father came. I didn't see him often, and I was nervous every time I did. This time, he brought me a painting. I remembered thinking it was very important because the case he brought it in had a lock. He took it out and said he thought that I could do an even better job learning if I could see and copy off a real piece, instead of an image."

"That's...something," Landon murmured.

Sofie shrugged. "When you're learning technique and testing out new mediums, trying to copy or recreate an existing piece is a good way to learn.

"He left the painting with me. Told me to make sure I paid attention to everything, even the edges."

Colette grinned at the mention of edges, but didn't interrupt.

"For a week, I worked. I spent the first two whole days just looking at it. Trying to mentally erase the cracks and discoloration in the varnish to see what it would have looked like when it was created. Then I started painting.

"My father came back, and I still remember the look of disappointment on his face. I was so scared. He smiled and told me it was nice, but the colors were wrong. Too bright. I told him my painting is what the original would have looked like when it was first painted, and I could prove it to him if he let me clean the original."

Sofie smiled, remembering the rush of pleasure and pride she'd felt with what came next. "Then he smiled at me, and I felt so talented and clever. He arranged for me to take a tour of a restoration lab, though I had to promise not to tell anyone I was planning to attempt my own restoration. He said it was because people would see how young I was and not understand that I was more than capable."

"That's probably not wrong," Landon said. "I don't think anyone would want a twelve-year-old taking solvents to an antique painting."

"I made a note of every chemical and tool they used and asked my father to get them for me. He did and when he came back a month later, I had cleaned the original painting. And I'd applied yellow-tinted varnish to mine to try and mimic the coloring or the original, because even after being cleaned, they hadn't quite matched.

"After that, he brought me new pieces almost every month, and each time, he'd ask for more. More detail. More accuracy. He brought me pages of notes on how to age varnish or mimic the craquelure. I later realized many of those notes were from confessions by famous forgers. One time, he brought a UV light and told me he wanted the paintings to look the same under UV light. That's when I learned how to paint not only what I saw but to paint time. To paint what came before—the images underneath. The corrections and overpainting."

"That's amazing," Colette murmured.

Sofie went on, the story flowing easily now as she talked about each new complexity her father brought her and asked her to recreate. The first time he brought her raw materials so she could make her own paints, along with period accurate paintbrushes. An X-ray, along with the original piece, the X-ray showing a whole figure that wasn't in the final.

"Did you realize what he was having you do? What he was doing with the copies you made?" Andrei asked.

"Not until I was in my artist residency. That wasn't my father's idea. I was enrolled at the university as a favor to my father, or maybe to the church. I was in the classes, but I don't think I was really a student, more I was…allowed to be there. I was focused on technique, and one of my professors, when they said I was struggling to find my own style, put my name forward for an artist residency. It came with studio time, supplies, mentorship, and access to an amazing lecture series."

Sofie shrugged. "My father wasn't happy about it, but he didn't stop me. It wasn't until I went to one of the lectures on forgery that I realized exactly how different what I was doing at home—creating exact, indistinguishable replicas—was to the way we learned technique by painting our own version of masterpieces in art school."

She winced, feeling a blush creeping up her chest at her naivety. "I was sheltered, and though they let me read and watch whatever I wanted, I was just a girl in a room with paint. And here was a lecturer talking about how art forgery was a billion-euro industry, and how art could be used as currency for crimes. That didn't seem to have anything to do with me…until he talked about the edges."

Colette murmured a noise of agreement.

"Until then, I didn't know how odd it was that my father brought me paintings without their frames. About how paintings are always in their frames, and when they're taken out and photographs are taken of the edges, those photographs are protected. That matching the edges used to be one of the only ways to spot a forgery. Then I remembered my father telling me to pay attention to the edges."

Sofie took a deep breath, held it, then released it on a sigh. "I wish I could say that the next time I saw my father I confronted him, but I didn't. Instead, I told him that if I was going to keep doing this, I would need more equipment. That the people who worked at museums had X-rays and chemical tests."

"So you acknowledged it without directly saying anything." There was no judgement in Andrei's voice.

She nodded once. "And it went on that way for several years, until he brought me a painting that I knew… That I knew was more than just a piece of art but of history."

"Wait, where was he getting these originals?" Landon asked.

"The Vatican archive," Andrei responded.

"No," Colette said, shaking her head. "The Vatican archive is documents. The Vatican museum has the art. The majority of the collection is in museum storage, but the museum and the archive are different."

"It upsets me that you know that," Landon muttered.

"Every art thief worth the title has imagined stealing art from the Vatican."

"You're going to hell," Andrei said in a bored tone.

But Sofie was sitting forward. "Yes! See, that's what I want."

They all looked at her, Andrei sitting up and slowly twisting to face her. She'd been right. It was much harder to focus on telling the story with his predatory attention on her.

"What do you mean that's what you want?" Andrei asked.

"I… Wait there's more. Unless you don't want to hear?" Sofie blinked at him.

"Tell me," he ordered.

She felt that command run down her spine.

"The paintings he brought me, they were all different styles. Nothing too modern, but not all Renaissance or old masters. During my residency, I leaned toward post-impressionist style for myself, but with more surreal subjects rather than everyday life. That becomes important in a minute."

Sofie twisted her fingers, nearly dropping the bottle.

Andrei reached out and clapped his hand over hers. The nervous, jittery feeling faded now that he was touching her again.

"Your father brought you a painting you knew was important," Andrei prompted softly, even as he took the glass bottle from her and set it down.

"He brought me Salvator Mundi."

Colette made a strangled sound, pressing the fingers of both hands over her mouth.

"The original," Sofie added with a knowing look at Colette.

Colette exploded up off the couch, shouting in French.

"Angel," Andrei said with a sardonic smile. "I want to freak out like Colette is, but I clearly don't know enough about art."

"Salvator Mundi is the most expensive painting in the world," Colette rushed to say, pacing behind the couch. "It sold for 450 million dollars, and that was more than a decade ago. With inflation…" She waved one hand in the air. "A lost masterpiece that was in the collection of an American businessman until 2005. Attributed to da Vinci himself. But!" Colette stopped, turning dramatically. "There's debate about who actually painted it. Some experts say it's possible da Vinci painted parts of it but not the whole. Many scholars theorize that there is an original that da Vinci created for his students and followers to copy. There are many versions of Salvator Mundi, credited to followers of da Vinci.

"Each has the same subject, composition, but different due to the different artist. The one that sold for a ridiculous sum sold for that much because it's supposedly da Vinci's original."

Landon had a phone out and was frowning at it. He held it out to Andrei who leaned in to look at the image—Christ in Renaissance attire, his right hand performing a blessing while he held a crystal orb in his left.

"But not everyone agrees," Colette continued. "It was probably mostly painted by Bernardino Luini, one of da Vinci's followers, with some help from da Vinci himself."

Sofie nodded enthusiastically as Colette spoke, squeezing Andrei's hand.

"If a piece with a tenuous claim on being da Vinci's original sold for 450 million, imagine what the true original would be worth." Colette sounded almost dreamy, and her eyes had taken on a faraway look.

"Who the fuck could afford to pay that?" Landon said with a shake of his head.

"A Saudi prince," Sofie answered.

"Ah, well. Okay, then."

"You're saying you saw the true da Vinci original?" Colette asked in an almost reverent whisper.

"Yes. It's beautiful," Sofie said. "The shoulders are twisted just a little like the Mona Lisa. And the orb is… indescribable. It's not just clear and flat. The fabric folds reflect the visual distortion of the curved surface of the orb."

Colette looked enraptured, and Sofie felt almost bubbly with excitement at sharing this information with some who could appreciate it. It was so nice to talk to people. Who knew?

"It took me a long time to replicate that part," Sofie added. "The sphere."

Colette braced her hands on the back of the couch and bent over. "You made a copy?"

"Oh. Um. Yes."

They all stared at her.

"And you didn't call me?" Colette demanded.

"We hadn't met yet."

"Oh, okay." Colette pointed at her. "Next time, you call me."

Landon reached up and grabbed Colette's hand. "No. Next time your friend is replicating a priceless piece of art, how about she not call you."

Andrei was ignoring the byplay between Colette and Landon, attention on Sofie.

"Your father brought you this painting. One you knew he shouldn't have. What did you say?"

"I saw it, knew right away what it was, and realized that anything involving that piece of art would be international news. Not just in the art community but to everyone. So I asked him what he was going to do with the copy I made, and if I would go to jail if I didn't do a good enough job."

Colette sobered, circling around the couch to sink down beside Landon.

"My father stared at me for a long time, and asked if I understood what we were doing. I said no, because I didn't really. But I said that I knew what a forgery was, and that if anything I made was presented as the original and not a reproduction, that I could go to jail.

"He said that all I was doing was making copies. Reproductions. There was nothing illegal about that. He brought me originals to work off because I was a gifted artist and deserved to be in the presence of the original pieces created by other gifted artists."

Sofie looked down at her and Andrei's joined hands. "I should have asked him where he got the originals. I should have asked him again what he was doing with the copies. I didn't."

"You were young and isolated. He was an authority figure in your life. It's understandable that you didn't question him," Landon said.

"It was smart," Andrei countered. "You protected yourself."

She smiled at him, but it felt shaky. "After that, I saw my father less, but other people started to show up. They would bring me things and ask me to make a copy. An exact copy. At first, my father would send a note with each stranger who came, so I knew he sent them. But then, after a few years, people started to show up who weren't referred by my father but by one of those first few strangers."

"I assume that's how you two met?" Landon asked Colette.

She nodded. "I'd heard whispers about a forger they called the new Dutch master. Able to make anything. A true artist. I worked for years to build trust with... well their name doesn't matter. The point is, it took me years to get that person to trust me enough to give me Sofie's contact information."

"By the time I met Colette," Sofie said, "most conversations I had were very frank. I knew that the copies I made would get passed off as the originals, but I was very careful to always say that what I had created was a reproduction."

"That's why you kept insisting I couldn't arrest you. You think you'd get off on a technicality."

Sofie cocked her head as she stared at Andrei. "I was wrong. Because you did arrest me."

"If it makes you feel better, if I do have to really arrest you, it will be for handling and possessing stolen goods. All those originals you had in your studio..."

Sofie opened her mouth, then closed it. "Is that a crime?"

"Yes."

"Oh."

Andrei's sly smile widened into a grin that made him look young and almost carefree.

"But the pieces your father brought you...those might not have been stolen." Colette bounced one foot as she thought. "At least not really. He might have been taking them from the Vatican museum storage. I know the museum storage and the secret archive aren't the same, but I bet he has access."

"That's what I think too," Sofie said. "At least for some of them. Maybe most. But once or twice, he brought me pieces that I knew were held in private collections or museums."

"What, exactly, is your father doing?" Andrei said. "Is he selling Vatican paintings on the black market, and putting your forgeries in storage in their place?"

"If I had access to a collection like that...that's what I'd do. Except I'd keep the original and sell the forgery," Colette added. "Sofie is very good. I expect her paintings would pass authentication tests, and if they came wrapped in something with the papal seal..."

"Collectors don't ask too many questions when they know the provenance is questionable," Landon said.

"The prefect of the Vatican Apostolic Archive is a black market art dealer." Andrei's use of the proper modern title for the archive startled Sofie.

It was a good reminder that just because he asked questions didn't mean he didn't know far more than he let on.

"And thief. Or broker." Colette shook her head in disbelief. "If he brought you originals of items you know weren't part of the Vatican museum collection, he had to get ahold of them somehow."

"Did you steal any of them?" Landon asked her, soundly only mildly curious.

"Do you want to know the answer?"

"No. I don't think I do."

Colette laughed, but then looked back at Sofie. "I don't think I ever worked with your father, at least not directly. I'm Catholic enough I feel like I'd recognize a priest, even without his collar."

A wave of exhaustion washed over Sofie and she pulled her legs up, curling them under her. The movement caused Andrei's hand to slip out of hers.

She reached out, trying to grab it back, but he was already turning away and standing.

Sofie tucked both hands between her thighs, hoping Colette hadn't seen that.

Landon and Colette were speaking softly. On one hand, Sofie was glad that Colette and Landon were here. Their presence dispelled some of the tension and made this more of a conversation, thanks to their periodic interjections and questions.

On the other hand, if they'd been alone, maybe Andrei would have had to interact with her more. He'd be the one having to ask every question.

Maybe if they'd been alone, he'd touch her, with more than just his hand on hers.

Andrei had gone to the bar, but now he returned with two open bottles of mineral water.

"Thank you," she said as he handed one to her.

He took a seat on the edge of the cushion, twisting to face her.

"What did you mean earlier, when you said that's what you want?"

His voice was low enough not to interrupt Colette and Landon's conversation, though once he spoke, they quieted.

"When did I say that?"

"When Colette was talking about robbing something."

He studied her feature by feature, and she felt as if she were behind museum glass, an object to be studied. "And you went with her to the museum, despite the rules you mentioned, and we have yet to talk about."

Sofie opened and closed her mouth, not quite sure where to start.

"Do you want to switch from forger to thief?" Colette asked. "I'll teach you—"

"No," Landon interjected flatly.

"—and you can come work at our new company where we only steal things when the museum says it's okay," she rushed to add.

Sofie shook her head. "It's not that I want to switch, but…well going with Colette, it was an adventure. And I'm tired of staying home. Of being alone."

Sofie grimaced, aware of how foolish that probably sounded to Andrei, given what he'd witnessed.

"But I did want to learn how to steal something from a museum."

Andrei closed his eyes, head dropping. "I know I'm going to regret asking this, but is there a specific reason?"

"Yes." Sofie squared her shoulders. "I'm going to rob the Vatican."

Landon started to laugh as Andrei switched out his bottle of water for another beer.

SIXTEEN

"WHY DID YOU SLEEP BESIDE ME?"

Andrei had heard her coming, so he didn't jump when Sofie spoke from behind him.

Two of the playrooms upstairs had beds. Landon and Colette were using one, and he'd given the other to Sofie. The couches down here in the half-finished lounge were long enough for him to stretch out on, so that's where he'd been attempting to sleep until he gave up ten minutes ago, opting to stare out the windows at the city lights in the distance. It was past the witching hour, and he'd taken comfort in imaging her upstairs peacefully sleeping.

She took another step, the swish of fabric only a whisper of sound. "Did hearing about what I am make it so you don't want to do it again?"

At that he turned, heart lurching.

Sofie looked like some long-ago fairy queen with a blanket wrapped around herself like a cloak, her hair loose on her shoulders. Moonlight made her ethereal. A creature of light not native to this dusty mortal coil.

"What do you mean?"

"Before, when I woke up, you were in bed with me."

Andrei shook his head. "I shouldn't have done that."

"Why?"

"Why?" Andrei arched a brow. "Do you think I nap beside everyone I arrest?"

Sofie's posture softened. "Only the ones you've already had sex with." She made a face. "Almost sex?"

He couldn't handle talking to her about sex right now. Not when the night had his defenses down, and the reasons he shouldn't, couldn't take her into his arms seemed weak and mutable.

If he did touch her, kiss her, he might not stop until he was inside her. Then he'd be the first one to touch her in *every* way.

"I'm sorry," he said again. "It was inappropriate. I'd intended to sit beside you and wait until you woke up to talk, but…" He shrugged.

"If you were awake and watching my house, it means you didn't sleep at all."

"Not an excuse," he said firmly, then relented a little. "But a reason."

"And now?" She closed the distance between them.

Andrei, coward that he was, turned his back to her, facing the view once more.

He felt her hesitate and closed his eyes, hating himself as he waited to hear the sound of her retreating steps.

Instead, she moved beside him.

"What did you mean?" he said after a moment. "You asked if my knowing 'what' you are caused me to not want to do 'it' again."

"Now you know that I am…damaged."

Andrei sucked in air. "Fuck. Angel, no."

"I am. It's not a bad thing. Just a fact. My life is not normal. You're right, I was trafficked for labor."

"You knew?" he asked gentle. "I mean, you'd heard the term human trafficking?"

"I knew that what I was doing was in some ways forced labor."

"In all ways. You were deliberately isolated and trained to perform a specific task."

"But I love what I do."

"Would you love it more if you were creating your own art? If you could show people, tell people what you created?"

That struck a nerve, he could see it. She started to say something but stopped herself.

Of all the things she'd created, how many bore *her* signature?

"Colette was right, I've made several passports. They're fun. I have a holographic printer."

"I'll pretend I didn't hear that."

Her lips twitched, and the ache in his gut lessened at that small sign of mirth.

"The point is, I could leave," she repeated. "But if I do…no one will bring me originals to paint."

"A passport isn't the only thing you need to leave. Do you have a bank account?"

"Yes. My father's friends, they pay their fees to him. But people like Colette, they pay me directly. Digital currency mostly."

"Digital currency isn't the same as having a bank account and debit card."

"My father has an account for me. There's always money in it for things I need."

"Meaning, your father can see every transaction you make, if it's an account you both gave access to."

"I get cash too. Colette once paid me a hundred thousand euros in cash. It came in a briefcase." Sofie grinned. "It felt like a movie when she gave it to me."

"And you have that money somewhere you can access it?"

"Yes. And my father doesn't know about it. I haven't used much. Mostly I use it to buy—"

She cut herself off, and even in the moonlight he saw the blush.

Andrei shifted closer to her, almost close enough to brush her arm. "Buy what?"

Sofie raised her chin but didn't look at him, instead staring resolutely out the window. "Toys."

The word hit him like a punch to the gut. He'd been trying, desperately, not to think about her in a sexual manner since realizing what was happening with her life. Maybe she was right; he was treating her as if she were damaged.

Yet she was the furthest thing from damaged he'd ever seen. She was pure. Flawless. Innocent.

And if he put his hands on her again, he'd drag her even further into the darkness.

Every part of him wanted to ask her about the toys she owned. Make her describe how she used them on herself.

Instead, he stepped back, running a hand through his hair. "I won't touch you again," he vowed.

She didn't move or react, but her stillness took on a brittle quality. "I know."

The words quavered with grief.

His heart cracked. "You know why I say that, Angel. And it's not because I don't want you."

"It's because I'm damaged. A victim too scared to leave."

"No," he snapped. "Don't say that about yourself."

"I tried to escape out the window, but then tried to run back into the house. I know how stupid that was."

"It wasn't stupid. You've been conditioned to think the only place you're safe is your house. For fuck's sake, he told you it was holy ground, and—"

Andrei cut himself off. There were a lot of pieces of

missing information in Sofie's story, but the middle of the night wasn't the time to start looking for answers. Especially because asking those questions might challenge what she knew and believed. Though she'd been matter-of-fact about her father's crimes, with no defensiveness or justifications, he hadn't gotten the sense she hated the man who'd turned her into his art slave.

He and Landon had sat down and come up with a list of questions after Sofie had gone to bed. Andrei had then done his actual job and started a real case file, sending off a detail-scarce preliminary report.

Rolf was now officially pissed because he'd never intended Club Alibi to be a safe house, and yet so far, that had been its primary use. First with Colette in London, and now with Sofie here in Amsterdam.

"It's okay. You were already done with me because I lied, and that was before you realized I'm—"

"Sofie, stop."

He couldn't bear the separation anymore. He hadn't held her, really held her, since he'd pulled her into the tree.

Andrei swept her into his arms, holding her against his chest. A chest that ached when she melted into him, molding her body to his.

"I swear I'm not broken," she whispered.

"Perhaps we're all a little broken, Angel."

"Even you?"

"Especially me."

Andrei rested his cheek against her head, content to just hold her for a long moment.

"My mother loved me," he said, surprising himself with the words. "That's the part people never believe when they hear the rest."

Sofie tilted her head, saying nothing.

"She was a prostitute. Not by choice. We lived in a one-room flat in a factory town in Czechia. Her clients all work at the manufacturing plant where they made cars. Every time I see a Skoda I think of her."

When he'd first pulled her to him, Sofie's arms had gotten trapped between them. Now, she wiggled them free, wrapping her arms around his waist and squeezing him. It felt good, not just to hold her but to be held in return.

"She'd tell me stories about the places we'd go when we had money. Someday we'd have money. We'd travel. Buy nice things."

"She sounds like a good mom," Sofie said.

"She tried. She made sure I was never sexually abused. Refused offers from men who were willing to pay enough to buy one of the Skodas they built to be the first to fuck me."

Sofie gasped, hugging him tighter.

"But she was less worried about the times the men were annoyed I was there and beat me. Or threw me out while they were with her.

"I ran away. First time, I was nine. Slept in a train yard for three days. I had no plan, no money, but I thought... Thought that if I left, I'd have control over something— anything."

"Did she look for you?"

"That first time, probably, when I didn't come back by the second day."

"Who found you?"

"No one. I always went back. I couldn't leave her."

Sofie took a shaky breath.

"So you see, I understand," he said softly. "Why you tried to leave, and why you tried to go back."

She nodded against his chest.

"When I was twelve, suddenly we had money. I didn't understand how or why at first. We moved into a house with lots of bedrooms. I got a room to myself. Then other women started showing up. They'd stay with us. Some spoke Czech. Some spoke Slovak, which we spoke too, because that's where my mother was from originally."

"The other women, they were..."

"They were being trafficked. The money was because she was helping force these women who originally came for cleaning jobs, into prostitution.

"She died when I was fifteen. Liver failure from Hepatitis B. A transplant could have saved her, I think. But they never even talked about it. Not for someone like her."

He took a measured breath, letting himself feel the grief and anger that he knew would never full fade. "I think part of me stayed there, in the hospital room where she died."

Sofie made a snuffly noise, and the idea that she was crying for him should have been absurd but wasn't. "What did you do...after?"

"I started working for the same people she had. Organized crime. It was survival. Nothing more. Until I got caught, and the authorities started offering me things in exchange for information. I realized that who I was, the life I'd led, had value. I could do things, go places, no one with a pretty childhood could. First, I was an informant, then, when I was old enough, I joined the state police. They sent me undercover almost immediately."

"That's how you ended up with Interpol."

"There were a few career moves and things along the way, but yes."

They stayed wrapped in each other's arms for a long time, enjoying the silence and the night.

"Andrei?" she whispered just as he was starting to think about scooping her into his arms and moving them to the couch.

He'd hold her until she fell asleep. Then he'd lay her out on one couch, and he'd take the other. That way, he could be with her, but removed the temptation of touching her.

"Yes?"

She pulled back, looking up at him. Her gaze was frank, her chin raised...but she was blushing.

"May I kiss you?"

SOFIE BRACED herself because she knew what his answer would be: no.

But she'd never forgive herself if she didn't ask. Especially now that he'd shared his own story. Now that she knew that when he said he understood, he meant it.

He'd said she wasn't broken, then admitted maybe they were all a little broken, but with him...with him, she felt whole.

With him, she was more the Sofie that craved adventure than the one who was a willing captive within the gilded cage her father had created for her.

Since Colette arrived at her house, she'd been Adventure Sofie, and was terrified to completely lose that person in favor of the Sofie she'd been just a month ago.

She almost had lost her. The feeling that she had to go home because it was the only place that she was safe—despite the evidence that wasn't true—had nearly overwhelmed her earlier. If she'd gone back into the house in that moment, she wasn't sure she'd ever have been able to bring herself to leave again.

Andrei had stopped her. Kept her safe from her herself.

He made her bold, daring. It was why she'd been willing to risk body and soul to submit to him.

And of all the people alive on the earth, he was the only one she wanted to kiss.

It would hurt to hear him say no, but the pain was worth it to know that she'd asked. That she was the Sofie who was bold and daring enough to go on adventures.

Becoming that Sofie over the past few weeks was a sign that she was ready. That she could do what was needed.

Though the Adventure Sofie voice in her head went silent as her body started to burn with embarrassment when the silence stretched on.

"There are a thousand reasons kissing you is a bad idea." Andrei's low voice wrapped around her like the silky dark of night.

Sofie closed her eyes, bracing herself to hear a list of all the ways she wasn't enough.

"And I can't remember any of them right now."

Sofie took a soft breath, hope blossoming. Slowly she raised her head, meeting his gaze. The moonlight was behind him, casting his features in shadow.

"My angel." He touched her temple, tracing two fingers along her cheek to her chin.

Gently he tipped her face up. She held her breath, scared that if she moved, she'd break the spell of this moment.

Someday she'd paint it. This moment of waiting for a kiss. She knew now why Klimt had used gold. She'd use silver.

Andrei lowered his head, brushing her lips with his.

It was a fleeting touch, and yet she felt it through every nerve in the body.

He groaned low in his throat, his arm tightened around her, and sealed his lips to hers.

This moment. This is what she would paint. A riot of color to show every emotion that flowed through her—joy, pleasure, nervous excitement, a prickle of worry that she was doing it wrong.

His lips moved—pressing softly, sliding gently. Then he opened his mouth just enough for her to feel the heat of his breath against her before his tongue gently touched her lower lip.

"Open for me, Angel," he murmured against her mouth.

She parted her lips, feeling foolish for not realizing that's what he'd been hinting at.

His tongue slipped inside. He traced the inside of her lower lip, then flicked the tip of her tongue. Tentatively she returned the gesture. It was intimate and strange. His mouth both hot and somehow cool. She realized she could taste mint—toothpaste maybe.

How strange and wonderful that by kissing him, she now knew things, even if they were as small and simple as his preference for mint toothpaste.

Andrei pulled back, resting his forehead on hers.

Sofie's throat tightened, and unexpected tears burned her eyes.

Her first kiss.

And it had been perfect.

Gently, Andrei eased her away from him, then bent to pick up the blanket that had fallen down around her feet.

She wondered if he'd spread it out on the ground, then lay her down on top of it. She wanted that—wanted the heat and weight of his body on hers.

Instead, he tucked the blanket around her once more, and strangely that felt right too, though she was a little disappointed. That kiss deserved to stand alone, the signature moment of this moon-soaked night.

"Goodnight, Sofie."

Maybe she should have worried the kiss hadn't been good. Maybe he'd kissed her out of pity, and she should be mortified.

But their gazes met, and what she saw in his eyes mirrored her own emotions.

What she felt as she looked at Andrei's dark, silent figure was neither worry nor embarrassment, but hope.

SEVENTEEN

"SOFIE, WAKE UP." The soft feminine voice was accompanied by a hand stroking her hair. It was comforting and strangely familiar. She didn't know why it was familiar, given that though her nannies had been caring, they hadn't been maternal.

Sofie snuggled deeper, trying to get away from the motherly touch because it did *not* compliment the dream she'd been having.

In her dream, she was with Andrei, and they were doing far more than just kissing.

"Sofie."

Dream Andrei held her by the throat, pinning her to the bed, the position at odds with the sweet words he whispered in her ear and the slow gentle thrusts of his cock into her pussy.

"Sofie!" The shout was accompanied by a shock of cold.

Sofie sat up, hair flopping over her face. She shoved it back and glared at Colette, who tossed the blankets she'd snatched off Sofie onto the floor.

"I was having a sex dream!" Sofie said in protest.

"Did you get to finish?"

"No, you woke me up."

Colette shrugged. "Sorry."

"Easy for you to say, you have someone to have sex with." Sofie flopped back on the bed. Her body was still humming with arousal.

Colette winced. "Ah, yes. That's true."

"Why did you wake me up?"

"Rolf."

Sofie sat up. "Who's that?"

"He's in charge of the Club Alibi project. He signed off on you being here."

"Andrei's boss?"

Colette shrugged again. "Close enough, I think."

"Is he…here?"

"He's on a video call and wants to speak to you."

"What time is it?"

"Nearly eight."

She'd slept in later than normal—often, she rose early to paint with the morning light. Still, her sleep schedule had been a mess for weeks. When Colette came to stay with her, there were nights they'd stayed up drinking and talking all night, while other times, they were up early to work on either their dresses or the necklace in preparation for the gala.

Sofie slipped out of bed. A cupboard door in the corner hid a sink, and Colette had gotten her basic toiletries. She applied toothpaste, then turned to look at Colette, asking, "Why does he want to talk to me?" before sticking the brush in her mouth.

"Andrei filed a preliminary report yesterday. That's why that other agent came. Rolf now has questions—actually I think Andrei and Landon have some additional questions too."

Sofie turned to spit. After washing her face, she scraped

her hair into a bun—it was tangled because she hadn't braided it before going to sleep, and brushing it would take too long.

She hesitated for a moment, briefly self-conscious, before stripping naked and digging into the HEMA bag full of supplies Colette had bought her.

"Rolf is a good man," Colette said as Sofie dressed. "He was with Landon and Andrei when they rescued me."

It was during one of those late drunken nights that Colette had told Sofie what had happened to her. Sofie knew that Colette had left things out, the pauses and hesitations in her story too obvious to be anything but gaps.

"He just wants information?" Sofie finished pulling on the loose camel pants and oversized white button shirt over a bralette and underwear. The shirt was similar to the ones she wore to paint every day, and she appreciated that her friend had found something that felt like her.

The lacy pale blue underwear and bra weren't at all like what she wore most days, but very much the sort of thing she would buy herself.

"Yes. They need to have all the information so they can decide what to do."

"They don't need to do anything." Sofie slipped her feet into ballet flats.

"Sofie…" Colette touched her arm. "You understand what's probably going to happen, don't you?"

"What do you mean?"

"What was done to you was a crime. A very serious crime. And I'm so sorry I didn't realize you'd been forced into it. I would never have come to you had I known that you'd been trafficked and groomed and…" Colette's eyes were bright with tears.

Sofie stared at her friend, a sinking feeling gripping her.

"Sofie?" Colette reached for her, but Sofie backed up, turning for the door.

"Where are they?"

"There's an office... I'll show you." Colette cast a worried look at her as she went first out the door.

Sofie paused for a moment in the open doorway of the office space, blinking as she realized it was just Landon and Andrei in the room. Rolf was on the large computer monitor.

"Jurisdictional issues will..." Rolf trailed off as Andrei and Landon both turned toward the door.

Sofie's stomach fluttered when Andrei's gaze met hers. A smile, softer than his normal sardonic grin, touched his lips, while a wicked glint still lingered in his eyes, especially when they flicked down her body in a quick assessment.

The outfit was comfortable and practical, but for a moment, she felt beautiful in it.

"Ms. Vermeer is here," Landon said, shifting so that there was a free seat between himself and Andrei, directly in front of the camera.

Sofie sat, nervous until Andrei reached over and took her hand.

He was holding her hand.

Something had changed last night when he kissed her. The problem was, she didn't know what it meant, if it meant anything at all.

"Ms. Vermeer, it's a pleasure to meet you." Rolf wore a suit and tie. The wall behind him was bookshelves with what looked like legal tomes as well as binders and a few pictures with what were no doubt important people.

Either his chair was small, or he was an exceptionally large man.

"Hello," she said, trying to act like she took meetings with people in suits and ties all the time. The way Andrei squeezed her hand made her think she wasn't doing all that well.

"I'm Agent Pederson. Agent Leonard and Agent... Rather, *Mr.* Malik have caught me up on your situation."

"There's no situation." She smiled. "I don't need anything from you." Sofie hesitated, fairly sure she needed to say something else. "So... Goodbye."

She started to rise, but Andrei put a hand on her thigh and pushed her back down into her seat.

"This isn't really a question of what you need," Rolf said. "A crime was committed. Several crimes in fact."

"I didn't do anything illegal."

Beside her, Andrei shifted, drawing her attention. "Angel, I know you think that saying you just made copies, with no intention of passing them off as originals, somehow makes it not a forgery, but the law is a bit more complicated than that."

Her stomach felt slimy. "What do you mean?"

"Forgery laws are nuanced and complex. But saying you 'just made a copy' of a painting, especially from an original, and didn't know what it was for, isn't a defense."

Sofie's breathing sped up as panic gripped her. "Are you arresting me, for real?"

"No," Andrei said vehemently, slanting a glance at Rolf. "We're not. But I'm telling you that you could be. That you could be arrested and convicted of forgery."

"But...but my father said..."

"He lied to you." Andrei twisted in his seat and took both her hands in his. "About a lot of things, I think."

Sofie's face heated with shame. She snatched her hands back from Andrei.

"I know that. I'm not a fool. I know my father isn't... I know." She swallowed. "I know."

"Ms. Vermeer," Rolf said gently, "you were trafficked as a child. Adopted and groomed for the sole purpose of using your skills for financial gain. Even now, what you're experiencing is forced labor."

Sofie shook her head but couldn't speak. Her cheeks and chest were flushed with shame. She wanted to curl up into a stupid little ball and hide.

"Work or service extracted under penalty of violence is forced labor."

"My father wouldn't hurt me. He may not be a good man, but he wouldn't hurt me." She barely got the words out through a tight throat.

Rolf's expression softened. "Ms. Vermeer, the men who attacked you weren't your father's enemies. They were hired by your father to scare you into compliance."

"No! They only came because I left my *sanctum*."

"Sofie, Angel, please listen." Andrei reached for her, but she leaned away and refused to look at him. "Even if he declared your house holy ground, that wouldn't stop someone from kidnapping you from there."

"It's not just my house," she snapped. "It's my house, the market, and the Basilica of Saint Nicolas. Those places I'm safe and no one can touch me."

"That's not true." Andrei's voice was no longer soft and caring.

She whipped around to look at him, shocked at the mocking smile on his face as he lounged back in his chair, legs stretched out and crossed.

"You're smarter than that. You know that those men weren't really your father's enemies." He arched a brow in challenge, as if to say *or maybe you aren't that smart*.

The soul-deep shame that had been burning her from within shifted to a different kind of heat. Anger.

"What I know is that if I leave, I'll never have the chance to get back what is mine," she snapped.

Andrei's eyes glittered. "Now we're getting somewhere."

"What my father is or isn't doesn't matter."

"No, what matters is what you are. And what you aren't is a thief."

Days ago, she would have been relieved to hear him say that, but this wasn't a confirmation of her lack of thievery. This was a taunt.

"Not yet, but I will be."

"Good enough to steal something from the Vatican?" Andrei's brow arched and he shook his head mockingly.

"Yes," she shot back. "I will. I'll get back what's mine."

"Please stop planning crimes." Rolf looked pained. "I can hear you."

"You're going to go steal back all those 'copies' you made?" The mocking way Andrei said copies made Sofie want to strangle him.

"No, I don't care about the copies."

"Forgeries."

"You said copies first."

"But they're forgeries."

Sofie cocked her head, studying him. "I didn't admit to that."

"But you did admit to having original artworks in your possession, many of which you either suspected or knew belonged in a museum?" Andrei tsked. "Your claim of innocence is getting harder to believe."

"Innocence?" She smirked. "I never said I was a virgin."

Andrei flinched at the word "virgin" and Sofie grinned in triumph. This was fun.

He recovered quickly. "The virgin maybe-thief," Andrei mocked. "Planning to steal all those pieces of art she forged…"

"*That* would be stupid."

"Then what are you stealing?"

"My paintings."

"Your forgeries."

"No, my art. *My* art." Sofie pressed a hand to her chest as she emphasized the second "my."

The mocking expression dropped from Andrei's face. "Your art…"

Sofie sighed. She hadn't planned to tell anyone, even Colette, this. However, the situation had gotten out of her control, if it had ever been in her control in the first place.

Sofie gestured at the computer keyboard. "May I?"

Andrei had to lean over and type in a password to unlock the computer. His arm brushed against her as he typed, and when he sat back, he placed his hand on her knee, even as she scooted forward in her chair to reach the keys.

A few seconds later, and she had a news article pulled up.

"Oh fuck," Landon breathed.

Andrei looked at her, back at the article, and then started to laugh.

"What?" Colette said as she burst into the room. "What is it?"

"Were you listening at the door?" Landon demanded.

Rolf sighed. "Will someone please share the screen?"

Sofie scooted to one side so Colette could share her chair, but Colette opted to perch on Landon's knee. It seemed like an odd and intimate position for her to take, given their audience. But then again, these four people shared a bond from when they rescued Colette.

Sofie rolled her shoulders to try and shrug off that familiar feeling of being left behind. Of being the one who stayed at home while others went out and had adventures. Though she was sure Colette would not have described it as an adventure.

"Vatican unveils four newly discovered artworks," Colette read out loud as Andrei shared what they were looking at with Rolf. "The collection includes an unfinished piece by da Vinci, two unsigned van Goghs, and a Cezan. These pieces, gifted to the church by devout Catholics either before or during the Second World War, were stored in the Vatican Apostolic Archive rather than the Vatican Museum's art storage. Their discovery is due to an initiative by archive prefect Father Noah Visser to conduct a complete inventory of the archive's contents.

"Previously thought to house only documents, the archive contains over 35,000 documents in the selective catalogue. The Vatican has stated it now expects to find other works of art hidden within the archive…"

Colette stopped reading as she reached for the mouse. Rather than scrolling down to continue with the article, she clicked on the image at the top. The grid layout showed four very different pieces of art, though each was easily identifiable as belonging to either da Vinci, van Gogh, or Cezan. A few more clicks brought up enlarged images of each individual piece.

Slowly, everyone in the room turned to look at Sofie.

She raised her chin, waiting for someone to say something. She'd assumed, based on Landon and Andrei's reactions, that they figured out why she brought up this article. But maybe they were the ones who weren't that smart.

"Angel…" Andrei said slowly. "Did you paint those?"

Sofie nodded, but what she said was, "Allegedly."

Colette made a snorting sound as she tried to stifle a laugh.

"Is your father trying to pass off your original art as undiscovered pieces by famous masters?" Andrei asked.

"I'm glad you're as smart as I think you are." Sofie tried to imitate his mocking tone.

Andrei shot her a look of warning and gentle threat that made her squirm a little in her chair.

"This is brilliant," Colette breathed. "The provenience is nearly impeccable. If the Vatican says that these were gifted to the church, who would doubt them? And so many art records were lost during the war, it wouldn't be hard to say that original sales records are simply missing."

"To be clear," Rolf said, "you did not intentionally paint those to be misrepresented as being pieces by the named artists."

"I painted them as I was trying to find my own style. That's what you do—you try every style, to see if that's what you love. And if you are going to do it, why wouldn't you try to do it in the way the masters did? Those—" she pointed at the screen, "—are some of the first pieces I made after my art residency."

Sofie's chest burned with anger and she had to clench her hands together to stop the rage from making them shake. "My gallery was full of my art for years. My father asked me if I needed somewhere to store them, but I said no. I wanted them with me. I was planning to, someday, go back to my mentor at the residency and ask for help putting on my own show. I wanted to wait until I had found my style, and had enough good pieces in it.

"My father would sometimes look at my original pieces, always complimented them. But one day, he came when I was rearranging, and I had all my favorite pieces out on display. He asked specifically about those and a few others. Asked me what pigments, brushes, and type of canvas I used. Then he asked if anyone else had seen them.

"A week later, I...I came home from the market and they were gone. All my original art, gone."

She could feel Andrei looking at her but kept her gaze on her hands, not sure she was ready to see what he felt about her confession.

"If you didn't create them specifically as forgeries, the authentication will show that they're modern, won't it?" Landon asked.

"Most of my paintings were created using only what the artists of the time would have had. Stretched my own canvas, and made my own paint for those ones they say are van Gogh and Cezan.

"I prepared my own poplar wood panel. Used charcoal first, then ink and watercolor, just like da Vinci did with *Adoration of the Magi*." Sofie twisted in her seat to look at Colette. "I know it's unfinished, but with da Vinci, I like those pieces best."

"It's stunning," Colette said. "And you're right, the contrast between the section—only sketched, inked in, shaded with the watercolor—is so striking."

"Thank you." Sofie's shoulders scrunched up in pleasure. "I loved making it so much. I wanted to see if I could create the same way they had."

"And you proved that you can." Colette was still studying the images on the screen, clicking back and forth between them.

"So the fact that they were in the Vatican archive and they won't find any modern pigment paints, means no one will look too hard?" Landon ran his hand up and down Colette's back as he spoke.

"It's more than that. Because some van Gogh expert will look at the brushstrokes and swear they were painted by Vincent himself." Colette looked first at Landon, then Andrei. "Sofie is that good."

Sofie's blush didn't burn this time, merely a pleasant heat at the praise.

"Van Gogh and Cezan both famously didn't remember to sign every single one of their paintings, so the lack of signature doesn't rule it out either." Colette's gaze was unfocused as she thought it through. "Any inconsistencies with the age of the varnish, or lack of dust and cracking, can be explained as previous restoration efforts, better storage…"

"Wait, you said he took *everything*?" Andrei's jaw clenched.

Sofie nodded.

Andrei made a sound that wasn't a laugh, not a true one. It was a sound that acknowledged how cruel people can be.

"Art is the thing you love above all, and he stole that from you."

Sofie nodded, but hesitantly. Once, she would have agreed with the statement that art was the thing she loved above all. But that was back when her world had been small.

An odd look of satisfaction crossed Andrei's face. "That's why you stay. Your father stole your art, and you're waiting. Waiting for…" Andrei paused, studying her. "For him to give you some sort of access to wherever he's keeping everything. You know you need information, and, if he's already moved everything to Vatican City, you need access. Once you have that, you'll steal back your original art. That's why you stay."

There it was, the truth of it all. The reason she'd been so desperate to be part of Colette's heist. The reason she didn't simply make herself a passport and leave.

She'd never admitted any of this before. Who would she have told? More than that, she only let herself think about all the pieces he'd taken once in a while, because thinking about it too often made her burn with frustration and rage.

To hear the words made it all seem more real…and her plan to somehow steal everything back and then disappear, foolish and best, and stupid at worst.

"Yes." Sofie nodded, because foolish or not, Andrei was right about her plan and her reasons. "All I have is my art, and I want it back."

ANDREI TUNED OUT what Rolf was saying in favor of studying Sofie's profile.

It felt as if he were seeing all of her for the first time. She'd been many things over the course of their short acquaintance. He thought that the last piece of the Sofie puzzle was understanding that she'd been groomed and trafficked to be exactly what she was—the best forger in the world.

But even after that revelation, he'd had a niggling sense that there was more.

Though Andrei understood better than most how being a victim of any kind could fuck with one's mindset, he had trouble reconciling the bold woman who dove headfirst into a BDSM scene with him despite never even having been kissed, with the woman who seemingly had been content to stay in her home, leaving only to go to the market and church, for years.

She had resources of money and skills, and while he was sure the fact that she'd been conditioned to think of her home as the only safe place played a part, it was the desire to get back what had been stolen that kept Sofie in her cage.

"No."

Sofie's vehement denial jerked his attention back to the moment at hand. Fuck. He hadn't been paying attention. Andrei leaned back to look at Landon behind Sofie's back as she argued with Rolf.

"Rolf wants to open a case against Visser for human trafficking," the other man murmured.

"Ms. Vermeer—"

"No." Sofie cut off Rolf. "You can't."

"I assure you, I can. Of the two crimes—art fraud and human trafficking—the latter is more serious."

"Don't do either. Leave him alone."

"Leave him alone so that you can perpetuate a crime

you insisted on planning while in Interpol custody?" Rolf asked archly.

Sofie nodded, but there was a hesitancy to it. She most likely loved her father, despite it all, and he knew how dark and heavy that love was.

"I'm afraid I can't agree to that, Ms. Vermeer."

Sofie flinched at Rolf's negative statement, and Andrei's jaw muscle flexed. He turned to face the monitor.

"We can't prosecute human trafficking without willing participation from the victim."

Rolf's eyebrow twitched at Andrei's challenge, but the resolve on his features didn't waver. "Then we'll pursue a forgery and cultural fraud case."

"About what?" Andrei asked. "What piece specifically?"

"In your report—"

"I made no mention of a specific piece of art we could examine and assess to build our case."

Now Rolf's expression cracked, showing his frustration. "Andrei, what are you doing?"

Andrei lounged back in his chair, knowing it made the straitlaced Rolf nuts. "I'm not doing anything."

There was a heavy silence.

"Come on." Landon patted Colette's ass. "I'm just a consultant and we're way outside the scope of my contract."

Rolf didn't speak again until the door had closed behind Colette and Landon.

"What's the endgame here?" Rolf said. "If there's no case, then this isn't an Interpol matter."

Andrei tensed. "What are you saying?"

"Unless we're opening a case, either into her human trafficking or art forgery, there's no reason for Ms. Vermeer to be in our custody, either as a protected witness…or a suspect."

"What does that mean?" Sofie demanded, then swiveled to look at Andrei. "What is he saying?"

"He's agreeing not to pursue charges against you for forgery. But if you won't help us with cases against your father, I can't keep you in protective custody."

"Protective custody?" Sofie asked softly.

"That's how we classified your arrest. A cover for taking you into protective custody. It won't show as an arrest on your record with local authorities," Rolf said.

"Oh, I…I didn't know." Sofie glanced at him uncertainly.

Andrei could have told her last night in the moonlight after he kissed her, but it would have broken the spell.

Last night, he'd felt the surety about how his life was and would be, fracture and come apart. He'd felt his surety about who he was—cynical, sardonic, carnal agent of the law who'd started life as a criminal—dissolve.

"Are we opening a case or not?" Rolf said.

"No." Sofie raised her chin, staring down Rolf.

He hid his grin behind his hand.

"Then it's time for your to leave Club Alibi, Ms. Vermeer. Today."

Andrei sat up, shaking his head. "No, we need a few days to plan where she's going to go."

"I'm going to go home."

Andrei whipped his attention to her. Swallowing his first words, he instead chose each one carefully. "I know that your home feels like a safe place, but it may not be. Your father may find out you were arrested or that you weren't at home last night. He may send those same men back to try and scare you again."

"My father wouldn't hurt me."

Andrei swallowed the panic that was clawing up his throat.

"I'll leave you to sort this out," Rolf murmured. "I'm

sorry we couldn't…I'm sorry. Andrei, I'll see you in two days in London. It's your week."

Andrei didn't acknowledge Rolf's words, and ignored the chime as the video call ended.

"I'm not stupid," Sofie said.

"I don't think you are."

"You do. At least a little."

"No, I think that your father has spent your whole life trying to isolate you. Conditioning you to think—"

"He won't hurt me, because if he if he hurts me, I might not be able to paint. That's why I don't think those men were my father's men. They hit me on the face." She pointed at her cheek. "What if they had damaged my eye? Then I couldn't paint."

Andrei's mouth snapped shut.

"I don't think he won't hurt me because he loves me. I think he won't hurt me because I'm valuable to him."

All this time, he'd worried about how to help her see the truth about her relationship with her abuser. But his sweet, innocent straightforward Sofie knew the truth.

Andrei suspected she still loved him in some way, because he had built that lovely cage he kept her in around the thing she loved.

"That's a very good point. But I think it's possible that your father's men know exactly how hard they can and cannot hit someone to do permanent damage."

Now, she looked a little uneasy. "No… No he wouldn't hurt me."

There was no point in continuing this conversation. She needed to have it with a licensed therapist.

Andrei backtracked. "We need a plan. You can't just go home."

"Why not?"

"Fuck, Sofie!" The panic that was now at the top of his throat, almost gagging him, made Andrei explode up out of the chair. "You're just going to go home and pretend none of this ever happened?"

"I won't pretend it never happened."

"So what? So you wait and hope that someday your father gives you a hint as to where all your art is and then…"

"And then I call Colette and she helps me plan how I get in and steal it back."

"Then what?"

"Then I have my art and I…I leave."

"Are you sure about that?" he snarled, aware his words were cruel.

Sofie flinched, but then got to her feet, standing toe to toe with him.

"I don't want to talk about this anymore," she insisted.

He needed to talk about this because the thought of letting her walk back in that house that wasn't a home but a guided cage, was going to drive him insane.

"We are going to—"

"No, Andrei. We aren't."

With a snarl of frustration, Andrei gripped her shoulders. Spinning her around, he forced her back step-by-step until he pressed her against the wall.

Sofie's breaths were shallow and fast, making her breasts rise and fall.

Andrei leaned down until his lips were almost on hers. She inhaled his breath as he exhaled.

"Andrei."

He closed his eyes, shoulder and arm muscles bunching as he fought for control.

"I've had very few choices in my life," she said softly. "Never asked for what I wanted."

"Angel…"

"But I want something."

"What do you want?"

"And I want to make a choice. Right here and now."

"What do you want and what do you choose?"

"I want to have sex, and I want it to be with you."

That wasn't what he expected her to say. For a moment, he considered saying no, not satisfied with the conclusion of their conversation about what she was going to do next. How she was going to be safe.

But then she pushed away from the wall, her breasts brushing against his chest as her lips touched his, and nothing else mattered except *now*.

Except being with the woman he was worried he just might love.

EIGHTEEN

"NO POWER EXCHANGE, no rules. You tell me what feels good. What you need."

Sofie nodded shakily. The boldness that had allowed her to declare what she wanted—to have sex with him—and then kiss him when it looked like he was going to insist on more talking had deserted her now that they were once more in the room where she'd slept.

She was sitting on the end of the mattress. The thin, heavy duvet was still on the floor where Colette had tossed it. According to a tag on one corner, it was leakproof.

And the fact that she was thinking about the duvet instead of sex was proof of how nervous she was.

Andrei was on the far side of the room, and the space between them somehow made her more nervous. But the way he looked, leaning back against the wall, his head tilted just slightly, his thick lashes partially veiling his eyes, was so sexy that arousal was quickly overtaking nervousness.

"I will," she rushed to say.

"I'm not sure I believe you, Angel."

"It's true. Now you know all my secrets. I don't have anything else to hide."

"That's a lie. Because there are things about you that I don't know and I want to."

"What things?"

Andrei pushed away from the wall, sliding his hands into his pockets. "You mentioned toys. What toys do you have?"

She was definitely blushing, but was going to pretend she wasn't. "I have a vibrator."

"Be specific."

"It's shaped like a rose."

"A clit sucker."

She'd never considered the word clit, sexy until she heard him say it.

"Y-yes."

"What else?"

"A dildo."

"How big, what shape, what color?"

"It's just…plain. Pink. Straight. It vibrates too, but not like the rose."

Andrei started toward her, step-by-step, like a big cat stalking prey. "And how do you use the dildo?"

"Like a dildo?"

"Do you slide it in and out of your pussy, or do you push it in and hold it there? Do you fuck yourself fast or slow?"

Sofie closed her eyes and swallowed, arousal flowing over and through her in waves. The sexual interrogation was embarrassing yet sexy.

"I usually push it in a bit and just…leave it there while I get the rose."

"And does the dildo stay, or is your pussy hot and wet?" His gaze slid up and down her seated form. "So wet that when you clench down because of the vibrations on your clit the dildo slides out?"

Sofie pressed the backs of her hands to her cheeks,

trying to cool the heat. The slight smile that curved Andrei's lips turned into a full grin.

"Answer me, Sofie."

"It slides out, but usually I try and go fast. I, um, insert the dildo and get the rose in place. Then I close my legs, and that holds them both in place."

Andrei was right in front of her now. She braced herself for his touch, expecting him to draw her to her feet and then help her out of her clothes.

Instead, he knelt, hands braced on the outside of each thigh. He pressed, forcing her legs that were already together, into tighter contact.

"Like this?"

"Y-yes."

"And do you lie there still and quiet? Waiting? Or do you work your hips? Do you hump the air, trying to imagine it's a real cock inside you?"

"I lie still. I tried one time, to move, but all by myself it felt…" She shrugged, not sure if "stupid" or "silly" was a better fit.

He didn't linger on that question, his next word drawing her right back into the sensual spell he was weaving. "And where are your hands? Are they playing with your pretty nipples? Clenching the pillow?"

"I play with my nipples first. Before the vibrators."

"Then where are your hands while the vibrators are working on your pretty cunt?"

"I…" She ducked her head. "This is embarrassing."

"There is nothing you can tell me that will change how I feel about you."

Her breath caught, and she slowly looked up. There was something stark in his gaze when it met hers.

He looked away first, but only for a moment.

"There is nothing you can say or admit that will lessen my desire. No kink I won't at least consider."

"I have a scarf. A long scarf. It's looped around a slat of my bed."

He watched her, attentive and nonjudgmental.

"I grab the ends and wrap them around my wrists."

His brows rose in surprised, but he nodded in encouragement.

"I make it tight, so I can feel the pressure." She gripped one wrist with the opposite hand. "I know it's just me, holding onto the ends to keep everything in place, but it feels so much better, easier, when I do that."

"Oh, Angel, you're going to love rope bondage."

She felt her own eyes widen. "Are we going to do that?"

Again, Andrei looked away. "No. Tonight, there's no toys. No kinks. Just us. What you like on your own might not be what you like with a partner."

She opened her mouth to ask if they could try rope bondage later, then.

Except there was no later. He said he understood, but he'd made it clear he didn't want her to return to her home. To her life.

Before those thoughts could derail her, Andrei brought her back to this moment by rising and pulling her to her feet.

"Any other toys you want to tell me about?" His fingers skimmed up her sides to her shoulders, then traced the line of her collarbones in and down until he reached the first button of her loose shirt.

"I bought a plug," she blurted out as he slipped the button free.

"An anal plug?"

"Yes."

"Have you used it?"

"Twice. I really like pushing it in and taking it out, but it was kind of boring just having it in."

Andrei took several deep breaths, leaning forward so he

could rest his forehead on hers as he did. "You're killing me, Angel."

"Killing in a good way?"

"The best way. And now, I know that you like having your ass fucked, not just filled."

"Oh. Yes, that sounds right. Fucked not just filled."

Andrei groaned low in his throat, slipping the last button free.

"Take it off for me," he murmured.

Sofie shrugged free of the shirt, her nipples hard inside the lacy bralette.

"Now the pants." His words were straddling the line between question and command.

"When you're ready," he added, almost as an afterthought.

"Please. You don't have to… I want this. I will tell you if I don't."

He watched her, a question in his dark gaze.

"Don't ask me," she blurted out, cheeks hot. "Tell me. Command me. I like that. It feels…right."

"You're so beautifully submissive. The things I would do to you in a full, working club…"

Andrei carefully gripped one wrist, pressing her hand against her own hip and guiding it down until her fingers caught the waistband of her underwear. A silent command to remove them.

She slipped them down her thighs, then wiggled her legs until they hit the floor.

"Now the bra."

Finally, she was naked before him, like she'd been that first night.

But there was a difference, because though she'd asked him to be dominant and commanding, he wasn't a Dom in this moment.

Sofie reached out, pressing her hands to his stomach.

He watched her as she watched her hands slowly draw his shirt up, exposing centimeter by centimeter of smooth skin. When she had the fabric up around his ribs, Andrei took over, reaching behind his neck to pull the shirt off with one smooth motion.

Sofie started to kneel as he had so she could undo his pants and pull them off, but Andrei cupped her elbows, keeping her on her feet.

"No, Angel. You don't kneel tonight."

He shucked his pants but kept on his boxers, which clung to his ass and thighs in a way she found wonderfully sexy.

They also showed off the very large bulge of his cock.

She felt him in her mouth, in her throat, but now imagining that cock in other places had a twinge of nervousness dancing up her spine.

"I've never done this before," she rushed out, feeling compelled to remind him.

"Now you tell me?"

Sofie giggled, then slapped a hand over her mouth. That wasn't a sexy sound. Quickly, she looked at his cock. It looked like it was the same size as a second ago. She relaxed, seeing that her comment hadn't killed his arousal.

Andrei tugged her hand from her mouth, then kept hold of it as he pulled her around to the side of the bed.

To her surprise, he climbed on first and sat in the middle with his back against the headboard.

"Come here, Angel."

Practically vibrating with nervous excitement, Sofie crawled across the bed to him, remembering the way she crawled across the floor when he ordered her to.

With soft words and firm hands, he guided her into position until she was straddling his thighs. Her own thigh muscles trembled in anticipation. Her wet, needy sex was bare and spread, the bulge of his cock close but not yet touching.

"Kiss me."

She blinked in confusion.

"Kiss me, Sofie."

Hands on his shoulders, she leaned in and down, pressing her lips to his. She was prepared for a quick hot kiss. A small appetizer before the entrée.

Instead, the kiss was slow and lingering. He teased and sucked her lips and tongue. The longer he kissed her, the more she relaxed into it, no longer focused on what would come next but instead on what was happening now.

She finally did the thing she'd imagine so many times, gently biting and sucking his full lower lip.

Gradually the kiss got more intense. His hand tangled in her hair to hold her still as his tongue thrust into her mouth, fucking her there the way he had with his cock.

His other hand cupped one breast, and when his thumb swiped over her nipple, she jerked free of the kiss to gasp.

"Please, Andrei. Please."

"Anything, Angel. Anything." He eased her back until she was sitting on his thighs, both hands on her breasts now.

He pressed them together, thumbing her nipples before switching to a gentle pinch.

"What feels better? This, or this." He gently scraped the very tip of her nipple with one blunt fingertip, while the other was pinched and rolled.

"I...oh, I don't—"

"Or maybe this." Bracing a hand against the middle of her back, he leaned in and sucked her nipple into his mouth. Teeth and tongue worked the sensitive nub, the constant stimulation making her hips start to rock back and forth. Her other nipple was twisted and tugged, the sensation occasionally tipping into the realm of pain, which only made it better.

Sofie tangled her hands in his short hair, anchoring herself to him the way she anchored herself to her own bed with makeshift restraints.

"Please, please," she whimpered.

"Let me see if you're ready," he murmured against her breast. "Hips up."

She lifted her ass off his thighs, making space for him to slip a hand between her splayed legs.

The first touch of his fingers on her slippery flesh was almost enough. Maybe would have been if she hadn't jerked hard in reaction to the feel of two fingers sliding over her.

"You're so wet. So ready for me."

"Yes. I am. Please."

"You come for me first."

"No, no. I want to come with you inside me."

"Maybe you will, but it's your first time, and penetration orgasms aren't guaranteed. However, I am very sure that if I do this…" He pressed his fingers on either side of her clit and started to rub in short up and down motions. "You'll come."

"Yes, yes, yes." She nodded so frantically she almost knocked their heads together. Luckily, he still had a hand tangled in her hair and pulled hard, forcing her head back, her upper body into an arch, before she could headbutt him.

The pressure against her scalp only made it better as his fingers worked her up and down, up and down. Not too hard or fast. Only pausing when he slid his fingers down to bring more of her arousal fluid up to her clit.

She'd transferred her hands from his head to his shoulders, holding on tight to keep her balance as he bent her back with a hand in her hair. Her leg muscles started to shake, and she didn't dare breathe deep, lest she deflate the slowly building pressure inside her.

Then he leaned in, sucking on the nipple that had before now, only had his fingers.

Pleasure washed over and through her. Clit and nipple both sending frantic pleasure signals racing through her body.

The orgasm was low and hot, rumbling through her like an earthquake. It made her teeth clench and her thighs tighten on his. The pinnacle went on and on as his fingers slowed but didn't stop rubbing her clit.

Finally, she collapsed against him, slumping on his chest. The air in the room felt cold against her sweat-dampened skin, but she didn't have to shiver for long.

Andrei wrapped and arm around her then rolled them to the side until she was on her back with him over her, his hips nestled between her thighs.

"Do you think you're ready for this?" His voice was rough, and as he braced himself above her, she saw that she wasn't the only one who was trembling.

"If you need to, we'll stop, and I'll use my fingers."

She nodded, nervous but still flush with pleasure.

Andrei sat up, first reaching around behind himself and grabbing the condom he'd apparently stashed in the waistband of his boxers.

He climbed off the bed for a moment to shuck his boxers, then was back in place between her spread legs.

He was beautiful.

Muscled but not muscular, with smooth skin that she wanted to lick. His cock was erect, the tip a deeper color than the shaft.

It looked huge.

She watched him roll the condom onto his dick, surprised at how sheer the condom was. When he was finished, she couldn't really see it except for the ring at the base of his cock.

With that done, he focused on her, looking over her naked, spread body with a casual possessiveness.

"Knees up. Brace your feet on the mattress."

Sofie repositioned herself, not looking away from his cock.

"Did you know that in classical antiquity, large penises were a sign of poor self-control and stupidity?"

Her nervousness had expressed itself as useless art facts. She winced.

Andrei took it in stride. "Is that why all the statues have small dicks?"

"Yes."

Andrei looked at his own cock, lips twitching before he shrugged.

"Call me a dumb brute, then."

Sofie giggled, then immediately worried she'd killed the mood.

"I love the sound of your laugh," he murmured.

A softer emotion slid through her, and she was getting ready to tell him that she loved his smile and his—

Andrei gently pressed her thighs open wider, bending a little to look at her spread, ready pussy. Worries about what to say and maybe killing the mood shifted to worries about what came next.

He stroked her sex from clit down to vagina. Gently he inserted one finger.

She sucked in a breath and held it, adjusting to the sensation.

Only to release that air on a gasp when his finger curled inside her and an unexpected throb of pleasure rippled through her.

"Does that feel good?"

"Yes... G spot?"

"Exactly. Have you ever touched yourself here?"

"No. I tried to angle the dildo one time but it didn't work."

"You need something curved." He thrust his curled finger, rubbing against her.

"Oh. Oh!"

"If we had time, I'd experiment on this sweet body. Try and see all the different ways I can make you come. Or at least bring you to that edge of pleasure and then use your sweet clit to push you over."

If we had time…

Andrei withdrew his finger and lowered himself on top of her. Braced on one elbow, he leaned slightly to the side, his other hand gripping his cock.

"Look at me, Angel."

Nervously, she obeyed, holding his gaze as he rubbed the tip of his cock up and down the valley of her sex. Her orgasm-sensitive skin gave a jolt every time the smooth, blunt head of his cock rubbed against it.

Finally, he placed the head of his cock at her entrance and didn't move it away. It felt impossibly big and blunt compared to her dildo.

She managed to refrain from asking if he was sure it would fit, but couldn't stop herself from stammering out, "Will you go slow?"

"Of course I will. Slow and gentle…until you need me to not be."

Andrei released his cock and shifted so now he was braced on both elbows above her. Even that small movement pushed his cock a little deeper inside her. She felt the stretch, a faint almost-burn.

But more than that, she felt a desperate need to be filled. To have him deep and hard inside her so that when her pussy clenched, she had that thick, hot flesh to clench around.

Andrei kissed her cheeks, eyelids, and finally her lips.

"Slow and gentle," he vowed as he gently eased his cock into her.

She had no idea how much of him was inside her when it momentarily became too much and she whimpered. The skin around her entrance felt too tight and though she knew it wouldn't, she was worried it would rip.

"I want you to tilt your hips. Don't arch your back, imagine pressing your lower back against the mattress. Yes, just like that."

All it took was a small adjustment, and the tight sensation eased, even as his cock slid deeper.

Andrei withdrew all the way, but before she could make a panicked noise, he thrust in. A bit faster, though not fast, and this time, it was much easier to take him.

"I'm almost all the way in." He was panting, and a sheen of sweat shown on his forehead. "Do you think you can take it all?"

"Yes. I want all of you inside me."

He groaned and thrust hard, seating the full length of his cock inside her. He was so deep that his pelvis pressed against her and she could feel his balls against her ass.

Andrei shifted his arm position, gripping one breast. He squeezed her nipple, harder than he had before, and a jolt of pleasure made her pussy clutch around him.

"I felt that, Angel. Felt you get so tight."

Maybe it should have scared her that he seemed to be at the edge of his own control. This was her first time, and perhaps it would have been better that he remained entirely calm and collected.

But she thought back to that thing she'd read—that being desired was the strongest aphrodisiac. She thought there might've been an addendum to that. One that said that seeing the effect you had on another person was the strongest aphrodisiac.

She felt both powerful and powerless watching him grit his teeth as he slowly withdrew. As if it took every fiber of his being to maintain a control that she was slowly shredding.

He started with a gentle, deep thrust. Pulling almost all the way out before easing in again.

It felt deliciously good. Both exactly the way she'd imagined, and so much more.

But the longer it went on, it wasn't just her arousal that built but a deep frustration.

"More," she begged. "I need more."

He stilled. "When you say more, do you mean harder…"

His hips pulled back and then slammed into hers, so hard it made a slapping sound and her body scooted up the mattress an inch.

"Or faster."

Again, he pulled back, only to thrust in once, twice, a third time. Not going as deep but moving fast.

Sofie wrapped her arms around him, nails digging into his back.

"Deeper," she demanded.

The slapping sound of flesh meeting flesh echoed in the room. Each time he thrust in, he ground against her, and sometimes, the angle was just right, and she felt a twinge in what she could now confirm was her G-spot.

A pleasure far deeper than the vibrator-induced orgasms she was used to, and even the clit-rubbing one he'd just given her started to build.

"I think…I don't know if I can come, but I feel like I can." She was aware that didn't make sense but hoped he understood.

"Slide one hand down between us and see if you can rub your clit."

They were both slick with sweat, making it easy to

wiggle her arm into position, her middle finger poised on her clit.

"I need to fuck you hard and fast. I want you to rub your clit until you come. If you come before I do, you can stop rubbing, but I want you to keep your finger on your clit. Gentle pressure. Then start rubbing again."

She nodded, past the point of being able to speak because she followed his commands, even as he gave them, her middle finger circling gently around her wet, swollen clit.

He tucked his arms under her shoulders, hands curling up from behind to hook over her shoulders and hold her in place as he fucked her hard and fast.

It was relentless and unforgiving. Again and again, his cock slid into her virgin pussy.

The orgasm took her by surprise, her eyes widening as her muscles started to shake. She almost jerked her hand away, remembering his order at the last minute and keeping her hand in place, fingertip pressing on the hood of her clit. Her pussy clenched around his cock, and orgasming around a thick, hot dick was exactly as wonderful as she'd always imagined.

"Again," he growled.

Her finger started circling her clit, once more almost without her conscious decision to do so. She was a creature of pure pleasure, more than willing to obey his every command because she knew in his words, she would find the path to that next peak.

His thrusts became uneven, his breathing unsteady. She watched him from beneath her lashes as his face tightened. When they'd come together before he'd been entirely in control and she'd loved that.

But she loved this too. Watching him succumb to this base desire and pure need.

"Fuck. Angel. Fuck."

He thrust both hard and deep, rocking her body with the force of it, and then he was shuddering above her, and she swore she could feel his cock twitching inside her as he came.

In that moment of climax, his gaze met hers, and dozens of sunrises and sunsets passed as time ceased to have meaning. It was only them. Only this moment.

Then Andrei lowered his mouth to hers, sealing this perfect moment with a kiss.

NINETEEN

ANDREI IGNORED the sound of his phone buzzing somewhere in the room. It was probably Rolf calling to tell him time was up. The sun was setting, and Sofie needed to be out of Club Alibi.

He'd take her out of the club, but not back to her house. According to her official records, she was a Dutch citizen, so it shouldn't be hard to get the local Interpol office to issue her a temporary passport.

Beside him, Sofie stirred. She'd fallen asleep almost immediately after sex, awake enough only to grumble about being cold.

He'd covered her up before leaving to take care of the condom. She'd curled into a ball and pulled the blanket over her head by the time he got back, but when he climbed in behind her and scooted against her back, she'd uncurled enough to mold her body to his until they were pressed together from chest to knees.

"Dusk," she murmured, stretching against him.

Her ass pressing against his cock only hardened his resolve—and his cock.

"Or dawn," he teased.

"No, the light is gold, not white."

Having never thought too hard about the tonal qualities of the light at dawn and dusk, the only response he could think of was to kiss her bare shoulder, then the side of her neck.

She gasped and shivered when he kissed her neck just below her ear.

"Sensitive?"

"Very," she whispered.

"I'll have to explore that more later."

She stiffened against him, then sat up. "I don't have to leave anymore?"

He sat up to. "You can't stay at this Club Alibi location. It isn't open to the public."

"I don't understand."

"The London club is up and running. It's a dance club on the bottom floor and a private BDSM club upstairs."

"Private or public? You've said both."

"Private, meaning membership based. But lucky for you, you know one of the Doms in charge." He winked.

Sofie didn't even smile. "I don't understand what any of this has to do with me."

Andrei rolled his shoulders to loosen the sudden tightness in his neck. "Sofie, you have to see that you can't go back to your house. Whatever you believe about your father, not wanting to hurt you, you were attacked in your own home. You have that elaborate security system that did nothing to stop them. That means that either they had the codes, or that system is incredibly weak."

"I can get a different system."

"Fuck." He rolled off the bed, gripping handfuls of his own hair to stop himself from screaming in frustration.

He took a minute to jerk on his pants before turning to face her. Sofie looked soft and rumpled. At one point, her hair had been in a bun, but he tangled his fingers in it, and now it was a cloud of messy waves around her bare shoulders. She pulled the blanket up over her breasts, but the smooth naked line of her back down to her ass was visible.

"Sofie, what is your plan?"

"You know my plan—"

"That's a fucking pipe dream and you know it. You're too smart not to."

She jerked back as if he slapped her. In a way, maybe a physical blow would have been kinder than his words.

"I'm sorry," he said immediately. "I'm sorry. That wasn't fair."

"What do you want me to do, Andrei?"

"I want you to not put yourself back in your father's power."

"You want me to just walk away. Right now. From everything. My whole life."

A panicky feeling that he was losing her made him lash out. "What life, Sofie? What fucking life?"

Her eyes widened in shock, and he pressed the heels of his hands to his eyes. He was an asshole. He'd always been an asshole.

Right now, he was the biggest asshole.

"It may not look like much of a life, but it's mine."

The rustle of fabric had him dropping his hands. She was off the bed, pulling on panties first, and then her shirt, which was long enough to touch the tops of her thighs. She held the fabric closed with one hand, gesturing with the other.

"I told you this morning that I've never had much choice in my life. And maybe when I did…do…have a choice, I make the wrong one." She raised her chin, even as it quivered. "But it's my choice. My life."

He had fucked this up and he was going to lose her. Clichéd as it was, the moment he slipped back into bed, pulled her body still flushed and warm from sex against his, he had no choice but to admit to himself that he'd fallen in love.

Being cynical and jaded were not the defenses he thought they were, because he was helplessly in love.

If he was lucky, this was just a case of really intense lust, and he was just too fucking emotionally stunted to realize that. He imagined it would be easy to mistake a mix of protectiveness and lust and think it was love.

But the part of him that always expected the worst knew that this was love. Because, of course he would fall in love with a woman who didn't love him back. A woman whose life was so tight and narrow that there was no space for him unless she chose to make room.

And it was very fucking clear she was not going to choose that. Not going to choose him.

But he had to try.

"Come with me," he said slowly. "Stay with me."

Sofie's expression softened, her gaze questioning.

"Right now, I'm stationed in London half the time, Budapest the other half. Both cities have world-class museums. I've got money saved up, enough that we can at least rent you a studio space in both cities."

Tears gathered along her lower lids. "Andrei…"

He felt like he was ripping himself open, trying to pull his very hard from his chest to offer it to her. "You can paint. Paint anything and everything you want. Your style, not copying someone else's. Original works, with your name on them."

"Yes," she whispered. "Yes, I'll come with you—"

He nearly went to his knees in relief.

"—while you're in London, and then I'll come home for a while and—"

"What the fuck? Sofie, no. No."

She stared at him. "What…did I do wrong?"

"You need to walk away."

"From my life?"

"From being under someone else's control. From being in fucking danger in your own home."

"So instead of my father being in control of my life, you would be."

"No." Andrei turned, slapping his hand against the wall to vent some frustration. "I don't want to be in control of your life. I may be a controlling asshole, but I limit how and when."

"Then why can't I come with you now, then come back here and—"

"Because I can't bear to watch you get hurt." He turned to look at her, leaning back against the wall, as the hope he'd been holding inside him continued to wither.

"I won't—"

"Don't lie to me, Sofie. Lie to yourself all you want, but don't lie to me."

She was trembling; he could see it from here, but she marched across the room to grab her pants, pulling them on.

He closed his eyes when she stripped off the shit to put on her bra before pulling the shirt back on.

"I told you I ran away. Again and again."

She paused to listen, fingers on the buttons.

"But I didn't tell you that I begged my mom to come with me. The last few years before she died, I realized what she was doing. What she'd become. And I knew it was bad. She was going to get hurt. Or arrested. Both. She was in danger, but no matter what I said, she refused to see it. No matter what I did, she refused to leave."

"It's not the same," Sofie insisted.

"Isn't it? You're in danger, but refuse to even acknowledge it. You don't have… You don't have to be with me. I'll help you, support you, even if we're just friends."

It would kill him to be close to her and not touch her and be with her, but he'd do it.

"Andrei…" Finally the tears that had gathered on her lashes fell, slipping down her cheeks. "I don't have much. My world is small. My life is small. But my art…" She swiped her cheeks with the back of one hand. "I know it sounds stupid, but of all the things that have been taken from me, all the choices I never had, my art is the one thing I might be able to get back."

Andrei nodded, though the fact that his heart was actively breaking made every movement feel dangerous and brittle.

"I understand. I truly do. But I can't watch you do this." He ran a hand through his hair. "I'll get someone to take you home."

He had his hand on the door when she called out, "Wait."

He didn't turn.

"When it's done, would you want…"

He was fairly sure he knew what she was asking. Someday, if she managed to steal back her art, and escape her father's influence, could they be together.

He should say no, because he wasn't going to wait for her. When he got to London, he was going to grab the first willing sub he could and control every breath she took until this desperate, broken, helpless feeling faded.

He should say no, but he knew that day would never come, so instead he said, "If that day comes, find me."

He heard a soft sob as he closed the door behind himself.

SOFIE CRIED, slept, changed all her security passcodes,

and slept some more before she was able to think past the grief.

She'd lost something precious when Andrei walked out that door, and it was entirely her fault.

She wanted to be brave, have adventures, but when he'd offered her a change for a true adventure—no, more than that, a life—she'd clung to what she knew. What felt safe.

It was Agent Baas who'd driven her home. The woman had let her cry quietly without asking questions. But she had talked. Agent Baas had talked about the psychological impact of abuse. How some people find it almost impossible to leave due to emotional ties, a safety in familiarity, or a sense they don't deserve love. She talked about how abandonment and lack of security at a young age could affect someone for all of their life.

And when she dropped Sofie off, she'd handed her an envelope full of papers—printed articles for her to read, a list of local resources, and on the top, a handwritten note with the name of several therapists who would be a good fit for her.

After a shower and lunch—it was less than twenty-four hours since she last saw him, though it felt like longer—she sat down with the papers Agent Baas gave her.

It was past time to admit to herself that getting back her art wasn't, by itself, going to be enough to make her feel like she'd taken control of her life. She'd built a shaky tower on the belief that if she could do that—become a woman capable of first manipulating her father and then pulling off an amazing art heist—she'd not only have her art but finally be a person brave and capable enough to leave everything she knew and start over.

Shockingly, none of the articles she read suggested committing crimes as a way to process her trauma. Apparently, art heists were not the kind of "work" that was meant when they said people had to do the work to get better.

Part of her wanted to cling to these papers as a different kind of excuse. That until she learned more, read more, and started going to therapy, she should just sink back into the life she'd been living before a heartbroken Colette showed up on her doorstep.

Then she wondered if this horrible hollow feeling in her chest was a broken heart. The fact that she ached to see Andrei again, even just hear his voice, made her think that it might be. She'd done an internet search for him, hoping she could find a picture, but Interpol didn't post their agents' pictures anywhere she could find.

Sofie put on water for tea, then carefully tucked the papers away. Therapy was on the to-do list, but she wouldn't use it as an excuse to avoid taking action.

She had to fortify herself with several cups of tea before she was brave enough to pick up her phone.

She called her father.

"*HALLO,* SOFIE."

After decades living in Rome, he had a faint accent when he spoke Dutch, though it was his native language.

"*Hallo, Vader.*" She sank down onto a box of canvas, hunching over as nerves jangled through her.

"It's late, is there something wrong?"

"I have a question. Do you know where my paintings are?"

He made a tutting sound. "Sofie, that's not something we talk about like this."

He meant over the phone.

"My original paintings." She stressed the important word.

There was a long silence.

Sofie moved the phone from her ear to check the call hadn't dropped. It was still connected.

"Vader?"

"Yes?" he said in the same smooth, kind voice he always used.

Apparent that long silence was his answer. Disappointing, but not surprising.

"Where is my passport?"

"Passport?" Now, he sounded genuinely surprised.

"I want to go to London."

"Sofie, it isn't safe—"

"It's not safe here anymore anyway. Men came into my home. They hurt me."

He sounded genuinely shocked and worried as he asked her what had happened, and for a moment, she doubted what Andrei and Rolf had said. Maybe he really did have enemies who respected and feared the church enough not to do worse than scare and slap her as long as she stayed at home.

He was assuring her that he would have her security fixed when she interrupted.

"Do I have a passport?"

She felt rather than heard his disapproval at her interrupting him. "Yes."

"Can I have it?"

"Is there something important in London?"

"Am I allowed to have my passport and travel?" She'd very carefully chosen those words, skimming the edge of the technical definitions used when referencing how human traffickers used documentation, primarily passports, to trap their victims.

"Of course," her father said slowly. "But I'm afraid I have your passport here."

"Can you overnight it to me?"

"When do you need it?"

"Tomorrow."

"Sofie, this will be very expensive…"

"Do you not have money?"

You should have plenty of money. The fee for those "friends" you sent to my home, and the proceeds for whatever black market and private sales you've made.

"You know I took a vow of poverty," he scolded. "But… yes. I can send it to you."

Relief made her almost lightheaded. "Thank you."

"Very good. I will see you soon, Daughter."

Sofie had to tap the screen twice to end the call her fingers were shaking so badly. She'd never spoken to her father like that before, and she thought she was okay until she went to take a sip of tepid tea and ended up running to the bathroom to vomit.

After a long time spent on the bathroom floor dry heaving and another shower, she shuffled back to her phone. This call was far easier to make.

"Sofie?" Colette sighed in relief. "I'm so glad you called. I didn't know if I should call you… How are you?"

"I will cry if I talk about it."

"Crying is good."

"I can't cry anymore. I called to tell you I have your things." She'd packed up Colette items since Colette herself hadn't been back to Sofie's place since the gala.

"Okay. How about I come into town tomorrow and we get lunch. We could go out, if that…feels safe?"

"I would like that." When Colette had stayed with her, the most Sofie had been willing to do was to stop in at the coffee shop between her house and the market. She'd only told Colette that she preferred to cook at home, not that there were no restaurants on her very short list of places that were "safe."

"I'm really glad to hear that."

"I have a question too." Sofie twisted the hem of her shirt between her fingers.

"What is it?"

"Do you have the address of the Club Alibi in London?"

TWENTY

"I'LL TAKE over for a bit. Take the rest of the night."

Andrei looked at Mateus Carvalho, one brow raised.

Mateus was one of the only people who knew the full scope of the Club Alibi project and Rolf's objective who wasn't an Interpol agent. As an investigator for the international criminal court, he actually had more access and authority that Interpol agents did in many ways. He and Rolf had worked together, and knew each other well enough that Rolf knew the other man was a Dom, hence asking him to help monitor and control the club.

This was Andrei's week, which meant being mostly sober and patrolling the public part of the club. The cutout in the center of the floor allowed the light and music from the dance club on the lower floor to flow and flash up into the dark, decadent space.

"I don't want to scene, so I'll stay," Andrei said.

"I think you might want to."

Andrei's jaw clenched. Despite his plan to grab the first willing sub, over the course of the two days he'd been here, he had yet to scene with anyone.

The idea of touching anyone but Sofie made him feel

vaguely ill, which only made his black mood worse. At this moment, he couldn't decide if he wanted to ask Mateus what the fuck he was talking about, or just skip ahead and punch him in the face.

"I'll take over. The last playroom on the left is yours for the rest of the night."

"Mateus, what the fuck are you—"

Mateus tipped his head toward the far side of the room.

An angel was walking through the club.

She wore white—a thin white slip dress with slits almost up to the waist on both sides. With each step, the fabric shifted, exposing the curves of her hip. The straps were strands of pearls, with more pearls set in the arched silver tiara perched atop her pale hair like a halo in a Renaissance painting.

Her feet were bare, and with each step she took, they curled nervously against the floor before lifting to take that next step.

"Sofie," Andrei breathed.

"She's beautiful. Congratulations."

"Thank you. Stop looking at her."

Mateus laughed. "I'm not the only one."

He wasn't.

All around the club, heads turned. In a sea of black, red, and neon, leather, latex, and vinyl, she stood out in her satin and white.

Her collarless neck would be like a catnip to some of these assholes. And he was chief among them.

Because he wanted her on her knees, his collar around her neck, the matching leash looped around his hand so that with a single tug he could pull her in for a kiss.

A Dom moved in, stepping in front of her, his hand resting on her hip. Thanks to the slit in the dress, two of his fingers were on her bare skin.

Andrei was already moving even as Sofie backpedaled with a gasp he could see but not hear.

She glanced around, her eyes wide, and his heart clenched. As brave and bold as she was, this club was far different than the empty, half-finished one in Amsterdam. And for someone who rarely left her home, the crowd and noise must be overwhelming.

He was three meters away when their gazes connected. He saw relief on her features, followed quickly by uncertainty, and then desire.

"Move," Andrei snarled, loud enough to be heard over the music.

The Dom, who put his hands on her, looked back over his shoulder, spotted Andrei, saw his own death reflected in Andrei's face, and got the hell out of the way.

Andrei scooped Sofie into his arms and turned, heading for the private playroom where he could have his wicked way with his very own angel.

SOFIE BURIED her face in Andrei's neck, hiding from the lights and noise.

Walking across that club with no idea where he was or what would happen when she found him, had been one of the scariest things she'd ever done. Scary and exhilarating.

She felt the eyes on her as she walked, and with each step was acutely aware that she wore nothing under the thin satin dress she'd quickly sewn, over the course of a half an hour, pausing to try it on and consult with Colette via video chat.

It was Colette who had suggested that since she needed to wear appropriate attire to get into the club—even with Landon intervening on her behalf with Rolf, who put her on the member list for the night—she dressed as an angel.

Sofie hadn't realized exactly how much she'd stand out until she had gotten here. With her face buried against Andrei's neck, she took a moment to process a few of the things she'd seen. Like the place in Amsterdam, this club had a large open space, but this one was fully outfitted with a variety of seating areas and stages.

One of the women on the righthand stage had been strapped to a St. Andrew's cross and was getting wax dripped on her nipples. A spanking bench on her left had a fully naked woman with a small crowd around her. The fact that at least five people held different implements, and even in the low light, the other woman's bottom looked incredibly red and sore, probably meant that people were taking turns spanking her.

She passed a woman kneeling between a man's feet. They hadn't been on a stage, merely lounging in a small cluster of armchairs. Well, at least the man had been lounging, his pants pulled down far enough to expose his cock, which his submissive was licking from base to tip in long, slow motions.

Sofie had nearly pointed and yelled, "I've done that!"

Though she was sure her attempts at oral pleasure were nowhere near as good as the other woman's.

The noise dimmed, even as the light brightened. Sofie lifted her head to see that they were now in a short hallway. Andrei turned left when it ended, walking past a series of closed doors. At the end of the hall, he bent his knees, just a little.

Though he didn't speak, she realized what he was doing, and reached out to turn the knob, pushing the door open.

Andrei strode into the room, kicking the door closed behind them before letting go of her legs.

"Are you here to submit, or are you here to talk?"

Sofie ducked her head. She knew it was a risk coming

here when nothing had really changed. She was changing, but her answers to Andrei's questions would be the same if he asked her again now.

That left her with only one answer.

"Submit, Sir."

His stillness was shredding her courage, and when he turned away, she squeezed her eyes closed.

She waited to hear the door open and close as he walked away once more.

Instead, there was a click, and the light shifted. The dim lighting that had been on when they walked in was gone. Now, several task lights illuminated a bondage chair, narrow bed with a tall four-poster frame that resembled a cage, thanks to the extra bars along the sides, and a table with a padded top and a series of straps dangling from each of the black metal legs. Outside the gold-tinted spotlights, the room was illuminated by recessed red lights built into the walls.

The effect was eerie and vaguely threatening, but in a way that made her nipples hard rather than inspiring her to run.

Andrei's hands brushed her back, her hips, as he moved behind her. "Take off the halo. It won't save you."

Hesitantly, she reached up, pulling the Kokoshnik-style tiara off.

Andrei took it from her, tossing it casually to the side. There must have been something soft in the corner because she didn't hear the clink of metal on wood. Now that her eyes had adjusted, it looked like it might have landed on a stack of blankets or pillows.

"I'm glad it didn't break," she said.

"Don't want me to break your halo."

"It's an antique Russian tiara worth forty million dollars."

Andrei's hands tightened on her hips and he let out a strangled shout.

"I'm joking! I'm... I'm sorry I'm nervous. I keep messing up the mood."

"Is that why you looked so worried every time you laughed?" He brushed her hair back on one side, his lips near her ear. "You thought you killed the mood?"

"Yes."

"Laughter, teasing, jokes…they're all a part of good sex."

"Oh."

Andrei's lips touched the point where her shoulder met her neck and she shivered. When he asked if she were here to talk or submit, she'd quickly prepared herself for this to be more like that first time, when they'd been strangers.

"Just to be clear, that that's not a $40 million antique that I just tossed away."

"No. I made it. To go with this dress."

"You made this one too?"

"Yes."

His hands slid up from her hips to just below her breasts, molding the fabric against her body.

"It's a beautiful dress, but this isn't how I want you, is it?"

For a heartbreaking moment, she thought this was the rejection she'd expected earlier.

Then Andrei spun her around so they were face-to-face, reached back, and flipped up the back half of the skirt and spanked her hard with the other hand.

She yelped, as much in surprise as pain. But the spank helped her remember what he said before.

"I'm not naked. I'm sorry, Sir."

"No, you're not." He slid one of the pearl straps off her shoulder. "You'll be punished for that."

Sofie took deep breaths, the soft, cool satin rubbing her

hard nipples with each one. She'd been too nervous both on the way here and walking across the club to get aroused. But now...

Her pussy was already embarrassingly wet, and she was aching to be used.

"A spanking?"

"It will be your ass that's punished, but no, not a spanking." He slid the other strap off.

For a moment, the dress stayed in place, clinging to her breasts. But then the weight of the pearl straps dragged it down, the entire thing slithering down and off.

Leaving her completely naked. It was almost starting to feel normal, being naked and vulnerable for him while he was fully clothed. Tonight, he wore leather pants with laces instead of a zipper, and a sleeveless black undershirt that clung to the muscles of his chest and left his arms exposed.

He looked dangerous and unapproachable. Unless she looked in his eyes, and then he was her Andrei, just as she was his angel.

His gaze swept up and down her naked body before he frowned slightly. Her hands curled into nervous fists at her side. Did he not like what he saw? She hadn't changed in the two days since she last seen him, had she?

"What else are you supposed to do, Angel?"

She didn't remember. Or maybe it was that she remembered a million different things. She searched his face for a hint, but there was no help there. He merely arched a cold brow, head tipping in that devilish way he had.

As he looked at her, even as panic for disobeying and disappointing him rose, her pussy clenched.

Oh. Oh.

With a gasp, Sofie sank to her knees and spread her legs wide.

"Good girl."

He positioned his booted foot between her thighs, and lifted the toe just enough to touch her sex.

"Show me how wet you are. How needy that pussy is."

It was degrading and embarrassing, but she did it, gingerly rubbing her pussy against the smooth hard curve of the toe of his boot. He lifted his toe a bit more, and her labia spread, her clit now rubbing directly on the hard leather. She bore down, grabbing his calf with both hands as she worked herself against him.

She should feel shame but instead, she felt like what she was—needy, desperate, and obedient.

Andrei's hand tangled in her hair. She was so desperately aroused that she felt almost lightheaded. When he tugged on her hair, she rose to her feet, gripping onto him to help herself get up.

And once she was on her feet, she leaned into him, taking deep breaths as she rested her face on his chest so she could fill her lungs with his scent. Her hands slid up under the back of his shirt, her touch at first soft, but then she raked him with her nails, scratching gently.

"I know, Angel. I know."

He picked her up, but instead of a bridal carry, he hiked her up with her legs hooked around his hips, his hands under her ass.

He only carried her a few steps before setting her down and spinning her around.

She was standing at one end of the padded table. For a moment, she was disappointed. It was the least interesting thing in the room.

He pressed gently against her ass until she moved forward enough that her lower belly touched the table.

He left her, but only for a moment.

"Arms up."

Instantly, she obeyed, and when she laced her fingers together on top of her head, he reached around from behind to play with her breast. He was slow but relentless. First gently squeezing, and turning then flicking in a quick up-and-down movement that made her take short, surprised breaths. Then he went back to squeezing, but harder this time. And when he twisted them, he tugged too, distending her nipples away from her breasts.

There was a moment where she thought she might come from just this. Her body so ready and primed that each tug and touch sent a bolt of sensation straight down to her sex.

When he released her breasts, it left her panting and needy.

A strong minty smell made her frown in confusion.

"This is a mix of spearmint and menthol."

"What is?"

"This." Andrei held his hand up in front of her face, showing her the slick oil on the pad of his middle finger.

"I...I don't understand, Sir."

"I know you don't, but you will. I wish I could be soft and gentle with you tonight, but I can't."

"I didn't ask for soft and gentle."

"You didn't," he agreed, "but remind me of your safe word."

"Rembrandt."

"That's right, Angel." He brought his hand to her breast and rubbed the oil into her nipple. It felt good, and she arched up into his touch.

But the second he pulled his hand away, a sharp cold bit at her nipple.

She gasped, looking down at her own breast in surprise, even as he reached around and applied the same oil to the other nipple. It took a moment, but that one too started to burn with cold.

"It's cold!"

"For now. Then it will get hot. And this will make it worse."

He showed her what "this" was when he put a hand on her back and bent her face down over the table.

The legs were a little too tall for her, the whole thing taller than a normal table, so she had to go up on her tiptoes.

Now, with her nipples squashed against the padded table top, the cold burn was fading in a favor of heat.

Andrei knelt and strapped her legs to the legs of the table, spreading them even wider as he did. Then he moved to the other end, stroking her arms from shoulder to elbow to wrist and drawing them straight as he did. Padded loops were slipped over her wrists and tightened, keeping her stretched out across the table. A final strap went over her waist.

A strange, lovely calm settled over her, even as she twitched in response to the burning sensation on her nipples.

Andrei gathered her hair which had fallen over her. "How does that feel, Angel?"

"Calm."

He'd been stroking her back and paused in apparent surprise. "I meant the oil. You're talking about the bondage."

"The oil feels hot. Burning."

"Too much?"

"No, Sir. I like the pain."

"But being strapped down like this, it makes you feel calm?"

"Yes."

He bent and kissed a line down her spine. "My perfect angel."

She floated in a happy peaceful place while listening to

him move around the room, undoubtedly gathering supplies he would soon use on or in her.

Something cold and round rested on the small of her back as he moved into position so she could see him.

"I told you your ass would be taking the punishment. This is perhaps less punishment and more preparation, but it will be uncomfortable and unfamiliar enough to serve both purposes."

"Preparation, Sir?"

"Preparing your ass for me to fuck. You need to get used to having something in you here." He reached out and gently stroked one finger along the crack, barely brushing her anus.

"Tonight, I'm going to use dilators." He opened a long case, tilting it so she could see inside.

A series of metal rods, one end rounded, the other flared to a wide base were arranged in size order. The smallest was the diameter of a pencil. The largest was thicker than his cock.

Sofie whimpered, staring at the fat metal tool.

"Tonight, you're going to take up to here." He pointed at one near the middle.

"What if I can't?"

"You can."

"What if it hurts?"

"You'll tell me. And you'll be specific as to how, and how much. It won't be comfortable, but it shouldn't be truly painful."

He set the case aside and pulled out the first three dilators. The thing he'd set on her back turned out to be a bottle of lube. He prepped each of the first three, coating them in lube, before slipping on a black medical glove and applying even more lubricant to the tips of his fingers.

"Your fingers are wider than the toys," she pointed out.

"Yes. The largest one I want you to take tonight is a bit

larger around than my thumb. You will feel it, but stretching you that much in one night isn't unreasonable."

Sofie moaned in arousal, his words touching her far more intimately than any toy ever would. To hear him say how he planned to use her, what he wanted from her body... It was bliss.

Slick fingers slid up and down, up and down the crack of her ass before finally settling against her anus. She tensed, bracing herself, but he only massaged her rear entrance with the pad of his fingers. Little by little, she relaxed until her body yielded slightly with each press of his fingers.

If she'd been able to move, she would have pressed back against him.

"Ready, Angel?"

"Yes, Sir."

The first dilator slid in with surprising ease. In an odd way, she almost didn't feel it after that initial pressure. He fucked her with it for several minutes, with the hand not manipulating the toy stroking up and down her back and hips instead.

Then he switched for the next size up. This time, she felt it a little more when he slipped it inside, but after only a few strokes, she felt her body adjust and relaxed into the sensation.

The third and fourth were easy enough as she floated in a hazy arousal-laced fog.

"You're taking this so well. You were made to be fucked here, weren't you?"

"Yes, Sir," she murmured, only to whimper as a far larger object pressed against her.

"Relax, Angel."

"It feels too big."

"It's not. You can take it for me, can't you."

Her mind was willing, but it took a minute for her to

convince her body to relax. He was applying more pressure than he had with the others, so when her muscles finally yielded, it entered her fast and deep. She yelped, her anus fluttering around the intruder for a moment.

"I'll give you a moment to get used to that."

The fingers of one hand stayed splayed across her ass as his thumb kept pressure on the base of the dilator. There was sound behind her, but it was muffled, thanks to the way her heartbeat thudded in her ears.

She hadn't identified that one of the sounds she heard was a condom packet being opened until she felt the blunt head of his cock rubbing against her clit.

"I want you to take both." His voice was low and dangerous. The auditorial equivalent of seeing the glint of a Jaguar's eyes in the night-dark jungle.

"Yes, please yes. I need you in me."

"I'll fuck you as long as you keep taking the dilators like a good girl."

His cock slid from her clit up to her entrance. He settled the head in place, then slowly began to work his cock into her.

She wasn't sure if it was the position or the dilator that made it feel so tight.

"Gentle, Angel," he charted as she tried and failed to wiggle her hips. "You're tight, but I'm going to fuck this pretty pussy."

That assurance that her body's tightness would not prevent him from using her, allowed her to settle down. The burning heat in her nipples had faded to a throbbing warmth that was almost indistinguishable from the drumming beat of her own heart.

Little by little, he worked his cock into her, stopping once to pull out and apply lube that felt shockingly cold when he slid back into her.

When he was fully seated with his cock deep in her

pussy, his belly applying pressure to the base of the dilator so it too was fully inserted, they both groaned.

Andrei pulled back, then started to thrust with small, hard pushes. Pleasure rippled through her in time with his thrusts, and she pulled against her restraints just to increase the feeling of restriction.

Andrei pulled out and she made a noise of protest.

"Time for the next size."

Though it was larger, it was easier for her to take this one. Her arousal was so acute that her body was like soft wax in his hands, ready to be molded and accept whatever he wanted to do to her.

She breathed through the feeling of the thick dilator sliding deep into her, then let out a groan as he reinserted his cock.

Now, his thrusts were slow and deep, his hips thumping against her ass. Again, she floated, spaced out on pleasure and submission.

"Last one. You'll feel the stretch, but your sweet little ass is made to take it."

"Yes, Sir."

She whimpered through the insertion of the final dilator, and he stroked her ass and thigh until her breathing evened out once more.

Then he started to fuck her with it.

He pulled the dilator all the way out and then forced it in again in one long push, not pausing to let her adjust to just the tip. Sofie's head lifted in a shocked shriek as sensation that she couldn't define as either pleasure or pain rolled through her.

Andrei's voice sounded ragged as his other hand moved to her pussy, thumb rolling her clit as he continued to relentlessly fuck her ass.

"Someday you'll call me master," he growled, so low she almost didn't hear him. "You'll wear my collar."

Again and again, he pulled the dilator all the way out only to reinsert it, forcing her ass to open and close repeatedly. It was wonderful and humiliating at the same time. The pure pleasure from her clit being stroked only made the sensations more confusing.

She didn't want him to stop; she never wanted him to stop. She wasn't even sure she wanted to orgasm. Perhaps it would be better to live in the state of submissive arousal for all time.

"Someday," he growled, thrusting the dilator all the way in and then grinding the flat disc base against her anus.

At the same time, his thumb stroked her clit in a fast soft rhythm that drove her over the edge. Her body quaked, the fact that she couldn't move somehow making the orgasm more intense.

Her mouth was open, but no sound escaped. That was until he thrust his cock balls deep into her pussy in one hard stroke. Her vagina now clenched down on his thicker girth, the double penetration shocking.

Now Sofie screamed, the restraints groaning as she pulled against them. Andrei fucked her hard and fast, almost animalistically, until he grunted through his orgasm.

They stayed that way, both panting and shivering, for several long moments.

Then he kissed her spine, whispering something against her sweaty flesh before gently withdrawing from her body and then quickly freeing her from the restraints.

"HOW DID YOU GET HERE?" Andrei asked lazily.

She had no idea what time it was, but was fairly certain several hours had passed since they finished their scene. That time had been taken up with aftercare.

First, he checked her over and cleaned her up,

including using a neutralizing solution on her nipples. Then they'd retreated to what had turned out to be a large pile of thick blankets. He'd unfolded and re-folded several making a large pad for them to lounge on while reserving one to throw over the top of them.

He held her in silence, and held her while they talked about nothing in particular. Both had been careful to avoid mention of art, thievery, or their fight.

Until now. Until he asked how she'd gotten here.

"I took a flight and then got a cab. Colette and Landon gave me the address, and Landon helped to make sure I'd be able to get in."

"I will do something horrible to him in repayment for him not telling me you were coming."

Sofie laughed, snuggling against him.

But Andrei sat up, forcing her to do the same.

"I mean, how did you clear customs?" He pushed to his feet as he spoke, still turned away from her.

"I have my passport now," she said softly.

Andrei whipped around, eyes wide with hope. But then the expression shuttered. "Have things…changed?"

"Yes." She wished she could stop there, but she'd almost ruined their chance at happiness once before when she lied. "Not…not the way you want them to. Not yet."

His jaw flexed and he was silent for a moment. "So you really did just come to submit."

"I came because I needed to see you. Touch you. Hear your voice."

Andrei stormed away.

"Wait! Please."

Sofie tried to scrambled after him, but she had to stop and pull on her vest and he was already out the door.

The hall was empty. "Andrei, wait, please!"

He emerged from a door near the short hallway, striding back toward her. The anger was gone from his expression, but the flatness of his features now was almost worse.

"I'm a fucking moron, but I couldn't stop myself from doing this." Andrei held out a white document-sized envelope, bearing the Interpol logo in one corner. "What I said before is still true."

She took the envelope, not understanding what it was he was giving her, but terrified to ask and to ruin what had been the best night of her life.

"Take that to Colette and…" Andrei trailed off, rolling his shoulders. "Be safe, Angel."

TWENTY-ONE

HE LOVED HER.

Maybe there would have been a hope, even a slim fucking prayer, that he would resist falling fully and madly in love with her. That chance evaporated when Sofie showed up dressed as an angel in a sea of sin, ready and willing to submit in every way.

But last night, she had shown up, and despite how it ended last night, he was hopelessly in love with her.

Andrei lay sprawled on one of the couches. It was the middle of the day and there was no one in the club. Club Alibi London was open again tonight, but no one would show up to start prep for at least another two hours.

He could have gone into the London Interpol offices to work, but he was too lazy. He'd been sleeping here at the club in the room Landon had used. That hadn't helped the situation, because he ended up staring at the connecting door, imagining what he would do if he had Sofie in the other room the way Colette had been just next door for Landon.

He was in love, cynical asshole that he was.

Still, he hadn't changed personalities. He loved her, but

God, he was pissed. He wasn't sure if he was angrier with himself for being the fool who loved her, or with her for being so stubborn and refusing to listen.

A more rational part of him said she had every right to be stubborn because, as she'd said, it was her life and her choice.

Would it have made a difference if he told her that he loved her, and it wasn't just her life at stake, but her life and his heart?

The part of him that was an absolute moron hadn't been able to let go of hope. The hope that maybe if she were able to take back even a few of her art pieces, that would satisfy her need to reclaim her life and she could move on from the mental place she was trapped in.

What he really wanted was to rescue her, but she didn't need to be rescued. She needed to be empowered.

And that's why he'd given her every single bit of information he'd been able to pull from Interpol's many databases about Father Noah Visser.

He'd started the file thinking it was merely performative. Something to do to make himself feel better.

But there was actionable intelligence in there.

The most critical was a customs declaration form that had been flagged for further assessment four years ago. The large shipment had been identified for further questioning due to the sheer size—seven oversized boxes, most one meter square.

The shipment was headed from Amsterdam to a large country estate in Lanaken, Belgium. Lanaken was just across the Netherlands-Belgium border from Maastricht, and the property was owned by Visser's brother-in-law. The notes as to what had been done when the shipment was stopped were sparse, and there were no additional notes to go along with the original declaration of "personal household goods."

Andrei was fairly certain that Visser had shipped all of Sofie's original pieces to his brother-in-law's house. Probably, he was planning to bring them in one or two at a time over the course of years, then periodically "discover" new art.

For their purposes, retrieving art from a remote estate in eastern Belgium was a far more doable task than stealing something from the Vatican archives.

When he first found this information, he'd almost said fuck it, and gone himself. Simply booked a ticket to Belgium, driven there, and busted in the door.

But doing that wouldn't help Sofie. She had a plan, had made a choice, and he would respect that.

Respect it and wait.

Well…wait as long as he could. Andrei wasn't a patient man. Assholes rarely were.

"Fuck it."

He grabbed his phone from his pocket and called Landon.

"Andrei?"

"Let me talk to Colette."

"Yeah, I'm good. How are you?"

"Are you being held hostage and trying to send me a message, or are you just being an asshole?" Andrei closed his eyes and pinched the bridge of his nose.

"I could only aspire to be as much of a dick as you are," Landon said.

"I don't like this new happy version of you. You were easier to deal with when you were brooding and tortured."

"I was never tortured. I do the torture. I am the torture," Landon muttered.

"This conversation is making me stupider."

"You didn't have far to fall on that front." Landon laughed at his own joke. "Here's Colette."

"Andrei?"

"Yes." He took a moment to switch mental gears. "I'm...I'm just calling to ask how it's going. With Sofie."

Colette was silent for a long moment. "What do you mean?"

"This is me calling as a friend, not as an Interpol agent."

"Very well..." She still sounded confused.

Time to be blunt. "How is it going planning the heist with Sofie."

"The heist? To steal from the Vatican? We haven't...I don't actually think it's possible."

Andrei sat forward, stomach now churning. "No, I mean stealing the paintings from the house in Belgium."

"What house in Belgium?"

"Fuck." Andrei jumped to his feet. "I gave Sofie a dossier on her father. The main thing, the thing I put on top of the stack, was about a house in Belgium. I think her paintings are there." He quickly ran Colette through the information he'd gathered from the custom's investigation.

"She didn't tell me any of this. I was waiting for her to call and tell me how it went when she saw you. I haven't heard from her. I had hoped maybe she was still there."

"She was here two days ago. I mean...she probably left yesterday since it was the middle of the night when..." Andrei realized he was starting to ramble and stopped, forcing himself to think. "I'll check if and when she booked a flight."

"Did she tell you that now she has her passport? She was so proud that she got it. She called her father and made him overnight ship it to her from Vatican City. Confronting him made her so nervous that she threw up, but she did it." The hopeful pride in Colette's voice was hard to hear.

The image of his sweet Sofie, so anxious and scared by a phone call to her father that she had to vomit made him in turn feel ill.

"She told me, but... Fuck. Colette, can you and Landon go to her house and check and see if she's there?"

"I'll call her too."

"Thanks." Andrei felt like a moron because for everything he knew about her, he didn't have her damn cell phone number and hadn't been able to find it in any of their databases. "Can you, uh, send me her number?"

"Of course. And I'm sure she's just at home. Hopefully she's painting. I don't know how long she normally goes without painting, but I don't think she's picked up a brush since that night at the gala."

That calmed his jangling nerves. Sofie probably was at home painting. Maybe she hadn't even opened the envelope he gave her. Or maybe she'd flipped through quickly, not realizing that he put the most pertinent piece on top.

"I'll call you when we get to her place," Colette assured him.

"Thank you." Andrei was up and moving too. To check her flight information, he needed to be in the office on a secure connection that could access aviation administration records for the EU.

"I'm sure she's fine," Colette said, but Andrei heard in her voice the same sinking dread he felt.

THE OLD HOUSE was bigger than she'd imagined. There had been no pictures of it, even on Google Maps. She'd expected something modest based on the one description she'd found of the property as a "stone farmhouse."

Instead of a single-story stone structure in disrepair, this was a three-story stone structure that felt and looked more like a country estate with a well-maintained drive. Off to the side, what looked like an old barn and several smaller buildings were in disrepair, more closely resembling what she'd been expecting of the house as far as condition.

She'd also expected it to be abandoned, but at first glance, it looked too well maintained for that.

After reading the customs report that Andrei had made sure was the first thing she saw, she combed through the rest of the information he provided until she ran across a property deed. From there, she checked the family tree that had also been included. From what she could tell, the owner of the property—her father's sister and the sister's husband, were both still alive, though in their nineties. She didn't imagine they were living here, unless they had help coming in every day.

Sofie hung back, watching from within a clump of thick bushes. Hours passed, but no one showed up.

Finally, she decided to be bold and approached the front door. Though it looked well maintained from a distance, up close, there were spiderwebs in the corners of the windows, dust thick on the panes, and the plants in the pot by the front door were dead.

Still, Sofie knocked and wiped her sweaty palms on her pants. She might be about to meet her aunt and uncle. Pathetic though it may be to think about them that way, given that her father had never truly been a father, some part of her couldn't shake this primal urge to find and hold onto a family.

She knocked again after a few minutes, and when there was still no answer, she decided to peer in the windows.

Most of the windows were newer double glazing, expertly fitted into the old stone frames. That meant that their locks were also the more modern kind. Until Sofie reached the back of the house. There was one small single pane window with the simple lock that Colette had showed her how to pick one wine-soaked night.

Sofie wriggled in delight as she dug into the satchel

slung across her body for a set of jewelers' tools, many of which could double as lock pics as she'd discovered.

It took her far too long, and she left one small scrape on the stone sill when her hand slipped, but it would disappear with the next rain.

Sofie tossed her satchel in first, then wriggled in the narrow window, grunting and groaning as she negotiated getting in without also falling on her head.

The landing wasn't graceful, but at least it didn't result in a concussion.

She climbed to her feet in a small, poorly renovated bathroom and carefully closed the window. Wait, what had Colette said about an exit plan? Maybe she should leave the window open in case she had to make a quick getaway. Then again, given how hard it had been to get in the window, it probably wouldn't be any easier to exit through it.

She waffled for several moments but ended up closing and relocking the window.

Now that she was inside, the excitement had turned to anxiety. This had been fun when she'd been doing it with Colette at a fancy party with champagne everywhere. Her nerves were already on edge after taking her first train trip, then her first time hailing a taxi, all just to get here.

Sofie lingered in the bathroom, taking deep breaths, until she felt both calm enough, and brave enough, to exit.

The house felt still and quiet as she tiptoed from room to room. The bathroom seemed to have been the very last room that hadn't been updated and remodeled. Every other room in the house was beautiful in a timeless way that meant it could have been done twenty years ago or two. The size of the kitchen and the fact that it had an island meant they'd probably had to merge a few rooms to get the square footage for that.

A dining room, office, and library followed the kitchen.

There were no photos or mementos to give her an idea of who lived here. Not until she came to the room at the very end of the house.

She wasn't sure what this room would be called. It was almost a conservatory, given that there were large windows on three walls that let in a massive amount of natural light. Two long tables down the middle of the room gave it an almost library-like quality, though if it were up to Sofie, she would much rather sit on the built-in padded bench under one of the large windows.

The ceiling was double height, the thick beams seeming small they were so high above her.

As lovely as this room was, it felt oddly unfinished, as if it hadn't yet found its purpose. Sofie turned to leave and that's when she saw them.

The one interior wall of the room was covered in canvases. From floor to ceiling, arrayed in neat rows and columns.

And she had painted every single one of them.

Sofie pressed her hands to her mouth. She'd expected to find her paintings locked up in crates and boxes somewhere, if she found them at all. Instead, they were on display in this massive room that now felt like a gallery. She walked up to the closest piece, and it felt like she was greeting an old friend.

"They're beautiful."

Sofie screamed, jumping back from the scene of Hades watching Persephone she'd painted with heavy chiaroscuro like Caravaggio favored.

Sofie whipped around to see her father standing in the doorway.

Noah Visser walked to stand beside her. For many years, he'd seemed ageless, but now…this was an old man. His hair was as white as his collar, and his cassock hung loose on his now-hunched shoulders.

He still used the heavy cane he'd carried for years, but now he seemed to actually need it. The handle was a large marble ball carefully carved with the continents as shown on the Behaim globe. It had made her giggle that the Americas were entirely missing when he first showed it to her.

"Father," she said, as much in greeting as in acknowledgment that it hadn't been all bad. There were times he had been a father to her.

Hadn't he?

She desperately wished she brought some of those articles Agent Baas had given her, because with her father standing beside her, smiling softly as he looked at her paintings, what had seemed so clear before no longer was.

"You are so talented, Sofie. A true gift from God."

Sofie clutched the strap of her bag, sending all of her tension into her hands where they gripped the strap so her voice stayed steady. "Whose house is this?"

"If you're here, surely you must know," her father chided.

"You never told me I had other family. An aunt. Uncle."

"Isn't the church, in all its glory, not your family?"

Her cheeks burned and she wished she could scream at him to stop.

"You should not be here," Noah said when she didn't respond.

"Why not, my art is here?"

"Safe. On display even. Isn't that better than leaning against a wall in your studio?"

"Better is where I say it is. I'm the artist. These are mine. Not copies, mine." She hated that she sounded like a child arguing over a toy or treat instead of piece of her own soul made material with paint and ink.

Noah shook his head in disappointment. "And what do you plan to do with them?"

"What any artist would. Sell them. Have a gallery show. Start a social media account and film myself painting."

"And what will happen when people see how good you are? When they realize that your brushstrokes are indistinguishable from those of Caravaggio and van Gogh."

"You mean, what happens if they realize I can paint like van Gogh, see that you are my father, and then remember that you just happened to magically find two previously undiscovered van Goghs. You care only because my art existing might threaten your scheme."

She wanted to see shame or maybe shock that she'd figured it out. Instead, he only inclined his head.

"Exactly."

It was too much. All of it, a whole lifetime building to that moment. "Why? Why couldn't you have adopted me and made me a real daughter? Why couldn't you have encouraged me to be a famous painter instead of a forger? Why did you take my paintings and try and pass them off as these lost masterpieces? Are you going to sell them?"

"Sell them? No. The items in the Vatican Apostolic Archive are not for sale."

"Then why?" She wished she could be calm and cool in this moment, but emotion leaked into her voice. "Why would you take this from me if you aren't even going to sell them?"

"Because, in future years, if anyone were to ever question one of your forgeries, I will offer these newly discovered pieces as a basis for comparison. The most famous paintings in the world have been cleaned, restored, and cleaned again. But I will show them a pristine van Gogh, preserved because it was forgotten, and that…that will be what van Gogh truly looks like."

Sofie stared at him. It made a twisted sort of sense, but she still didn't understand why.

"That might work in the short-term, but longer-term someone will ask questions. Or there will be some new test that will prove they're too new."

"And when that happens, all art will be questioned."

Perhaps he was mad. Perhaps the reason for all of this was that simple.

"Father...that makes no sense."

"It does, because when they begin to doubt the art that hangs on their walls—and certainly many of them will be the copies you made, their doubt will not be misplaced." He paused, apparently regathering his train of thought. "We will take it, those beautiful things now deemed worthless. They will be returned to the church, which is where they should always have been."

Thinking he'd lost his mind might actually be better than this truth.

"Everything you've done is to sow doubt among the art community so that someday they'll think everything is worthless, and give those pieces to the church?"

"Too many of the things in museums are Catholic art. They were created for the church. The church was their patron. The artists themselves were devout."

"What's the point of the church having all these things when you already have more than you could ever display? Vatican City itself isn't even big enough for the museum you'd need to display all the things already in the museum's archive."

"Enough, Sofie. They were made for the glory of God and are being used for the greed of man."

"But I've made copies of paintings with no religious content. Not painted by Catholics. You keep mentioning van Gogh, but only a handful of his works depict anything religious."

"I said enough." Noah tapped the metal tip of his cane hard on the stone floor. The sound rang like a shot.

Sofie flinched, curling in on herself, but only for a moment. She was brave and this was an adventure. A terrible, terrifying adventure, but an adventure nonetheless.

"What about the money? People paid you for the paintings I made. Where did that money go?"

"To do good works."

"To do good works, or did you give it to your sister so she could remodel this house?"

Again, she hoped for a gotcha moment, but Noah just shook his head.

"I did not want you to feel so alone. That's why I let you live in the city where there were people all around. But I feared that the protection I gave you was not enough."

"Protection? The men who came into my home...you sent them."

"That place is not your home anymore. I think it's best you live here now. It will be less convenient for those who wanted to work with you, but I will find an intermediary."

Sofie shook her head. "I'm not staying here. And I'm not staying in Amsterdam either." She raised her chin. "I'll keep your secrets, Father. I have to because I now know that you lied and what I've been doing is a crime, even if I never knowingly created something so it could be sold as the original. So I know that if I try to go to the authorities, I will end up in prison.

"But I'm done. From now on, I will only paint for myself. For my own joy." She looked up at the wall, at the near sum total of her life's work. "I will come back for these and then I'll disappear."

Noah tapped his cane on the floor again, this time twice in rapid succession.

"No, Daughter," he said kindly. "I'm afraid you won't."

The door opened, and three men appeared. There was

something terrifyingly familiar in their builds, though this time she could see their faces.

Noah gestured to her with one hand. "Please take my daughter upstairs."

She still hadn't really believed that it was her father who had sent those men to hurt and scare her. Still doubted that he would do her any real harm, even as they chased her through the house, one punching her in the stomach when they finally caught her. She doubled over on the floor, mouth opening and closing as she desperately tried to get air into her lungs.

"Take her upstairs," her father said. "I'm sad it has come to this, but I'm glad we prepared."

TWENTY-TWO

"NO ONE HAD SEEN HER. I asked at the market, and at that church." Colette's voice was tight with worry.

Andrei paced his gate at the airport. It felt maddeningly like he could have walked to Amsterdam in less time than it took to fly there from London. He'd bought the ticket this afternoon, but the only flight with space was this late-night one that was currently delayed an hour.

The fact that he didn't know how long she'd been gone, let alone where she was, was killing him.

"She definitely flew back here yesterday?" Landon's voice was distant. Colette must be holding the phone.

"Yes, confirmed with immigration on both ends. She landed in Amsterdam yesterday morning. She must have gotten on the first flight out."

He felt slightly sick, thinking of her going from the club immediately back to the airport. Probably sore. Maybe in sub drop. He'd done hours of aftercare, but she deserved better.

His angel who'd rarely done more than go to the store and church but was so terrifyingly fearless at times.

"Did you see the papers I gave her in her place?" he asked. "Interpol envelope."

"No. I didn't. She might have tucked them away. She has secret vaults and safes in some of the walls." Colette's tone brightened, but if was forced. "Maybe she went to a hotel. Or a spa. I wish you'd been able to track her phone."

Andrei closed his eyes. Once he'd had her number, he tried to track her phone, but she had ridiculously high security on it that prevented him from getting access. A panicked call to Rolf hadn't helped as even Rolf's clearance wasn't high enough. She must have somehow been given diplomatic level credentials on that phone to prevent tracking. He doubted she had any idea, but it was another way Visser had isolated her.

And as for Colette's suggestions…they both knew she wasn't at a spa or hotel.

When he gave her the envelope, he'd expected her to go to Colette. It's the only reason he'd given it to her. Not only was Colette competent and dangerous, but Landon would go where Colette went.

"Fuck this," he snarled. "I know where she is, because I fucking sent her there like a lamb to the slaughter. I'm changing my flight to Dusseldorf or Brussels."

"We'll meet you there."

"No, you stay in Amsterdam in case she comes back."

Andrei ended the call, pulling up the airline app on his phone. Storms over Central Europe earlier in the day meant many of the flights were delayed, and if he was lucky…

Yes! There was a flight to Brussels, delayed and leaving in half an hour. He raced through the airport, changing his ticket as he ran.

She'd left yesterday morning. Probably that meant she spent most of yesterday catching up on her sleep, and then maybe reading through the packet he'd given her. That put her in Belgium sometime today, probably afternoon at the earliest with travel time.

How long would she spend looking around? A few hours?

More than likely he was wrong, she'd found nothing, and was on her way back to Amsterdam. And that was fine because Colette would be waiting for her.

But what if she had found something. What if she found the headquarters of the organized crime ring her adoptive father was running and was there right now. Realistically the soonest he would reach her would be just before dawn, assuming he could get a rental car when he landed.

Nearly forty-eight hours after she'd left London.

A lot of bad things could happen in forty-eight hours.

WITH HER THIRD ESCAPE ATTEMPT, Noah Visser's patience ran out.

It was somewhere around three a.m. when one of the guards hauled her back inside. This time, she'd managed to go out a second-floor window, creep along a ledge, and then climb down a tree. She never would have been brave enough to attempt it if she hadn't jumped out her own window into that tree with Andrei there to catch her only days ago.

This time, there was no one in the tree to catch her. Unfortunately, there had been someone out smoking, despite the hour, and after her a heart-stopping chase through the dark, he caught her.

She'd escaped from bedrooms on both the second and third floors. The money hadn't extended to a full remodel on the upper floor, so the doors and windows were both older, and apparently, she had done a very good job listening to Colette's instructions.

"This is unacceptable, Sofie," her father said, looking even older than he had earlier, thanks to the rumpled bathrobe he wore.

"Yes, it is," she snapped back. "Let me go. You cannot keep me here."

Noah sighed. "I had wanted to wait and show you this tomorrow. It's best in the morning light." He chuckled softly, shaking his head. "But I guess it is tomorrow, and close enough to morning.

"Bring her to the studio."

There was one guard on each side of her, their hands too tight around her upper arms as they marched her down the long third-floor hallway. At the far end was a heavy wood door.

Her father opened it with a key, revealing a large room with windows on three sides. It must be the room directly above the gallery.

Unlike other parts of the third floor, this room had been remodeled. The windows were new as was the concrete tile flooring. Off to one side was a small kitchenette, and on the other, a half wall delineated a bedroom space with a bathroom beyond that. It was a little apartment.

With a door that locked from the outside.

Not just an apartment though. The majority of the space was a painting studio. Many parts of it were a near replica of her first-floor studio back home in Amsterdam. Long metal tables. Her preferred brand of easel. She saw jars of umber and lapis lazuli on bookshelves. There was even an apothecary's cabinet.

It took her a moment to process the implications of this room existing.

"You made this for me," she said as the guards released her.

"Yes. Everything just the way you like it." He smiled

indulgently. "You started telling me exactly what you wanted when you were just ten."

"You made this for me because you knew someday the threats and scare tactics wouldn't be enough and you'd have to lock me up." She started to shake. "This is a prison."

"This is a home. A place where you will be safe and you can do what you love."

"No! No. I love art, but there's something I love more." She caught herself before she said "someone."

"This is your home, Sofie. I have always made sure you have a home, and this is it."

"No!"

Noah shook his head. "I'm needed in Rome, which means we cannot take any more time with you than we already have. We cannot stay so you..." He sighed again. "I will have to make it so you cannot leave, even if you get the door open."

What did that mean?

Sofie yanked free of the men's hold and started backing toward the windows.

"Perhaps it is a good lesson anyway." Real regret touched Noah's face. "Put her on the ground please and hold her legs."

Sofie fought, even though she knew it was hopeless. She tried to punch, kick, run around them. She couldn't stop them from doing what they wanted with her, lifting and carrying her to the center of the room and facing her down on her back.

Once they had her on the ground, one man pinning her arms beside her head, the other pressing her shoulders into the ground, while the third held her ankles, her father stepped up beside her.

Then he slowly and deliberately reversed his hold on his cane, the heavy marble ball dangling.

He was going to hit her with it.

She stared at the gray and green marble ball, about the size of a billiard, and it loomed larger and larger the longer she looked at it.

"Let this serve as mortification of the flesh. With each step, the pain will remind you of your greater purpose here. Let your spirit grow in strength, as your physical body feels the pain."

Noah was no longer a strong man, but he had physics on his side as he brought the cane up and back like a golf club and then swung, the heavy marble head cracking against the side of her knee.

Sofie screamed at the tearing sensation. Finally, finally, stupid girl that she was, she believed what everyone else had tried to tell her.

Yes, her father would hurt her.

"I don't have the strength for her other leg. Help me."

Her other leg? Tears tracked from the corners of her eyes into her hair. She thrashed, but not hard because every movement sent shards of pain up and down her left leg.

She begged and whimpered as the man holding down her shoulders rose to his feet and took the cane.

"Please, Father! Please no! I won't…I won't leave. I'll stay home. Like you told me. This is my home and I won't leave home."

"I know, my child." He smiled down at her, then nodded to the man, who swung the cane high as he grinned.

This time, she heard bone crack.

TWENTY-THREE

ANDREI WAITED and watched as the dawn light brightened to full morning. There was a single rental car parked by the house, and so far, he'd seen two different men step out at various points to smoke.

Without knowing how many of them there were, or if Sofie was even inside, he didn't dare move any closer.

He had a horrible kind of déjà vu, to the point that he even eyed one of the trees and considered climbing it. But there was too much open ground between where he now crouched in the heavy vegetation along the property line and the one good tree.

Finally, what he'd been hoping for happened, and two men walked out together.

They were speaking Italian, but a parabolic mic app on his phone and live translation software took care of that.

"We have to leave in an hour, but she's barely started painting," the shorter one said.

"I don't want to be stuck here in this fucking shit hole." The taller man gestured around at the beautiful estate, which was far from a shit hole, but was in the middle of the Belgian countryside with not much to do.

"If one of us has to stay, we should get to fuck her."

The taller man laughed and the cold sound carried to Andrei. "You know, all she needs are her hands and her eyes to paint." He made a cutting motion with two fingers. "Her other parts? We could start removing them."

"You heard the father, we can't risk infection if we cut off a toe or two. Elio already hit her too hard."

Andrei closed his eyes. He'd once been a criminal, and his switch to the other side of the law had more to do with security and quality of life than deep moral convictions. It was why he never really cared that Sofie was a forger.

And looking at these men now, he decided that there was no greater good than protecting the woman he loved. And protecting her might mean every man here had to die.

SOFIE'S HANDS shook with pain as she tried to sketch out the outline of the image her father had just described to her. He wanted it in the style of da Vinci, as that was the piece that had attracted the most attention.

There were no poplar boards in the supplies, but she was terrified to say that, in case that earned her another strike. She'd snapped at one of the men earlier when the pain became too much, and he'd shown her what too much really was when he pressed on her right knee and she momentarily blacked out.

Her left leg throbbed, but her right felt like it was on fire. They'd had to lift her off the floor onto the stool. Carry her to the bathroom, though she'd been able to stand on her left leg long enough to use the toilet without assistance. She'd had to bite a fold of her shirt to keep from screaming when she lowered herself onto the toilet, and by the time she was done, had been weeping with agony.

Now she was at an easel, sitting on a tall stool which

allowed her to keep her leg mostly straight. Her father was sitting beside her, hands on the head of his cane. He watched her with rapt fascination as she sketched the image of St. Gerolamo Emiliani walking among those dying of the plague. He'd requested this specific subject.

St. Gerolamo was the patron saint of orphans and abandoned children.

If she hadn't been so scared, and in so much pain, she would have laughed.

"You have always loved to paint," he said wistfully. "Makes me sad to hear it is no longer your first love."

"I fell in love," she whispered, voice shaking, her mind hazy with pain and possibly shock.

"With…a person? A man?"

"Yes."

"How did you meet him?"

It didn't matter if she told the truth. She would never walk again. Never see Andrei. Never leave this room. She had been the worst kind of fool and now would pay for that stupidity. Not just with her life but in suffering.

"He arrested me."

"I saw that you were arrested. I was shocked, Sofie."

"I wasn't really arrested." She hated herself for reacting to the disappointment she heard in his voice. "He saw through the window in my bedroom when your men came in and started hitting me. He tried to rescue me, but I…I panicked. Tried to run back inside because." She glanced at her father, head swimming a little—she shouldn't look around too much. That was dangerous. "Because I'm not safe unless I'm at home."

Her voice broke as she obediently parroted the words.

"That's right." He patted her shoulder. "But you're home now."

A whimper crawled up her throat but she swallowed it.

"How was it not really an arrest?"

"He arrested me to put me in protective custody. Because I kept insisting on going home even though it wasn't safe."

Her father made a displeased noise.

"He... I..." Sofie bowed her head, pencil falling from her fingers. She stared at where it lay on the floor. She wasn't sure if she could get it.

Her father bent down and picked it up, placing it on the tray of her easel.

"It is good to know love, though only the love our God has for us is eternal."

Her father stood, placing his hand on her shoulder. "I must go, Daughter."

As much as she wanted him gone, she was terrified for him to go. "You're leaving me like this? I can't walk, I can't..." She was breathing too fast, but she couldn't seem to make herself slow down. "It hurts so much."

"I will send one of them back tonight with perhaps a wheelchair for you and something to help you with the pain. But remember, pain and suffering—they teach us. They help us reach a spiritual place."

He bent over and kissed her head, patting her shoulder once before turning to make his slow way to the door.

Sofie let the pencil fall from nerveless fingers and watched it roll across the floor.

"WHO MOVED the car into the barn?" Taller Asshole asked as they strode across what had once been a farmyard toward the small outbuilding. The morning sun was cheerful, the sky a brilliant blue. Not exactly murdering weather, but Andrei made do.

"That idiot Elio must have. Where is he?"

Dead in the car.

Andrei followed them at a safe distance, having confirmed with Elio before snapping his neck that there were three men and Father Noah Visser here.

And that they had the father's pretty blonde daughter locked in a studio on the third floor.

Andrei gave up on the translator app, tucking his phone back into his pocket as Shorter Asshole opened the door into a small shed, exhaust billowing out. It was a small space, and the running car was wedged in there—he'd broken off one of the mirrors getting it in.

Both men reeled back, coughing. Though he no longer knew what they were saying, Andrei could guess.

What the fuck is this? Why is the car on? What is he doing?

They'd never get answers.

Andrei shoved both men hard against the boot of the car, then slammed the shed door closed. He had to shove, given that their legs were now pinned between the door and the bumper. There were screams of pain as he dug in his heels and refused to let the door move even an inch. Grabbing the shovel handle he'd found for explicitly this purpose, he wedged the door closed using a crack in the cobblestone farmyard.

Once he was sure it was secure, he stepped back, watching the heavy wood door—they just didn't make things this way anymore—shudder with their futile attempts to escape.

Andrei made a quick circuit of the shed. He'd already used spare rags to close up cracks in the old stone to make sure all the exhaust fumes were trapped inside.

He kept watch as the men thrashed and shouted. Soon the shouts turned to coughs. He wouldn't wait here until they died—he was burning with the need to find Sofie, and all that coughing would have weakened them enough that at this point, he had full faith in the shovel handle keeping them inside.

Andrei turned, shocked to see another figure standing halfway between the house and the shed.

Sofie's father.

He wore the collar and cassock of his office, both hands braced on the round head of a heavy cane.

They regarded one another for long moments.

"You're the man she loves," Father Noah Visser said after a moment.

That surprised him more than the other man's presence.

Noah smiled. "You look surprised. She didn't tell you."

"She never had the chance because you locked her up here the same way you locked her in that house in Amsterdam."

"Here, yes, there are locks."

"You made sure she never had a chance."

"I made sure her life had meaning."

"Yours won't. They'll never find your body." Andrei smiled. "And if they do, I'll make sure evidence of every scandal you have and haven't participated in comes to light. They won't make you a martyr or a saint. They'll strike your name from the books and pretend you never were."

That got a reaction, a flare of anger in the old man's eyes. "God will know—"

"I hope he does. If there is a God, you'll burn in hell for what you've done to her."

"My soul is clean."

"If that's true, then so is mine." Andrei stalked toward the other man, done with this conversation. He needed to find Sofie. He knew they'd hurt her, but didn't know how badly, and it was killing him.

Andrei stopped in front of the old priest.

"I think death is too good for you." He backhanded the old man—he wasn't ageist so didn't feel bad about it. Bending, he rummaged through the man's pockets. The father moaned in what Andrei thought was Dutch and clutched his side. Broke a hip maybe.

Andrei took the man's phone, wallet, and cane, then straightened.

"Goodbye, Father. If this is what sends me to hell, it's a just price to protect Sofie."

Leaving the old man on the ground, probably immobile and with no way to call for help, Andrei walked away.

SHE FLINCHED at the sound of the key in the door. Sitting here with nothing to do had been worse than trying to sketch, so she managed to get herself up on her left leg and lean over just enough to reach the cup of pencils on the long counter under the window.

She was nauseous with pain by the time she sat down. Some small part of her wanted to simply give up. It would be so easy. Those windows may be new, but they weren't bulletproof. She could shatter them and then… A fall from this high would hopefully kill her.

Those thoughts had occupied her in the time immediately after her father had left.

But now… Without them looming behind her, and now that she was holding perfectly still and not exacerbating her injury, a ribbon of hope was coiling behind her heart.

Andrei.

Andrei would come. Maybe not right away. But he would wonder what had happened to her. He would go looking.

Colette. Colette wouldn't need forgeries anymore, but they were friends, weren't they?

Colette would realize she was missing before Andrei tried to look for her. A week or two maybe. Hopefully Colette called Andrei to tell him she was gone, and he'd tell her about the file of information. They would come to look for her. All she had to do was survive.

Yet as the lock clicked, terror swamped her, blotting out that fragile curl of hope. And with the rise of terror, the calm, rational thoughts that had been saving her sanity were sucked down beneath the surface.

Sofie gripped the edge of the canvas, bracing her right hand and touching the canvas with the pencil lead, though she couldn't draw even a line. Instead, what appeared was a squiggly dot created not with intention but because of how badly she was shaking.

"Sofie."

The sound of his voice was a cruel trick. She closed her eyes. Andrei wasn't here. Not yet. She had to suffer more before she could be rescued.

"Sofie, Angel…" He inhaled. "Sofie, what the fuck did they do to your leg?"

Footsteps thudded across the floor, but she refused to look. This was some cruel yet wonderful hallucination.

"Angel." His voice broke. "Angel, can you look at me? I'm going to take you out of here. I'm… Fuck, I should have come in earlier."

Now his voice was starting to shake as badly as her hand.

"I can't leave," she breathed. "This is home and I have to stay at home."

"This is not your home."

"I'm safe if I stay home. I left. I went to other places and now I-I-I…" She stuttered to a stop.

"Home," he said. "Okay. Home. You don't have to leave home."

At that, she opened her eyes. Andrei, her beautiful Andrei was here.

"Andrei."

"Yes, Angel, yes."

"If I leave home…"

"You're not leaving home," he assured her. His gaze was fervent or earnest. His soul laid bare. "Because I'm your home. Or I will be if you let me. If you want."

She cupped his cheek with her left hand, still thinking maybe it was a hallucination until she felt the warmth of his skin and the scratchy stubble along his chin.

"I love you. I didn't think I would ever love someone. Not in the way…" He smiled softly. "Not the kind of love that you could paint. But I love you. And if what you need to feel safe is to be at home, let me be your home."

"You're really here."

"I really am."

"I love you, too."

"I know." Now his grin was cruel. "Your father told me."

"He's still here?" She whipped around to look which jolted her leg. Sofie screamed, gripping her right thigh.

Andrei was there, staring at her leg, his hands raised but not touching her. "What did they do to you?"

"My father has a cane."

"I've seen it."

"He hit me. My left leg and I think something tore, but I can stand on it. But one of the others used the cane on my right leg and I…I heard it break. The bone. My knee."

Andrei visibly swallowed as if trying not to vomit. "I should have killed them slower."

That unexpected statement cut through some of the shivery fear that gripped her. "Killed them?"

"The three younger ones are dead. Your father is lying in the yard incapacitated with no phone or way of calling for help. And we're leaving him there."

"I think murder is a crime," she said, bemused.

"It is." Andrei was up and moving through the studio, looking for something.

"You can't say anything to me about forgeries anymore, if you're doing murder."

"A fair trade." He raced back over to her, holding two long canvas stretcher bars and a roll of packing tape.

Andrei knelt and looked up at her. "I have to carry you out of here. If I'd known, I would have murdered them off site so we could call an ambulance, but it's too risky, so I'm going to carry you out."

Anticipation of pain made her stomach roll, but she nodded.

"I'm going to splint your leg the best I can first. He reached up with one hand and cupped her cheek. "Stay with me, Angel."

"Always. Why would I leave?" She touched him with tentative seeking fingers, asking silently for him to rise. Somehow he understood and moved so that she could press her lips to his. It was only then that she began to truly believe she was safe.

"Why would I leave?" she said again. "You're my home."

TWENTY-FOUR

PAINTING exhibition at the new Beaumont Gallery.

JOIN us for the world premiere exhibition of exceptional paintings by Sofie Leonard showcasing the transference of mastery across mediums and styles.

SOFIE LEONARD first appeared on the art scene as a child nearly a decade ago. Now painting under the married name Leonard, she first made a name for herself by successfully submitting three of her own original works to the auction house Christie's where all three were verified as being lost masterpieces by Cezan, van Gogh, and da Vinci himself. It was only when the artist herself encouraged the auctioneers to use a new fluorescing test on the back of the canvas that her signature and a note describing why she worked so hard to learn to emulate the masters was discovered. During her hiatus from the art world, Sofie worked as a restorationist and is currently working with the Malik

Beaumont security group to help museums and private collectors not only strengthen their security but assess all current inventory.

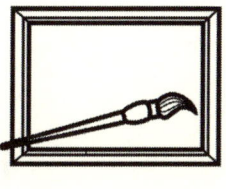

EPILOGUE

World Premier Art Show at the New Beaumont Gallery.

JOIN us for the world premiere exhibition of exceptional paintings by Sofie Leonard, showcasing the transference of mastery across mediums and styles.

SOFIE LEONARD *first appeared on the art scene as a child nearly a decade ago. Now painting under the married name Leonard, she first made a name for herself by successfully submitting three of her own original works to the auction house Christie's where all three were verified as being lost masterpieces by Cezan, van Gogh, and da Vinci himself. It was only when the artist herself encouraged the auctioneers to use a new fluorescing test on the back of the canvas that her signature and a note describing why she worked so hard to learn to emulate the masters was discovered. During her hiatus from the art world, Sofie worked as a restorationist and is currently working with the Malik Beaumont security group to help museums and private collectors not only strengthen their security but assess all current inventory.*

ABOUT THE AUTHOR

Lila Dubois is an award winning, multi-published, bestselling author of erotic, paranormal and fantasy romance. Her book *J is for…*, the tenth book in the bestselling checklist series, won the 2019 National Readers' Choice Award. Additionally, she's been nominated for the RT Book Reviews Erotic Novella of the Year for *Undone Rebel* and the Golden Flogger.

Having spent extensive time in France, Egypt, Turkey, Ireland and England Lila speaks five languages, none of them (including English) fluently. Lila lives in California with her own Irish Farm Boy and loves receiving email from readers.

Visit Lila online:
www.liladubois.net
author@liladubois.net

facebook.com/AuthorLilaDubois
instagram.com/liladuboisauthor
bookbub.com/authors/lila-dubois
tiktok.com/@liladuboisbooks

Manufactured by Amazon.ca
Bolton, ON

45780253R00173